"How long have you been wanting to kiss me?"

It was tempting to fling the truth at him—the truth that they had *already* kissed. It would feel good to catch him off guard and watch him absorb that fact.

She couldn't do it, of course. After the satisfaction of shocking him wore off, she'd be left with the awkwardness of him knowing she was the idiot who had kissed him in the boathouse while he thought she was someone else.

"You were stroking my lips," he reminded.

"I was checking to see if you were breathing."

He whirled her around, sending her colliding into his chest.

"Oh!" Her hands came up to his chest, palms flattening on the very body she had only moments ago felt at her leisure. Now it felt different. Now he was awake. Alert . . . his eyes as sharp as a hawk's gaze on her. Now his heart pounded swift and hard beneath her touch.

By Sophie Jordan

BEAUTIFUL SINNER

A DEVIL'S ROCK NOVEL

SOPHIE JORDAN

AVONBOOKS

An Imprint of HarperCollinsPublishers

BEAUTIFUL SINNER. Copyright © 2018 by Sharie Kohler. All rights reserved. Printed in the United States of America. No part of this book may be used or reproduced in any manner whatsoever without written permission except in the case of brief quotations embodied in critical articles and reviews. For information, address HarperCollins Publishers, 195 Broadway, New York, NY 10007.

First Avon Books mass market printing: November 2018

Print Edition ISBN: 978-0-06-266659-8
Digital Edition ISBN: 978-0-06-266660-4

Cover design by Nadine Badalaty
Cover illustration by Aleta Rafton
Cover photograph by Michael Frost Photography (man); © miroslav_1 /iStock/Getty Images (fence); © Johnny Adolphson/Shutterstock (pasture and mountains); © Ivan Mikhaylov / Dreamstime.com (sky)

Avon, Avon & logo, and Avon Books & logo are registered trademarks of HarperCollins Publishers in the United States of America and other countries.

HarperCollins is a registered trademark of HarperCollins Publishers in the United States of America and other countries.

FIRST EDITION

18 19 20 21 22   QGM   10 9 8 7 6 5 4 3 2 1

For my Kiawah Island retreat crew:
Thanks for cheering me on as I finished this book. I love all of you!

BEAUTIFUL
SINNER

ONE

*T*HE THING ABOUT small towns was that everyone knew your business.

Even now, at the age of thirty, Gabriella Rossi's life was still fodder for gossip. She thought she left this town for good after high school. She thought she escaped it years ago. She thought she had moved on to better things. But here she was, walking into her former high school, a place where hope went to die, a place that held few fond memories and smelled of stale body odor and mothballs—a place she had thought to never step foot inside again.

She inhaled a deep breath as she prepared to walk into the sprawling two-story structure.

You can do this. You're not seventeen anymore. You're not the brunt of jokes or bullying. You're not Flabby Gabby.

"Come ON! We're going to be late!" Tess snapped

and charged ahead toward the looming building, tugging her seven-year-old son by the hand as her heeled boots beat out an angry staccato.

"That girl needs a good whippin'," Nana Betty grumbled as she rolled her walker another step forward. It had been five weeks since her knee surgery, but her grandmother was gradually regaining her mobility.

Gabriella grinned as she held on to her grandmother's elbow and guided her up the curb and onto the sidewalk. "She's a little old for spankings now, Nana."

"All the more reason. She should know better than to be such an asshole."

Gabriella had to bite her lip to stop from laughing. She couldn't help it. Hearing her diminutive eighty-year-old grandmother use such language was funny as hell. "Tess just wants to get good seats."

Nana Betty grunted. "What for? So we can see your brother up close? I see his face enough. Bah." She lifted a gnarled, heavily veined hand from the bar of her walker and slapped the air.

"Nana," she chided, even if she was secretly amused. Their brother was the principal of Sweet Hill High School. That pretty much made him a town celebrity. Parents who wanted the best for their child curried favor with him like he was the crown prince of Sweet Hill. He reveled in it.

But today wasn't about Anthony.

Tess's daughter was being inducted into the National Honor Society. Their brother just happened to be officiating over the ceremony.

As they entered her old high school, Gabriella told herself returning to this place was no big deal. Her niece would get a certificate and a shiny pin and then their family would leave and go eat dinner at Applebee's or some other place her mother selected.

Gabriella's phone rang in her bag. She fumbled for it, pausing in the hallway.

Her heart lifted a little at the sight of Cody's name. Finally. He was calling her back.

She gave Nana Betty an apologetic smile. "Give me a minute, Nana. I need to take this. Hello," she answered a little breathlessly.

"Hey there, Gabs," he returned.

She winced. She hated when he called her that, but at least she had him on the phone. She'd left her boss at the *Austin Daily Reporter* multiple emails and voicemails over the last two weeks without a peep from him. Jerk.

"Thanks for calling me back, Cody. Have you had time to look over any of the proposed topics

I sent you?" It was a courtesy question. He'd had plenty of time to look over her proposals. Just like he had plenty of time to post pictures of himself water skiing with friends at the lake. She wasn't stalking him. Really. They were Facebook friends. He posted those pics for the world to see.

"Yeah, those aren't going to work. Send me some more."

All the air expelled from her lungs in a deflated rush. It probably wasn't a great idea to come off as annoyed or desperate. Even if she was.

"Cody . . . you said I could still work while I helped out with my grandmother." She had taken her sabbatical with the understanding that she could freelance for him remotely at her own pace. She wasn't being paid, so any additional income would be helpful. Except Cody had accepted none of her proposals in the five weeks she had been here, forcing her to get a part-time job at a coffeehouse. Cody had agreed to the two-month sabbatical, but she was starting to wonder if her job would be waiting for her in three weeks.

"Then give me something I want. You're not writing for your high school paper anymore, Gabs. You're supposed to be a real reporter. So prove it. Prove you're good enough for this paper."

It stung. She thought she had been doing that.

She had spent the last three years as a reporter for the *Austin Daily Reporter*. It had been a step up from her previous job as a copy editor at a paper in Fort Worth. When she first went to work in Austin she had thought her career was finally taking off. Recently, however, she felt like she was stuck in a rut. Maybe it was turning thirty. She had taken a hard look at her life and realized that Cody kept most of the good assignments for himself or his more veteran reporters and stuck her with all the fluff pieces.

Her silence must have been telling. He tsked and adopted a consoling tone. "Now hang in there, Gabs. You're a good writer. You just need the right story—"

"Is this because of us? Because we broke up?" The caustic retort slipped out before she could help it.

Nana Betty lifted both of her gray bushy eyebrows.

Her cheeks flushed in embarrassment. Not one of her best decisions—dating her boss—but she wasn't some bitter ex. She had thought he wasn't bitter either. When she had taken that hard look at her life, she had also realized her relationship with Cody wasn't something she wanted anymore.

When you're thirty and you can't imagine the

man you're dating as a potential husband, then what was the point in dating him?

His friendly tone vanished. He laughed harshly. "You're not that special, Gabriella. You're definitely *not* the kind of girl a guy can't get over."

She flinched, remembering another reason she had ended it with him. In any disagreement or fight, his temper flared. "Gee. Thanks."

"This isn't personal. It's business. If you want to keep working for me then give me what I want. And you know what that is."

She sighed. Yeah. She knew.

She knew exactly what he was asking of her because he'd asked it ever since he learned she was from Sweet Hill.

Ever since he learned her cousin was Shelley Rae Kramer and ever since the man sent to prison for killing Shelley Rae was exonerated and released. It was big news. National coverage kind of news, and Cody wanted the inside track.

As far as he was concerned, Gabriella had access to the inside track.

She took a step away from Nana so she couldn't be overheard. "I won't exploit my family like that." She regretted ever confiding in Cody about her family. It had happened in a stupid moment of weakness when they'd been dating.

The murder of her cousin had hit her family hard, and the recent discovery that the wrong man had been sent to prison for the crime had only ripped open the wound. Her family's emotions ran the gamut—from denial to anger. Any closure they'd managed to achieve had been shattered. Her aunt and uncle couldn't cope anymore. They'd bought an RV, packed their things and left town. That still didn't stop the reporters from harassing the rest of the family though. They wanted interviews from anyone connected to Shelley Rae.

"Jesus, be a professional, Gabs. I don't give a shit about your family. I want Cruz Walsh. *He's* the story. What kind of person confesses to a murder he didn't commit? Find out. Go get it."

She chewed the inside of her cheek, mulling that over. He was right. She could do the story on Cruz without focusing on her family. But . . . *could* she? This was Cruz Walsh they were talking about. She didn't know if she could be objective when it came to him.

"Fine," Cody snapped into the silence of her thoughts. "Then some other reporter will do it. They'll get the story you're sitting on. They'll publish it. And it may or may not even be the truth."

She winced at that because over the years there had been a lot of untruths spread about the night

Shelley Rae died. The wrong man had been convicted for the crime, after all. The truth mattered to her. It always had . . . in every story. Cody knew that about her. In the beginning of their relationship he had called it endearing. Now, it just annoyed him.

Maybe she should consider writing the article.

"Gabriella!" Her sister marched down the hall, her boot heels clacking on the tile and her oversized designer handbag swinging wildly from her elbow. "What are you doing? You know I want good seats and you're jawing on the phone." Shaking her head, she snatched Gabriella's phone out of her hand.

Gabriella tried to snatch it back, hearing the faint tinny echo of Cody's voice as he repeated her name. "Tess! That's my boss!"

"What boss?" Her sister dropped Gabriella's phone into her bag with a derisive snort. "Last time I checked, you didn't work. You live in Nana's garage apartment."

"I work for the *Austin Daily Reporter*," she said between clenched teeth. She'd said as much to her sister before. "You know I took an unpaid sabbatical to come here and help Nana after her surgery." Because she gave a damn. Her brother and sister might be local but they were too busy with their lives to help out with Nana on a daily basis.

She helped care for Nana alongside a part-time in-home nurse and physical therapist. In addition to that, she worked at The Daily Grind. She didn't really have a choice. She needed the money. And it wasn't as though any of the family thought to pay her for putting her life on hold and coming to Nana's aid. They just figured her life was the least important. She had no husband or kids and they didn't consider journalism a real career, so she should be able to drop everything. Because her *everything* didn't amount to *anything* in their eyes.

Tess squared her shoulders with a sigh and leveled a stern look on Gabriella. "I mean a real job. A career."

Of course.

The barb stung. A *real* job. Like Tess had. Meaning a job that garnered a large salary.

Tess was one of the most successful real estate agents in town. Her billboard greeted you as you drove into Sweet Hill. She always liked to lord her success over Gabriella, dropping how much money she made on her most recent sale. As though making a lot of money made her a better person. Ever since Tess divorced last year, she was even more driven, and more obnoxious over her perceived success. As though it somehow made up for the part of her life that was broken.

With a disgusted sigh, her sister spun around and charged down the hall, still dragging her son.

"Don't pay her any mind. That girl has been as mean as a rattler since she caught her man diddling their housekeeper," Nana Betty chimed in.

It was true. She'd caught Jason in bed with their nanny/housekeeper. Actually having sex together in their bed. Tess had come home early to change clothes because she'd spilled food on her blouse at a lunch meeting and she caught them together. After that shock, Tess discovered her husband had had a string of affairs with women all over town. Their housekeeper. Their dental hygienist. Their daughter's piano teacher. Even one of Tess's former sorority sisters. He would sleep with her when he went to Amarillo on business. Apparently there was no actual business in Amarillo. Just Tess's sorority sister.

"Well. Wouldn't you be in a bad mood, too?"

Nana sniffed. "I would have shot him in his special place."

Chuckling, Gabriella took her grandmother's elbow. Together, they advanced down the hall and turned the corridor to the auditorium.

The double doors loomed open and students stood there, handing out programs to the large crowd of people gathered waiting to go in.

"Looks like we're not getting front row seats." No doubt they would hear about that later from Tess.

"Nana Betty. Aunt Gabriella." Trent, Gabriella's eighteen-year-old nephew, approached them with a smile. His father could be a pain, grilling her on her life choices even more than Mom and Dad did, but Trent was a good kid. Laid-back and generous. He lacked his father's intensity.

"There's handicapped seating up front. I can take Nana there," Trent offered.

"Sounds great." Handing Nana Betty off to her nephew, Gabriella glanced around her former stomping grounds warily . . . like she needed to be on guard. Just like old times. She'd always been on guard in high school.

She may have skipped her ten-year high school reunion, but she knew she'd have to come back here someday. She had nephews and nieces that went to this school. Her brother was the principal. Trent was graduating in a couple months. It was an eventuality.

Only she had hoped it would just be to visit . . . and then she could flaunt a cute boyfriend or maybe a husband. Oh, and by then she would have won a Pulitzer, too. Yeah. That was the dream. Reality fell short. Substantially short. The last thing she wanted was to run into someone she went to school with.

"Oh my God! Gabriella Rossi. Is that you? You haven't changed a bit!"

Earth.

Open.

Swallow.

She heard the voice and knew immediately who it belonged to. Twelve years had passed but that voice hadn't changed. It was still shrill and had that air of no-one-cares-if-I'm-loud-because-I'm-so-cute.

Gabriella was beset with a flash of Natalie's face. Laughing and always taunting as she looked around to see if her audience was suitably impressed. If Natalie was shouting a greeting, Gabriella guessed she had forgotten it had been her habit to torment her.

But Gabriella hadn't forgotten. No, she would never forget.

The heaviness in her chest expanded. She couldn't look. She didn't want to. She didn't want to see Natalie right now or ever. It seemed the height of unfairness that she should have to. Wasn't living through high school with the likes of Natalie enough? Did she have to experience her as an adult, too?

She couldn't do this.

She thought she could return here with a sense of accomplishment for her big city life and career to boost her, but she hadn't taken into account that she might see Natalie again. People like her weren't supposed to be real. Past tormentors should be relegated to the past. Bullies lost to childhood, never to surface again. They weren't supposed to materialize in the here and now.

Before she could consider what she was doing, Gabriella spun around and ran. Heat flushed through her. Forget about how stupid she must look. The past—*fear*—was a powerful motivator.

She took a corner, rounding it sharply and colliding with a body that felt like a mountain. The velocity launched her back and gave her whiplash. Hard hands clamped down on her arms, saving her from hitting the ground.

"Oh!" she breathed, her gaze jerking forward and locking on the guy in front of her.

Speaking of people who weren't supposed to materialize . . .

She had thought coming face-to-face with Natalie was bad. But this? *Him?* This was so much worse.

She cocked her head to the side, staring intently into the pair of dark eyes staring back at her. Even if he wasn't holding on to her, she couldn't go anywhere. She was trapped. A bug pinned beneath a jar from the power of his stare alone. Her mouth dried and her pulse fluttered at the skin of her throat.

She knew those eyes. Knew them from long ago and knew them from recent news footage.

Knew them from her dreams.

Some things were impossible to forget. His face was one of them.

The thin white scar bisecting his right eyebrow and slashing his cheek was new. It didn't detract from his good looks though. On the contrary, it seemed to enhance the beauty of his face, add a bit of harshness to all that masculine beauty.

In high school, all that masculine beauty (minus the scar) had made her heart race. Of course, her heart betrayed her now . . . still racing.

The big hands holding on to her arms flexed. The heat from his palms and fingers singed her through her sleeves and into her flesh. She felt that heat everywhere. All the way to her core. To nerves she didn't even know she possessed.

Her gaze stalled on his lips. She knew that mouth, too. Intimately. He didn't know that, of course. No one did. She'd sat on that secret for years, burying it deep, taking it out only at night. Alone in her bed with her fantasies.

But here she was.

Here they were.

Face-to-face.

Of course, she never expected to see him again.

Never expected that Cruz Walsh, the man sentenced to prison for murdering her cousin, would ever be free to walk the streets, much less collide with her in the hallway of their old high school.

TWO

IF CRUZ HAD to choose between prison *or* returning to the halls of Sweet Hill High School, it would be a tough decision.

Both had been their own form of hell on earth, but if he were honest with himself, he'd been more at home in prison than he ever had been in high school, so there was that.

Yeah, he knew that didn't speak well of himself. Especially considering he had been an innocent man sitting in prison. It shouldn't have felt right. Prison shouldn't have felt like a place where he belonged, but Cruz had never felt at home in polite society.

And he didn't feel at home in these halls either. Not years ago, and not now.

At least in prison there were no masks. You were who you were. No facades.

High school had been full of deceptions. People pretending. No one was honest. Except his teachers. They were pretty up-front, letting him know how little they thought of him and that they only expected trouble from him. With the last name Walsh, he was branded the moment he stepped into a classroom.

As for his peers . . . the guys either looked up to him or wanted to kick his ass because of his reputation. Girls? Well, they were always around. Always available. At least the ones that liked the bad boys like him . . . and there were plenty of those that did.

"Pardon me," the female in his hands said in a gust of shaky breath.

He steadied her, his body still rocking from the sudden contact with hers.

"It's okay." His hands lingered on her arms as he stared at her. A slow warmth spread through him as he inhaled her clean, floral scent and assessed the brown eyes and the dark wavy hair. She wore minimal makeup. Brown freckles dotted her nose and cheeks. She was pretty in a fresh-faced girl-next-door kind of way.

His hands flexed on her arms. He should let go of her. She'd done nothing to invite his touch, and still his hands remained on her after it was clear she had regained her balance.

Since he'd been released from Devil's Rock, he'd been with a few women. He had a lot of time to make up for, after all. Years of celibacy. Things hadn't changed much. He might have been exonerated but he still had the bad boy reputation that women wanted. *Certain* women anyway. Certain women not like this one.

He knew that instantly from how wide her eyes grew as their staredown continued. She looked like a fucking Disney princess. He would never approach such a sweet-faced girl. He never *had*.

His gaze dipped, looking her over, trying to assess her shape beneath her boxy blouse.

"Excuse me." She glanced at his hands still on her arms.

A sneaking suspicion began to grow in him. "Do I know you?"

It couldn't be . . .

"Umm . . ." The way she dragged the word out hinted that they did know each other and she knew it. "No, not really. I mean, kinda. We graduated together. From here." She waved vaguely around her.

Could it be her? What were the odds?

"Oh." He studied her face, a strange tightness wrapping around his chest. Their graduating class hadn't been that large. But it had been several years ago. A lifetime ago, really. He'd lived and died and been born all over again in that time. He couldn't expect her, of all people, to still be here in Sweet Hill. She had been destined for great things outside of this town.

"It was a long time ago," she muttered, color rising in her cheeks.

"Yeah," he agreed, and glanced around the hallway he once roamed. This place felt like something from a dream. "A long time."

"You're probably thinking of someone else." It was like she didn't want him to remember her. She continued, "People change." Her tongue darted out to moisten her lips. "Not that you've changed that much. Just older . . ." Her voice faded. The blush in her cheeks deepened, making her freckles stand out even more. All of a sudden, he wanted to touch them.

He knew. There was no doubt. The invisible band around his chest tightened until it finally snapped. He exhaled. Gabriella Rossi. "Can't look eighteen forever," he replied.

"Of course not. None of us can."

Gabriella. His body had known, had recognized her instantly. It just took his brain longer to process.

"You're . . . You sat behind me in health class." It seemed safe to admit that. They had more than health class together, but he didn't need to let on just how much of her he remembered . . . how much she had affected him back then.

She blinked thick lashes over her brown eyes. "You remember that?"

"Yeah." He remembered everything that had to do with her.

She nodded. "We had a few other classes together, too."

So that meant she remembered him. That meant she knew where he had been all these years and yet she was still standing before him, letting him put his hands on her. She was still talking to him like they were ordinary people. Like *he* was an ordinary person and not the man that had gone to prison for killing her cousin.

Something sank and twisted inside his chest. Everyone knew. He should be used to this by now. Most people in this town didn't treat him like he had been exonerated. People still looked at him like he was a guilty man walking the streets. Like he had gotten away with something.

There would always be that. He'd always be marked and he needed to get over giving a damn about it.

Except she knew.

She would look at him the way everyone else did. Seeing contempt in her eyes shouldn't matter. *She* shouldn't matter. He wasn't the same boy as before who cared about the same things. He grimaced. Hell. Did he even have it in him to care at all?

He quickly dropped his hands from her. "What was your name again?" As if he didn't know.

"Gabriella. Gabriella Rossi."

He nodded slowly as though the name struck a vague chord. "Yeah. You wore glasses."

"Just readers," she said, a touch defensively.

"You were smart. Always had the answers when the teacher called on you." His gaze skimmed the fall of her hair. It was still the same shiny dark color. Back then it had been long and she always wore it in a ponytail. Now she wore it loose and it hung just a little past her shoulders in artless waves.

"We had art sophomore year together, too," she reminded.

"Mrs. Henke," he recalled. The teacher wore scarfs and flowery skirts and liked to play music as they worked. Sinatra.

"You were good. I still remember your drawings."

He smiled. "Only class I got an A in."

"Art was never my subject," she said.

He had a vision of a freckle-faced girl with glasses sighing as she worked on a sketchpad. Every few minutes she would rip off the paper, wad it up and toss it aside in frustration.

A beat of silence passed between them. "And are you still Gabriella *Rossi*? Or have you married and started having babies like everyone else?" He posed the question casually, like her answer didn't matter.

"Me?" A shaky laugh spilled out of her. "Oh, no, no, no. I've been building a career."

She said it like it was such an unlikelihood. She might not be for him, but this girl was exactly the kind you brought home to Mom. Cute, clean, fresh-faced . . . and she had a hell of a rack. Even better than he remembered.

He was trying hard not to notice, but then he had always noticed. He was aware that under her boxy blouse she hid a considerable chest. He'd been aware from the moment she ran smack into him and he got a bounty of soft breasts cushioned against his chest.

"Me either."

"Yeah. I know." Her eyes widened as soon as the words slipped out.

He stiffened. So he had confirmation. "I figured you knew. Who doesn't in this town?"

She swallowed. He actually saw her throat work. "I just—"

"It's okay. Anyone with eyes and ears in this town knows about me." He nodded.

"I—I—"

He left her stammering and walked around her, continuing on to the auditorium. Really, there was nothing else to say.

For a moment he'd felt normal talking to her. A mistake. He wasn't normal.

Nothing about his life would ever be normal.

SHE CLOSED HER eyes and wondered if that couldn't have gone any worse.

She'd come face-to-face with Cruz Walsh. The man had been convicted for a crime he didn't commit and she knew that people in this town weren't going easy on him. She knew that firsthand.

Various members of her family still thought he had been involved in Shelley Rae's death. The ones that didn't believe the right man was now in prison for the crime, but that Cruz was responsible for the delay in justice. If he hadn't owned up to the crime in the very beginning, then the true killer would have been caught sooner.

She simply didn't see the sense in *still* blaming Cruz. Even if she hadn't crushed on him all through high school, even if he had been a complete stranger, she couldn't fault him. She couldn't hate him. The facts were all there. He hadn't killed Shelley Rae and he had suffered more than any man should for a crime he didn't commit. How could she hate him after all he'd been through? Seven years in prison . . . God. She couldn't even imagine the horror of it. Maybe she should write that article just so the world could see things from his side.

She returned to the auditorium. Her brother's voice droned on with the aid of a microphone. The ceremony was well underway. At least she wouldn't be cornered by Natalie now.

She slipped inside the cavernous room and flipped down a seat in the back row, easing into it. She tried to focus on the students seated on the stage, easily identifying her niece . . . but her gaze drifted over the crowd, searching until she found *him*.

He was seated facing forward, his gaze fixed on the stage. A man and woman sat beside him: his sister and her new husband, the sheriff of Sweet Hill. That had caused a good amount of a stir. Those two getting hitched was unexpected. A Walsh and the good sheriff. It was scandalous and every gossip in town was agog with the news.

No match could be more shocking.

It was almost as unimaginable as Gabriella and Cruz hooking up. That would rock this town . . . and get her disowned by her family. Good thing nothing like that would ever happen.

At least not again.

THREE

*S*HE WOULDN'T HAVE *gone if it wasn't graduation night. If her parents hadn't looked at her with the full expectation that she would go—that for once she should party like every other teenager.*

As if that didn't make her feel like a loser. Her parents actually wanted her to party. They probably wouldn't even mind if she got into a little trouble. Nothing too serious, mind you. Just minor shenanigans. Something that would make her more like other kids. More like her brother and sister. Tess had been a cheerleader. Her brother had lettered in every sport: football, basketball and baseball. To say that Gabriella was the odd duck was putting it mildly.

Don't get her wrong. She was celebrating inside. She'd graduated. She was leaving Sweet

Hill. Finally. Going to college where she could start fresh. Where she could be anyone she wanted to be.

Her mother even forced her to wear a skirt tonight. It's a party, Gabriella. Put on makeup. Dress up a little. Look festive.

So here she was. Showing more leg than she liked or probably should. It wasn't like she had the body for skirts. She wasn't tall and she was too curvy. That's what her mother called her. Curvy.

The kids at school just called her fat.

The student population of Sweet Hill High School had made it abundantly clear over the years that Gabriella Rossi was not one of the pretty people, and the pretty people are the ones who mattered.

"C'mon, Bri. Let's dance." Kari grabbed her hand and dragged her out into the living room where a few other girls they knew danced. The furniture had been pushed to the far walls to make room for a dance floor.

All two hundred and nineteen members of their graduating class were crammed into the house and trickled out onto the lawn—along with a scattering of the more popular underclassmen.

She wasn't cool. Not by a long shot, but every

graduate was invited, so she didn't have to meet that criterion for once.

The couple of drinks she'd consumed in the back seat of Kari's car on the way here had helped loosen her inhibitions. She let herself dance with wild abandon. She'd be gone soon. Who gave a damn what anyone thought of her anymore? She didn't have to care about these people for the rest of her life. My, what a freeing thought! God knew they had never cared about her.

Kari watched her bad dance moves, laughing in approval. "There you go. Shake it!"

"I'll be back," Gabriella shouted to Kari over the music. Apparently those drinks had gone straight through her. She exited the living room and got in line for the bathroom.

Natalie, the party's host, was in line in front of her, whispering loudly to her friend, oblivious to Gabriella standing behind her. Thankfully. Gabriella had suffered enough of her attention over the years. Indifference was the kindest treatment she could expect from her. If Natalie wanted to play her usual role of bully, Gabriella would have gotten out of line. As it was, she hung back, arms crossed over her chest, trying to remain unobtrusive.

"I told him I'd meet him in the boathouse but

that's before Jack showed up. Can you believe it? He wanted to surprise me." Natalie rolled her eyes as if a hot college boyfriend popping up unexpectedly was such a bummer.

Everyone knew Natalie was still dating a guy who graduated last year and went to college in Oklahoma right now. Everyone also knew that she was hooking up with other guys while he was away at college. Apparently she had made other arrangements for the night and her boyfriend's arrival had ruined those plans.

"So what are you going to do about Cruz?"

Gabriella's ears perked up right along with her heart. There was only one Cruz and she had been achingly aware of him for years.

He might have a bad reputation and be a troublemaker by everyone else's estimation, but he'd never bullied her, and that was saying something since she'd endured a lot of that over the years. No, Cruz had left her in peace. Occasionally, he even smiled at her. The bullies had been the good kids who came from good families and, ironically, went to church. Her parents were friends with their parents. They attended PTA fundraisers together.

Gabriella knew to look past the outer shell. She had learned that before she learned to fingerpaint.

"Well, I can't go out there to talk to him now. Jack is in the next room."

"So you're going to just leave him out in the boathouse?"

Natalie shrugged. "Maybe I can sneak off after a little while when Jack starts talking football with the other guys. That won't take long. It's all he talks about."

The other girl laughed. "Oh, you are bad, Nat. You would sneak off to hook up with Cruz Walsh with your boyfriend nearby?"

Natalie and Cruz Walsh were hooking up.

Gabriella felt an irrational pang in the center of her chest. They were both beautiful. It shouldn't be so surprising. Beautiful people flocked together. And it shouldn't feel like such a betrayal. She had no claim on Cruz.

"What can I say? Cruz can do things with his hands and mouth, and oh my sweet heaven, his dick . . ." Her voice faded with a sigh. "Well, let's just say boys like Jack are missing that gene or something."

"Yeah. I guess being raised in a gutter gave Cruz a leg up or something."

"Or something." Natalie giggled. "You have no idea."

"Oooh. You do like the dirty ones." The two girls high-fived amid further laughter.

Natalie's friend sobered enough to say, "Yeah. Well, what makes you think he will wait for you?"

"Have you seen me tonight?" She motioned to her body. "And don't forget he's had a taste before. He'll wait for this."

Gabriella glanced from Natalie's tight little body to her own and back at Natalie again. Natalie wore a skin-tight dress that left nothing to the imagination. It showed off her narrow waist and long legs. Every line, dip and curve of her body was on full display. Gabriella wouldn't be able to squeeze a thigh into that dress.

The girls entered the bathroom together and shut the door, sparing Gabriella from the rest of their conversation.

She stood there for a few moments until they exited. They paused when they spotted her.

"Gabby! I didn't know you were coming," Natalie exclaimed, eyeing her up and down.

"You invited the entire class," she reminded, hoping this wasn't going to be one of those moments where Natalie decided to make a scene, singling out Gabriella for attention.

She smiled slowly, looking genuinely pleased. There was so much deception in that smile. "That's right. I did. But you never come to any parties. I didn't expect to see you here."

She resisted asking if Natalie really thought about her at all—when she wasn't in the act of bullying her.

Natalie stepped closer and draped a slim arm around Gabriella's shoulders. "Have you found the buffet yet? We had Sammy's BBQ cater. I'm sure you'll love it. There are so many ribs and just slabs of brisket."

From anyone else the comment would have been harmless. But not Natalie. Her eyes danced spitefully and she took a deep sniff of air. "I'm sure your nose can lead the way."

Her friend laughed, and Natalie preened, proud of her cleverness. Slipping her arm from Gabriella's shoulders, she moved away with an air of "my work here is done."

Gabriella hurried inside the bathroom and shut the door. She breathed deeply, despising Natalie, despising being made to feel so awful—so very small.

Somehow it was all compounded with the knowledge that Natalie was going to make out with Cruz in the boathouse. She shook her head. It was wrong that she should even care.

As she leaned on the sink, head hanging, she realized Natalie wasn't even with Cruz right now. Right now, Cruz was alone in the boathouse. Wait-

ing. Being stood up. Unless, of course, Natalie managed to slip away and see him. Then she would be with Cruz. The idea of that . . . the image of them together . . . made her sick. And angry. Why should awful girls get dreamy boys like Cruz Walsh?

She lifted her gaze to the mirror, staring at herself. She felt ridiculous, dressed up in a blouse and skirt. She'd never made such an effort with her appearance before, but Mom had talked her into it. The makeup on her face was subtle, but that too felt over the top. She lightly rubbed beneath both eyes, collecting any mascara dust.

Telling herself that this would be the last time she had to suffer the likes of Natalie, she emerged from the bathroom and returned to Kari on the dance floor.

Kari was dancing and making calf eyes at a guy from her Spanish class that she had crushed on all year. Apparently now she finally had the courage to make a move.

Suddenly Gabriella noticed Natalie waving at her. She was standing with her friends, her college boyfriend in their midst. Catching Gabriella's eye, she pointed in the opposite direction, stabbing a finger repeatedly through the air. "The ribs are that way!" she hollered.

Natalie's friends laughed.

Gabriella's face burned.

That did it. She tapped Kari on the shoulder. "Hey," she called over the music. "I'm going to go outside. It's too hot in here." Not a lie precisely. The room was warm—especially with her face flaming.

Kari nodded distractedly at her, still gawking at her crush.

Gabriella pushed through the press of bodies until she stumbled outside into the crowd. It was still tight, but there was free-flowing air, at least. She lifted her chin up to the night and drew a deep breath, her hands opening and closing at her sides, yearning to grab hold of Natalie's hair—or do even just one thing that would make her feel half as bad as she made Gabriella feel all these years. Just one thing that would disappoint or crush her. Even if just for one night.

A very drunk girl stumbled up beside her and bumped into her. She was one of the pretty people— part of Natalie's circle. "Heyyyyy there. It's Flabby Gabby. What are you doing here? Never see you at parties."

Gabriella ignored the hated moniker. Natalie had invented the nickname in kindergarten and people had been calling her that ever since. She was done reacting to it even if it still stung. She'd *gotten good at overlooking slurs and insults. She had it down to an art form. She donned a mask. Kept the hurt inside.*

One time she'd bought an ice cream sandwich in the cafeteria. She had been sitting with Kari, talking and eating her ice cream when a couple guys stopped directly behind her and made smacking sounds with their lips. She'd looked over her shoulder at them.

"Mm-hmm. Are you enjoying that? Is it gooooood?" There was something so cruel in the exaggerated questions. In the way they nodded their heads at her like she was some simpleton. One of the guys rubbed his belly for further emphasis.

She had whipped her head around and stared straight ahead, waiting until they moved on. She tried to act normal and calm and unaffected in front of Kari even as Kari asked if she was okay. Gabriella couldn't finish her ice cream sandwich. She dropped it on a napkin in front of her like it was poison.

Her lunch turned to rocks in her roiling stomach and bile rose up in her throat. She held herself together until the bell rang and then she disappeared into the crowded hallway. Into a bathroom. Into a stall where she threw up. Not because she was deliberately trying to purge or anything. No. Those boys' brutish faces swam in her mind and their taunts echoed in her head, making her sick.

She braced a shaking hand on the stall wall. Tears choked her. Snot rolled from her nose. She wanted to go home. She wanted to curl up on her bed and hug herself until she didn't feel so marked, so tainted, but she was stuck.

Stuck at school for the rest of that day.

Stuck for three more years. Until tonight. Graduation night.

Tonight she was finally free. She should feel great. Instead she was reflecting on that day in the cafeteria.

It was funny how that one memory stood out in a sea of memories. The bad ones always did. The bad ones left scars. Even now, standing on this porch, she felt the puckered flesh of that scar. The skin had never knitted back together in quite the same way. All it took was some little bitch pointing her in the direction of the buffet and another one calling her Flabby Gabby and she felt that scar throb and split open again.

Gabriella strode past the girl. Did she think she was so special? So very funny? She wasn't even remotely original. Originality fell to Natalie and jerks that taunted her as she took a bite of ice cream.

Soon she would never have to see Natalie or any of these people again. She wouldn't have to hear the words "Flabby Gabby" uttered ever again.

Gabriella kept walking, circling around the house and heading down the sloping lawn toward the boathouse sitting beside the river. Suddenly, she knew what she could do. She knew the one thing she could do to spite Natalie. The one thing she could do to disappoint or crush her. Even if only for tonight.

The boathouse beckoned, calling to her. It was like an invisible string pulled her there.

She could see Cruz there in her head, waiting for Natalie . . . and she just couldn't stay away. Cruz didn't deserve to be used by such a nasty piece of work.

The building was dark. There was no indication of Cruz or anyone inside. Water lapped the shoreline in a soft, rhythmic slap. Noise from the party was a distant growl on the air. She glanced back up the incline to the house where the lights were tiny dots. It felt very far away and she wanted it that way. She wanted it to disappear.

She stepped onto the narrow wooden deck that ran along the boathouse. The river flowed underneath the dock and building. She peered over the railing at the water, black and fathomless below.

Her shoes, strappy contraptions that Kari insisted she borrow, gave her a good two inches. They clomped loudly over the wood slats as she walked. If Cruz was still inside, he definitely heard her coming.

She stopped before the door and inhaled a breath. She always got nervous around Cruz. Considering they'd had at least one class together every year of high school, it really was pathetic. She shouldn't feel so rattled in his presence. She should at least be able to string a couple coherent sentences together.

The door creaked loudly, the rust-worn hinges protesting as she pushed it open.

"Cruz?" She stepped inside.

The place smelled of wood. Cedar coupled with the faint underlying odor of motor oil.

She had a vague sense of large darkened shapes. Boats, obviously. She'd actually been in this boathouse before. She and Natalie had been in the same Girl Scout troop and Natalie's dad had taken the entire group out on the river. Mom made her go.

"Cruz," she whispered. She didn't know why she was whispering. She was here to find him and tell him that Natalie was standing him up because she was busy with her boyfriend.

Despite the warm air, she shivered a little. This

had the makings of a C-grade horror movie. And yet here she stood in the dark, calling the name of a beautiful boy as though finding him was the only thing that mattered.

She jerked when the door slammed shut behind her, carried by the wind.

"Cruz?" she called out again, louder.

She was here to tell him that Natalie wasn't coming. At least she wasn't coming any time soon. It was the courteous thing to do. The decent thing. The guy shouldn't have to wait out here for her.

"I just wanted to—"

"Hey." A deep voice curled around her as a hand simultaneously circled her arm. Not just any hand. Cruz's hand. He whirled her around. She released a startled cry. Her hands came up, flattening on his chest. "Took you long enough," he husked.

It was dark. It was dark and he thought she was Natalie.

The realization stunned her. And repulsed her.

In no reality was she Natalie. Not even close. She couldn't squeeze her fat toe into Natalie's jeans. Only utter darkness could account for that confusion.

She tipped her chin up—even in these heels he

was tall—and opened her mouth to correct him of that misapprehension.

She had no warning. No hint of what was coming. Just the slight tightening of his hand on her arm . . . and then his mouth was on hers.

Searing-hot lips slanted over hers and it was the shock of her life.

She had never been kissed before. She'd fantasized about it plenty of times. Listened as other girls huddled together and giggled about what went on over the weekend with boys. She read about it in her mom's romance novels that she snuck off her nightstand. She even practiced it on a stuffed animal a time or two. She was heartily, achingly, mortifyingly aware that she had reached the ripe age of eighteen and never been kissed.

Until now.

The fantasy was all she ever had before.

But now she had the reality. The reality of Cruz Walsh's mouth on hers.

It was unbelievable. No. It was more than that. So much more than that.

His lips moved over hers, expertly, skillfully, coaxing a response. A response she did not know how to give. Because she was hopeless like that. Hopelessly inexperienced.

She trembled, her hands still trapped between their two bodies. She didn't know what to do. Even with his skilled mouth pressing so hotly over hers, she froze like a block of marble.

He pulled back slightly. "What?" She could feel the warm breath of his words fall on her lips. "You not into it anymore?"

Her racing heart lurched in her chest. Not into it? Was he kidding? This was Cruz Walsh. She'd been into him for years.

However, the question reminded her that he had done this with Natalie before. Clearly Natalie would be responding differently. Gabriella winced. For starters . . . she would be responding.

She shook her head and made a sound that could be interpreted as no.

"What's the matter then?"

"Uhh." A beat stretched between them as she floundered for speech.

Play it cool. This is the moment you explain to him that you're not Natalie.

His arms loosened around her enough so that she could move her hands. She splayed her fingers wide on his chest, ready to push. To put proper distance between them.

But it never happened. She couldn't do it. She was too weak. Too caught up in the fantasy that had somehow miraculously, insanely become her reality. Too caught up in his warm breath so close to her face and the sensation of his chest under her hands.

She'd seen him shirtless before so she could visualize his chest. She'd spotted him out the second-floor window of her Spanish class sophomore year. He'd been playing basketball with a bunch of guys. All his sweaty, glistening, perfectly toned skin on display as he played with disgusting agility. What sixteen-year-old looked like that? He deserved his own CW show. She'd admired him alongside every other gawking girl in her class. Admiring him from a distance had felt safe. Nothing about this felt safe. Everything about this shouted danger.

Cruz Walsh had just become her first kiss. Unbelievable as that was.

She couldn't let this moment fade away, knowing she had stood stupidly frozen as it happened. She had to make it count.

She had to kiss him back.

But her chance was slipping away.

He stepped back with a sigh, obviously taking her frozen muteness as unwillingness. "More games, Nat? You wanted me to meet you out here. I didn't even want to come to this party."

Her lips worked, but she could produce no sound. The moment she said something it would be over. He would know she wasn't Natalie.

Another sigh. "I'm so over this." He turned to leave then.

Move. Do something!

She grabbed his arm, stopping him.

He waited, pausing as he faced her in the dark. An edge of impatience sharpened the air . . . and something else. Something taut and thick.

If she wanted to keep him here with her, she was going to have to persuade him . . . and persuading boys wasn't exactly her forte.

She flexed her fingers on his forearm and slid them down to his hand. Just like she had never kissed a boy, she had never held a boy's hand either.

His hand was much larger than hers, with calluses on the pads of his fingers. She ran her fingertips over the rough patches and gave his hand a squeeze. Then, guided by some kind of instinct, she turned his hand over and bent her head, pressing a lingering kiss to his palm. She put all her yearning into that kiss, a plea, hope that he would not walk away.

He didn't move. She took that as a good sign.

Emboldened, she reached for his other hand

and did the same, pressing a long, savoring kiss to that palm, visualizing him in her mind. The boy she had secretly crushed on for so long she could not even recall when it had all began. Cruz Walsh had simply always been there. Larger than life in her mind.

His breathing changed ever so slightly as her lips moved over his skin.

She lifted her head from his hand and stared straight ahead, blindly into darkness. She had only a vague sense of his face above her.

For the first time she had his full attention on her. Sure, he thought she was someone else—someone awful who had tormented her all her life—but she shoved that aside for now. She could have this . . . enjoy this for a little while longer.

"Please don't go," she whispered, keeping her voice low and indiscernible. Indiscernible but not inaudible. He heard her. "Will you stay? For a bit?"

"You're acting . . . different."

Her heart tripped with excitement. He was still here so "different" couldn't be all that bad.

"Different . . . how?" Her chest fluttered. She wanted to be different. She didn't want to be like Natalie. She didn't want to be like any other girl for him.

"For starters . . . you never say please and

you've never asked for anything. You take, Natalie. That's what you do."

A slight smile curved her lips. That sounded like the Natalie she knew, too.

Still holding on to his hands, she lifted up on her tiptoes and pressed her mouth to his, this time determined to prove she wasn't a chunk of marble.

He hesitated only a beat and then started kissing her back.

Worried he could detect her lack of experience, she followed his movements, kissing his top lip, then his bottom, determined to come across as a competent kisser. Given this was her first kiss, she knew that might be a stretch.

The good news was that after a few moments she didn't have to think about what to do. It was just instinct. Passion.

She slid both hands along his cheeks, cupping his face, reveling in the sensation of his skin, the bristle of an incoming beard scratching against her palms.

When her tongue grazed his, she felt a hot bolt of electricity dart down her spine. She shot straight up in his arms and leaned into him with a moan, opening her mouth wider to him.

He froze and pulled back slightly, and she felt a flash of fear that it was over, that he was stopping, that he was pulling away from her. Maybe he had figured out who she was. Or rather who she wasn't.

"Cruz," she gasped, holding his face between her hands like they were glued there and couldn't let go. God. She was going to have to get over that because she couldn't cling to him forever.

His breath tangled with hers. "You've never kissed me like that before."

"I . . . know?" Okay, that sounded more like a question than statement of fact.

He flew into action like a sudden storm. His hands slid down to her ass, each of his hands gripping one of her cheeks as he lifted her off her feet and carried her.

She gave a little yelp and dropped her hands to his shoulders, hanging on for dear life.

His feet thudded across the wood planks. The boathouse was dark but he clearly knew his way around it. She tried not to think about how many times he had been in here with Natalie. She didn't want to think about Natalie at all. This was her moment. Her time with Cruz.

Right now he was here with her. That's all that mattered.

Suddenly he lowered her onto a table, wedging his body between her open thighs. Her legs dangled off the side. His hands settled on her knees. Her bare *knees*.

Somehow he managed all this without ever breaking their kiss. As far as she was concerned, this proved all the rumors of his prowess. She had always suspected as much. Now she knew. The boy was a god.

"Nice skirt," he said as his fingers played with the hem, tickling her skin.

That's right. She was in an easy-access skirt. The one Mom had bought and insisted she wear. She wondered what her mother would think of her wearing it now. And then she forgot all about her mother.

She hissed a breath as his hands slipped beneath the hem, skating along her thighs. *Thank God she had shaved.*

His hands are on your thighs. His hands are on your thighs. *The refrain ran on repeat in her mind.*

"You feel different," he drawled, and she tensed. Of course, her body didn't feel like Natalie's body. She had just hoped that he wouldn't really absorb that fact. It wasn't as though he and Natalie were exclusive, after all. She knew there were other girls in his life.

"Different?" she choked.

"Yeah. Better than I remembered."

She gasped. Had he really said that?

His fingers inched along the tops of her thighs and then slid around to her hips, fingering the sides of her panties. She tried to visualize what underwear she was wearing in her mind, but then she figured it didn't really matter in here. It was dark. He would never see them. And the swift way his hands moved over her and how her body trembled in reaction, she wouldn't have them on for long.

Oh. God. Was she already losing her panties? Just like that? She was really about to go from her first kiss to getting naked with him in the blink of an eye?

But this was Cruz. It wasn't like her infatuation with him sprang up overnight. And it wasn't like she had planned on being a virgin forever.

Gabriella always figured it would happen. She imagined it would happen when she left Sweet Hill and Flabby Gabby behind. The right guy would come along, probably in college, and it would simply happen.

And yet what guy could be more right than this one that her legs were wrapped around?

Of course, there was a very minor flaw to this scenario—to doing this with him. To doing IT with him.

He thought she was someone else. He thought she was Natalie. Awful Natalie. Once the idea was there, she couldn't shake it. It sank its teeth into her.

He must have felt her withdrawal. He pulled back, his breath fanning her face warmly. "What's wrong?"

She lifted both her hands to his face again and simply held him, her thumbs grazing his bristly jaw in small circles. She wanted to relish this . . . memorize it.

Except he thought she was someone else. She couldn't shake the wrongness of that.

The table was tall enough that their faces were level. She lowered her forehead to his until their noses touched and lips brushed. Meanwhile his hands still kept their delicious hold on her hips, his thumbs hooked inside her panties, burning an imprint on her skin.

They had to stop. Or she had to come clean about who she was.

Either prospect turned her stomach.

The door to the boathouse suddenly creaked open, its oil-starved hinges groaning. "Cruz?" The door banged shut. "Cruz? You still in here? Where are you?" Natalie's heels clomped over the floor as she walked deeper into the boathouse.

Cruz tensed, turning slightly away from her, in the direction of Natalie's voice.

"Natalie?" he murmured, the bewilderment clear in his voice. His fingers fanned out on Gabriella's hips as though assuring himself of her presence, that she was real . . . flesh and blood in his hands.

"Where are you?" Natalie sang out. "It's so dark in here. Cruzie . . . are you hiding from me?" She giggled.

Cruzie?

Gabriella rolled her eyes.

His hands loosened on her hips and he stepped back. "Who are you?" he demanded. It might have been dark but she could feel the intensity of his stare on her.

She wasn't about to be discovered. Not by Cruz. Not by Natalie. This would be her secret.

Rather than answer, she came to life, flying into motion. She jumped down from the table. She remembered enough of the boathouse to know there was another door at the opposite end of the building.

She took off, crying out when she slammed into the corner of a table. Biting her lip against the pain, she quickly shoved it aside and kept on going as though the hounds of hell were after her.

"Wait!" Cruz called after her, but she kept going, her legs pumping hard and fast. She could hear Natalie's voice, too. She didn't process the words, but they didn't matter. She slammed out of the back door of the boathouse and ran up the hill toward the house, diving into the partygoers spilling out onto the lawn and losing herself in the crowd.

Natalie was with him now. The girl he wanted.

The girl he thought he'd held in his arms. Not her. Not Gabriella.

He'd forget all about the anonymous girl he'd kissed now that he had the one he really wanted.

FOUR

*S*HE HARDLY PROCESSED the ceremony happening around her. She was too caught up in memories of that night in the boathouse. She had trained herself not to think about it over the years. At least not a lot. She had succeeded. *Mostly.* It was her first kiss, after all, and still the best to date. Kind of pathetic, but there it was. The truth.

Cruz's kiss was unforgettable.

She hadn't seen Cruz since that night in the boathouse. Well, except for on the news.

When it came to light that he had been wrongfully imprisoned, they juxtaposed pictures of a young twenty-something-year-old Cruz with Cruz today . . . hardened, big-bodied, unsmiling but still mesmerizing as he walked out of the courthouse into broad daylight.

She'd watched that clip of him over and over,

staring at his body. The lines of his face. She'd tried to read his expression, to get some idea of what he was thinking . . . of who he was now after seven years in a cage for a crime he didn't commit. *What kind of person did that make you?* She wanted to know that and not for some interview. She wanted to know it for herself.

She shook off the troubling thought. She was never likely to know the real him, but seeing him again brought the night in the boathouse back with alarming intensity. His mouth. His hands on her thighs and hips. The shape and texture of his face under her palms. The velvet curl of his voice in her ear. His voice when he had pronounced that her body felt *better* than he remembered. Heat swamped her.

Applause shook her just as her memories threatened to suck her back under again. She pressed a hand to her overheated cheek and released a ragged breath.

The clapping subsided and everyone rose to their feet and started filing out of the auditorium amid rumbling conversation. She stood and hurried out of the large room before everyone exiting spotted her in the back. She definitely did not want that much attention.

Gabriella sped ahead to the cafeteria, hoping to take position in a corner where she could observe undetected. It was about more than avoiding Natalie now. She wanted to avoid Cruz, too. That seemed the most pressing concern at the moment. *Avoid Cruz. No more encounters.*

Adults and students flowed in a stream into the lunchroom and ebbed toward the table laden with refreshments.

Gabriella leaned against the wall near the door, unobserved. Nana Betty and Trent entered the room at a slow pace, moving right past her. She didn't join them. Instead she shrank back. Anthony and Tess followed close behind them, and she felt no eagerness to mingle with her brother and sister. As two people prominent in the community, people flocked around them.

Her parents were there, too. Mom preened, reveling in the people, the attention gained through her important children. This was precisely the type of event she loved. An event where she got to showcase her family. She loved her high standing in the community, loved showing off her children and grandchildren. Dad, however, wore his usual expression, which translated to: how-soon-can-I-get-out-of-here-and-into-my-recliner.

Her niece, the reason they were here, stood off to the side chatting with friends who were also being inducted into the honor society. Gabriella sighed. She needed to make her way over to Dakota and congratulate her. It was the reason she came, after all. She could rationalize hiding from Natalie and Cruz and even her siblings, but she had to step forward to greet her niece at the very least.

"Still hiding in the shadows, Gabby? My, my . . . how some things never change."

She tensed at the sound of Natalie's voice. It was inevitable, she supposed. Once she'd been spotted, Natalie wasn't going to let her slip away without a reunion.

She had to bite back the response she wanted to say. *You're right. Some things never change. You still manage to make all the old scars throb.*

Fixing a smile to her face, she feigned nonchalance and faced her old nemesis. "And how are you, Natalie?"

"I'm great." She nodded doggedly. "Wonderful. I'm married to Jack Brewster. Remember him? He was a year ahead of us. He's an orthodontist. We live on ten acres and have two kids. My daughter Lily is an amazing gymnast. She'll make cheerleader when she tries out in a few years, for sure."

It was crazy. It was like she had no memory of the past. No memory of the bullying. No conscience at all.

Natalie's grin turned blinding bright and she cocked her head at an angle. "Like mother, like daughter." More laughter. "That's what everyone says."

"Lovely," Gabriella returned, wondering how a simple "how are you" merited a highlights-of-the-last-decade reel. If this was the kind of thing she missed at her high school reunion, she didn't miss anything at all.

"And what about you?" Her gaze flicked down to Gabriella's bare wedding ring finger. "Still not married." She tsked. "Such a shame."

"I've always been career-minded. There's still time for marriage . . . kids."

Natalie wrinkled her nose. "Really? Is there?"

"Time enough," she returned, her gaze flitting out to the cafeteria, searching for any excuse to break free of Natalie. For a reason to pardon herself without looking like a coward running away.

"If you say so." Natalie's skepticism rang ripe in her voice. "Just don't wait too long. You'll be one of those dried-up career women who have to go to a sperm bank when they're forty." She whispered *sperm bank* and the word *forty* like they were something filthy on her tongue.

"I'll keep that in mind."

"Oh! Would you look at that?" Natalie's gaze drifted over Gabriella's shoulder, widening in delighted disgust. "There's your cousin's killer, walking the streets bold as you please."

Gabriella flinched, her gaze landing on Cruz as he entered the cafeteria alongside his two sisters and brother-in-law. His expression was like marble, revealing nothing. Not so much as a flicker of emotion crossed that brutally handsome face. Her lungs constricted, the air freezing inside as she devoured the sight of him.

He really was beautiful to behold. Other than the sheriff, who was hot in his own right, Cruz Walsh stood out in this crowd. He cast every man in the vicinity into shadow. The way his shirt settled against his chest, hugging well-formed pecs . . . the way his strong biceps peeked out from the short sleeves of his shirt. Her mouth went dry looking at him and her face flushed hot. She knew what that meant. All her freckles would be standing out against splotchy skin. Her reaction made her feel sixteen again . . . and she did *not* want to feel like a teenager again. Those had not been good years. She did not wish to relive them. Well, minus the kiss in the boathouse. That had been the one highlight.

With considerable effort, she tore her gaze from Cruz Walsh and looked around the room. Natalie wasn't the only one staring. Several people paused amid conversations, watching him as he made his way across the cafeteria. He had to be aware of it. She wondered what that was like—to have everyone stare at you wherever you went. And not because you were someone famous like Brad Pitt. No, because they thought you were scum who had gotten away with murder.

Why had he stayed in Sweet Hill? He'd been out of prison for at least a year. Why hadn't he moved away where he could start fresh? Well, fresher than here anyway. There might be a few people who would recognize him in Anytown, USA. He had been the subject of national news, after all. But he wouldn't get near the amount of negative attention as he did here. And out in the world at large, people would generally believe in his innocence, unlike here where people only saw the stigma of his last name.

"Cruz Walsh was exonerated," she reminded, her voice a little sharper than she intended.

Natalie rolled her eyes. "Yeah. Sure. But you remember him from high school. Did he ever strike you as innocent? C'mon. No way. That guy has blood on his hands, mark my words. Your poor cousin." She shook her head as though saddened.

Gabriella rolled her eyes. Natalie didn't know her cousin. She was several grades below them in school. Hell, Gabriella hardly knew her cousin. She'd been a pretty, popular girl, and as an only child, she'd been horribly spoiled by her parents.

When she was a teenager, Shelley Rae hardly ever attended family events with her parents. When they did manage to drag her, it was clear it was against her will. She pouted and plopped down in some corner with her nose buried in her phone. Whenever Gabriella tried to talk to her, she only got grunts and one-word answers.

Gabriella probably should just let the subject of Cruz drop, but she couldn't. "He never struck me as a killer."

Even when he was convicted of murdering her cousin, Gabriella had grappled with a sense of wrongness over it all. Deep inside she'd had her doubts, which had made her feel guilty because Shelley Rae was dead. Even though she hadn't been particularly close with her younger cousin, it had crushed the family and she should have been loyal to Shelley Rae. Since all evidence pointed to Cruz—and he had confessed to the crime—she should have felt like everyone else. She should have wanted his head on a pike.

Instead she had wondered if Cruz had somehow been railroaded into confessing.

In her bones, she had felt like it all had to be a mistake.

She'd held her tongue, of course. The last thing she had wanted to do was upset her family more by voicing her unfounded theories. Especially since she couldn't have been sure her theories weren't fed by a long-nurtured crush.

Even in college, that crush had still been there, buried like a festering splinter she couldn't claw out. She'd thought about him in her dorm room late at night, secure in her bed. She'd thought about him every time she kissed another boy.

Remembering him was easy. Forgetting less so.

When the news had hit that he was actually innocent, she'd felt relieved to know her judgment wasn't so totally skewed. She might not have had great luck choosing men, but she hadn't been totally off the mark with Cruz Walsh. He was no murderer. Her first crush and first kiss hadn't been totally ill-bestowed.

Adolescent infatuation or not, he had been innocent.

Cruz Walsh was incapable of murder.

"Don't tell me you believe he didn't do it? He's a Walsh, Gabby. Everyone knows they're trash in this town."

Everyone except the sheriff, she resisted sarcastically pointing out. Her gaze skipped to where he stood across the room, one hand resting possessively on the small of his wife's back. His wife, a former Walsh.

She kept the observation to herself, instead saying with mock innocence, "Weren't you and Cruz Walsh special friends? I'm almost sure that you and he . . ." She let her voice fade suggestively.

Natalie went still. All joviality fled her face and she more resembled the stone-cold bitch from high school that Gabriella remembered. "Well, you heard wrong. I don't know who told you that, but I never associated with trash like Cruz Walsh."

She flinched.

Natalie continued, "The guy is a criminal who deserves to be behind bars."

"They wouldn't have released him if that were true."

Natalie did that annoying tsking sound again. "So naïve. Perhaps that's why you haven't married yet. All the city boys in Austin must play you. Take advantage of a . . ." Her gaze skimmed Gabriella. "Overweight, aging woman with no bank account to speak of if those shoes are any indication." Natalie shook her head as though sympathetic. As though she had not just dealt an insult.

The woman hadn't changed. This conversation was pointless unless she wanted to stick around and let Natalie offend her some more. "Ah, excuse me, I need to check on my grandmother."

Natalie opened her mouth, but Gabriella turned away before she had to hear another word.

She ducked out into the hall, craving a moment to herself. She walked down the empty corridor lined with lockers and inhaled the nostalgia.

She paused in front of Mrs. Mooney's classroom and peered inside the small window beside the door. Same desks arranged in a circle. Yearbook had been her favorite class. She smiled. At least all her memories in this place weren't bitter ones.

She moved on and turned down another corridor until she arrived at her old locker. She brushed a hand over the cold metal door. She stood in front of it like she had countless times and glanced to the right. Exactly nine lockers down, separated by one classroom door, loomed Cruz's old locker. She had spied on him beneath her lashes, acting as though she were searching for something in her locker.

Voices drifted behind her.

She stilled, listening. Damn. It was Natalie's voice. "She went this way. Oh, you have to see her, Meredith. She's the same ol' Flabby Gabby."

The air left her in a rush. She felt as though someone had just punched her in the gut. She shuddered and sucked in a bracing breath. Her mind tracked back. Meredith from high school—one of Natalie's flunkies. Gabriella remembered her well enough and she had no desire to see her again.

Ah, hell. Didn't they have anything better to do than look for her? Children to wrangle? Husbands to torment? Botox to inject?

"I heard she's working at a coffee shop and living with her grandmother," Meredith contributed gleefully. "So much for being salutatorian. Second in our graduating class got her nowhere, didn't it?"

Meredith had been a cheerleader like Natalie. Also like Natalie, she loved to pick on the girls with less. Less friends. Less popularity. *Less*. Period.

Nuh-uh. She wasn't going to let the mean girls from high school have another go at her. She didn't have to endure it anymore.

She took off at a light run, but the hallway was long and she could still hear them. The stretch of corridor seemed longer now than it ever had when she attended school here.

A door suddenly came into view on the right. Finally!

It wasn't a classroom. It was windowless. She tried the handle and it gave easily, the door swinging open. Yes! She plunged inside.

Shutting the door, she collapsed back against it, breathing heavily, her heart beating hard in her chest, less from exertion and more from adrenaline.

She swallowed back a frustrated giggle. It really was absurd. She was running down the halls of her high school from former bullies and ducking into closets like it was some game of hide-and-seek. She should be beyond this.

Their chatter floated closer, carrying through the door. They were still out there, which meant she wasn't going anywhere. She was stuck in—she glanced around to confirm her location—a storage closet. Various equipment occupied the space. Cleaning paraphernalia. A few old projectors. A podium.

She waited for the voices to pass. And then she waited a few minutes longer just to be safe. When they didn't find her, they would probably circle back around. The last thing she needed was to be caught easing out of a storage closet.

Sure enough. Their voices soon returned, drifting past the door.

Then, after a while, nothing. Releasing a breath, she grabbed hold of the door handle and turned it.

Only it wouldn't turn.

She froze a long moment, her heart seizing in her chest. Denial flashed hot through her. The knob wouldn't give in her hand. She shook it and rattled it as her stomach plummeted to her feet.

Oh. God. Oh. God. NO. She was locked in. Stuck in a closet in her old high school. She dropped her forehead to the door. "Please. This isn't happening. Not here."

It took all of thirty seconds for her to debate whether or not she should make some noise to attract attention.

Of course, she should. It was Friday night and she did not relish spending the weekend stuck in this closet. Her mind quickly strained to remember how long a person could survive without water. Would she even make it until Monday when the building opened again? God. She could just imagine that headline. Sweet Hill Alum Found Starved to Death in Closet. Not happening.

Telling herself she would come up with some explanation for whomever opened the door, she started pounding, calling through the barrier, "Hello! I'm locked in! Anyone out there? Can you open the door please?"

She knocked until the side of her fist throbbed. After a few minutes, she took a break and let her forehead drop against the door in defeat.

No one could hear her. No one was out there in the halls. Everyone was either in the auditorium or worse. A cantaloupe-sized lump formed in her throat. Maybe they had all left. Maybe the building was truly empty.

Her family would think she had left. Gabriella and Nana Betty had caught a ride with Tess, after all. They were probably all heading to the restaurant for dinner.

"No," she groaned. Her stomach grumbled. Great. She was hungry, too.

How had this happened to her? Tess had her phone. Damn it all. How could she have let her sister take away her phone? Now she was locked up minus a way to communicate with the outside world. And no food or water.

She slapped her hand weakly a few more times against the door, almost falling forward when the door was wrenched open.

"Oh!" she cried out, catching her balance on a nearby shelf and staggering back several steps in the closet. She looked up. "You!" Her stomach quivered. Suddenly she was wishing she faced Natalie and Meredith again. Bullies would be better than this.

Better than him.

FIVE

"**W**HAT ARE YOU doing in here?" He looked at her with mild curiosity as he stepped inside the closet, clearing the threshold, his big body wedging the door open. "Is someone else in here with you?" He peered around at her surroundings. "Or do you just enjoy closets?"

"No one is in here with me," she said hotly, backing away. What did he think of her? That she snuck off at her niece's school function to make out with a stranger in a closet?

"No?" He angled his head, and then she realized that her answer just made her seem even odder. If she wasn't in here for sexy times, then why was she in here all by herself?

"I was avoiding someone, if you must know."

"Ah." He nodded his head slowly. "A hiding spot."

She flinched, not liking the word *hiding*, however accurate it might be. It had a cowardly connotation to it, and standing this close to Cruz she felt self-conscious enough without appearing weak, too. This was a man who didn't know a thing about weakness. Not after what he went through. There was only strength and endurance within him.

Her gaze flicked over him. The guy had staying power. Her cheeks burned at the double meaning behind that thought.

Not that kind of staying power. Of course, she wouldn't know about that . . . about him. She could only guess. Fantasize.

She shifted her weight beneath his scrutiny, backing up another step and bumping into something that gave way behind her. Then she was falling, gravity sucking her down. "Oh!" Her hands flailed, desperate to grab onto something.

He lunged forward, seizing her arm.

Then fear of falling fled as she watched the door swinging for home behind him.

Noooooo.

It happened in slow motion. He grabbed hold of her just as the slam reverberated in her ears. She heard a prolonged cry and realized it was coming from her as the door slammed shut into place, just inches away from them.

She squirmed free of him and lunged forward. She gripped the knob. Maybe this time it wasn't—

Nope. It was locked again.

Growling, she yanked and pulled and attempted to turn the stupid knob.

"Yeah. Pretty sure that's not going to help."

Turning, she glared at him. "You locked us in," she accused.

"You might have mentioned when I first opened the door that you were locked in here."

She pointed to herself, refusing to accept that logic. She'd been confronted with *him*. Clearly that had rattled her head. "Don't blame this on me!"

He arched a dark eyebrow and crossed his arms over his chest, clearly unimpressed with her. "Okay. I'll just blame the door then."

"Do you have to blame anyone?" she shot back.

Ignoring her, he moved to the door and ran his hands along it. He touched the hinges, assessing.

After a few moments of watching him, she asked hopefully, "Can you get us out of here?"

He looked back at her grimly. His expression was answer enough.

"Well." She crossed her own arms over her chest.

"We'll just have to call for help. Someone will hear us. You heard me," she reminded.

"I don't think there are many people left in the building. I spotted everyone heading to their cars from the second floor. I was heading back to the cafeteria when I heard you through the door."

"Heading back? Where were you?"

He paused a beat. "Just walking the halls."

Walking the halls. More like avoiding the cafeteria like she had been. She made a snort of skepticism. Maybe he had his vulnerabilities, after all.

"What's that?"

"I beg your pardon?"

"That sound you made? You want to say something? Say it."

"I don't know what you mean," she lied.

"Right." Shaking his head, he went back to studying the door. Dragging his hands through his hair, he cursed. "Fuck. Didn't imagine I'd ever be stuck in a box again." He looked back at her in disgust. "With a relative of Shelley Rae Kramer."

Of course. That's the only way he saw her. Shelley Rae's cousin. A random girl who sat behind him in high school. He didn't know her as a friend or classmate.

Sighing, she pushed past him. "Excuse me. I

have to try at least." That said, she started pounding on the door. "Helloooo! Can anyone hear me? I'm locked in the closet." *With a guy that radiates heat and has no concept of personal space.*

She didn't know how long she pounded. Until she couldn't feel her hand anymore. Until he moved off somewhere out of her vision, where she couldn't feel the heat of him quite so much. That was some relief, at least.

Tired, she stopped beating the door and turned to face him.

"Done?"

"Don't you have a phone?" she snapped.

"Don't *you*?" he returned.

She nodded. "Of course. My sister has it. What about you?" She looked him over as though she could glimpse a phone on his person.

"I don't have one."

She blinked and stared. "What do you mean you don't *have* one?" As in *at all*? No way.

"I. Don't. Own. A. Phone."

Who doesn't own a phone? She inhaled sharply through her nose. "Why?"

He shrugged impatiently. "I've gone without one for this long—"

"Because you were in prison," she snapped

as though that would help the point sink in. "You went without a phone because you were in prison."

"I know where I was," he bit out. "Don't need reminding of it."

His eyes were cold as he glared at her, and she realized that was worse.

Worse than when he'd simply looked *through* her all those years ago.

Worse than when he was all heat and passion and intensity in the boathouse.

Coldness from him was worse than any unkindness she'd ever been dealt from others. God, she'd always wanted him to look at her. Notice her. She just hadn't anticipated he would look at her with . . . dislike.

"Of course. Sorry." She leaned back against a shelf. Several inches separated them, their shoulders parallel to each other. No more staring face-to-face and that was probably for the best. She'd annoyed him. "I don't guess you'd forget that."

"No, I wouldn't."

"Phones have really . . . advanced since you went away," she offered.

"Really?" Sarcasm edged his voice. "I hadn't noticed how everyone has one glued to their hand every hour of the day."

"And you still don't want one?"

He sighed. "Seven years I was locked up, inaccessible to people. Kind of used to it. I don't need to be in constant touch with anyone."

Several moments passed, the silence throbbing between them. "What are we going to do?" She glanced up at the window set high in the wall. It was rectangular in shape, not very large.

"You won't fit through there," he said, following her gaze.

She flinched, all the old reflexes kicking in. Immediately, she felt like he was making a crack against her size, although she shouldn't take it so personally. A ten-year-old wouldn't fit through that window.

"I know that. Just looking at the light. It's going to be dark soon."

Then she would be trapped in here.

In the dark.

With him.

Her breathing hitched. He must have noticed because he asked, "You okay?"

"What? Me? F-fine. Yes."

"You're not afraid of the dark, are you?"

She heard the wariness in his voice . . . as though he was worried she was going to have a panic attack. "No."

"So is it the prospect of staying locked up all night with me then? That would make a lot of women nervous in this town."

"No. I'm not nervous about that," she lied, not bothering to point out that she was not like most women in this town.

"I get it. I'm Cruz Walsh. You're Shelley Rae's cousin. Seems pretty obvious you'd be nervous."

"Why should that make me nervous?" She laughed lightly and damn if the sound didn't ring nervously even to her ears.

It actually didn't bother her. Sure, she couldn't bring him home for Sunday dinner, but there was no chance of that happening anyway. He would never want to go to dinner with her. She had never been his type. And that was okay. *He* wasn't her type either. She was an adult now. She'd moved well past crushing on the town bad boy.

"C'mon." He looked at her with ill-concealed annoyance. "You don't need me to spell it out. Your family wanted my head on a platter since the day I was arrested." He shrugged. "I didn't blame them. They needed someone to blame."

"Yeah," she agreed, recalling that time in her life. It had been ugly. She had been away at the time, out of college and working in Fort Worth, but she'd still felt it—felt her family combusting from afar. She'd come home for the funeral. It was every bit as awful as a funeral for an eighteen-year-old girl could be.

She'd steered clear of the trial. All of her family had attended. She stayed in Fort Worth. She didn't need to be there, too. She couldn't have sat in a courtroom as Cruz was sentenced.

"But you're not responsible for what happened to Shelley Rae," she added.

"Doesn't matter. I'll never be good with them." He shrugged like it didn't faze him.

She wanted to tell him he was wrong, but that wouldn't be true. He was forever tainted in her family's eyes and there was no changing that. *She* wouldn't change that.

"Do you want to be? Good with them?" she clarified, turning her head to stare at him, curious for his answer.

Curiosity was ingrained in her nature. She wanted to know everyone's story and the more interesting the person, the more she wanted to know. That's why she became a reporter. In the back of her mind, she heard Cody's voice: *You're not writing for your high school paper anymore, Gabs. You're supposed to be a real reporter. So prove it. Prove you're good enough for this paper.*

Her chest squeezed uncomfortably. Easier said

than done when she had history with the subject. Also, Cruz didn't know she was a reporter. She should probably disclose that. It was the ethical thing to do.

Except she was *not* doing a story on Cruz Walsh, so she didn't need to confess anything to him.

Great. She was playing the justification game now.

"I guess I should say I care, but if I cared what others thought of me . . ." His voice faded and he finished with a shrug. "Well, my life would have turned out a lot differently."

"Why are you still here?" God. She couldn't help herself. She told herself she wasn't digging for a story. She wasn't peeling back the layers on Cruz Walsh. He had simply always fascinated her.

He glanced around the closet, his big shoulders flexing under his shirt in a way she just didn't get to see these days. At least not on any of the men in her orbit. Cody had been slim. She'd always felt self-conscious about that. As though she might crush him with her weight.

She'd never crush Cruz. He was big and strong. She almost felt small beside him. Good thing the light was fading fast in the closet. He wouldn't be visible for much longer and then her senses wouldn't be so overloaded with him.

"Uh. We're trapped," he replied.

"No. *Here.* In Sweet Hill." She was pretty sure he knew what she meant. He was simply deflecting. He didn't want to talk about himself. She knew that much already since he'd turned down countless interviews. "You could have started over anywhere else."

"I don't remember you being so chatty."

She tilted her head to the side. "I thought you didn't remember me very well." When she ran into him in the hall earlier it had taken him a while to even place her in his memory. He had to ask to clarify her name.

"I don't," he said gruffly. "Only a little."

"I talk more now," she acknowledged after a few moments, trying not to let it bother her that he could barely remember her. It was kind of hard to be a reporter and not talk to people. "People change," she added.

He studied her then, his hard-eyed gaze inscrutable. Finally, he answered, "My family is here. And it's the only home I've ever known. Changing towns won't change anything that happened. It won't change me."

She sucked in a breath. Wasn't that what she had always thought? Always hoped. Changing towns. Moving far away. She'd thought it would change her. *Save* her. Keep her from being Flabby Gabby.

She stifled a pained laugh. And yet today she had been called that *again*. Twelve years later and she felt like she was in high school again.

Suddenly the similarities between the night in the boathouse and this one struck her hard. Her head whipped around in the darkening space. Here they were again. Alone in the dark. Soon-to-be dark anyway. Sure. They'd both done a lot of living in that time, but right now she felt as young and vulnerable as she did then.

Except this time there would be no escaping out the door. She was trapped with him. The reminder spiked dread deep inside her. She'd be stuck here for days. *Days.*

She advanced on the door with renewed zeal and resumed pounding on it. "Anyone out there? Hello! I'm locked in here."

"I think they're all gone," he said after several moments, his voice calm. Too calm. As though he feared he was dealing with someone unhinged.

She turned back around and slumped against the door. "How long until starvation sets in?"

"We won't starve." Exasperation tinged his voice.

"What about water? There's nothing to drink in here."

"It won't be pleasant in here . . . *together*." At that word, he sounded truly aggrieved. He didn't want to be in here with her any more than she wanted to be locked in here with him, and that was a mortifying reminder. After all, he hardly knew her. She was just a girl he went to high school with. A nobody. "But we should be fine until Monday."

She couldn't help wondering if he would be annoyed if he had gotten stuck in here with Natalie. Probably not. They'd probably pick right back up where they left off and resume their old habits. *Once a fuck-buddy . . .*

Natalie had been lying through her teeth. She totally remembered hooking up with Cruz, and Gabriella didn't doubt she would hook up with him again given the chance. She'd never had a problem going behind her boyfriends' backs before. Gabriella doubted she'd suddenly developed any scruples in that regard.

She closed her eyes for several long moments, marveling at how she could be in this situation. This morning she'd cleaned Nana Betty's house, worked a shift at The Daily Grind and then headed to her niece's ceremony expecting to end her night at Applebee's with her sister scrutinizing her dinner choice. Any time she ordered anything other than a salad, Tess lifted an eyebrow and said something snarky.

Instead, she was trapped in an eight-by-ten space.

When she opened her eyes again it was darker. The light spilling through the small window was a deep indigo blue now, only slightly lighter than the air in the closet.

His face was cast in deep shadow, reminding her again of the night in the boathouse. "We should try to make ourselves comfortable," he suggested.

She nodded jerkily. "Right. No sense standing all night."

"Let's see what we can find." He started examining shelves.

She followed suit, moving around a podium and digging through a box. "Here's a drop cloth. It should offer some comfort from the hard floor."

She dropped the cloth under the window, spreading it on the floor as he continued rummaging around.

She lowered herself to the floor. "So. How are you enjoying your newfound freedom?" She winced. If that didn't sound lame. Like she was her mother asking the neighbor how she was enjoying the new azaleas she planted in her garden.

Or even worse. It sounded like she was leading up to an interview. Cody would be proud. She could almost hear his voice in her ear, telling her to seize this opportunity. *Be a reporter. Don't let this chance to interview the elusive Cruz Walsh go to waste.*

"Oh. Is this where we do small talk?" he asked from across the space, moving a ladder and setting it aside so he could better explore the shelves behind it.

"It's something to do. We have the entire weekend, after all."

He groaned softly. "Don't remind me."

That stung. Something told her he'd rather be locked up alone than with her.

She stretched her legs out in front of her and leaned back against the wall, trying to act like she didn't care. She stared at the dark shape of him. "Conversation will help pass the time."

He sighed, but offered no comment. Okay then. So he was going to ignore her.

"Fine." He surprised her by agreeing. "We can talk. Yes. I'm enjoying my newfound freedom. A lot. Your turn. Who were you avoiding in this closet?"

She released a puff of indignant breath. "You call that an answer? Hardly satisfying."

"If you want more than that you're going to have to tell me who you're hiding from in this closet."

Sigh. "Natalie Markson."

He was quiet for a moment. "Short cheerleader?"

Of course, he remembered her—and her cheer-leader status.

"That's her." The girl he had thought he was kissing in the boathouse.

"Yeah . . . she was—"

"A bitch?" she supplied. She couldn't help it. The girl had just called her overweight—*to her face*.

He laughed softly and she realized it was the first time she had ever heard the sound of laughter come out of him. "Yeah, something like that."

"What about you? Why were you walking the halls? Running from someone, too?"

"I don't do crowds." All levity left his voice.

"Why'd you come then?"

"For my sister."

"Same here. I came with my entire family for Dakota." She shook her head. "And I didn't even get to congratulate her."

"Your entire family was here? And you don't think anyone will notice you missing?"

"I drove with my sister. And there were so many of us here, all in multiple cars. Tess probably thought I went with someone else."

"Or they'll have the police out looking for you."

"Doubtful. But what about you? No one wondering at your whereabouts?"

"No. My sister knows I'm not a fan of crowds.

I saw Malia get her award. She probably assumed I slipped out."

He fell quiet then. It was fully dark now. There was just the general outline of him. She couldn't hear him rustling around within the closet anymore. It should have made her feel better. She didn't have to stare at his face or body any longer. Except now she had that deep, disembodied voice that traveled over her skin like a velvet hand.

She moistened her lips. "Are you going to stand all night?" She patted the drop cloth. "You can sit."

Was she actually coaxing Cruz Walsh to sit down beside her? It was like something out of one of her dorm room fantasies.

His shoes scraped over the floor as he approached and lowered down beside her. Not that close, really. No part of his body touched hers.

She folded her hands in her lap and stared straight ahead into the opaque air. The building was quiet. Empty. Just the hum of the air-conditioning and the two of them. Not another soul in the school. "You think we'll be okay?"

"Yeah. It won't be that comfortable . . . or fun. We'll have to figure out bathroom arrangements in the morning . . . or sooner."

"Oh." That was going to suck. She hadn't even thought about that.

"I noticed a bucket earlier."

A *bucket*! God. Peeing in a bucket in front of Cruz Walsh definitely wasn't part of any previous fantasy. Maybe that's what she needed. A dose of reality with this guy. He wasn't into her. He was the *opposite* of into her. He barely remembered her and she annoyed him. Why not top it off by doing her business in a bucket five feet from him and making sure she killed any chance of him seeing her as a woman?

"There are worse things," he said.

Worse things than being locked up for a weekend with her? Or worse things than peeing in a bucket? "I'm not sure about that."

"I'm sure," he said dryly, and she suddenly felt foolish. Of course he would think that and now he thought she was a naïve, over-privileged diva.

He'd been in prison. Prison was worse. He was saying that being stuck with her was better than prison.

She winced. Well. That was heartening.

She let her head fall back on the wall and closed her eyes again. She doubted she would fall asleep, but it would be nice. Nice to close her eyes and wake up Monday morning free of this nightmare.

"So what do you do?" The question came

abruptly. It was grudgingly asked. She knew he didn't really want to know what she did for a living. He didn't care. He didn't want to talk, but they were here, stuck, no relief in sight. It was as though he surrendered to the inevitability of small talk. She could almost hear his internal *fuck it*.

"What do I do?" she repeated . . . more for herself. What was she willing to admit to him?

"Yeah. Since high school. Obviously you know what I've been up to. What about you?"

She didn't want to lie. She blew out a breath, aware that the truth probably wouldn't go down well. Not with him. Not considering that he had ignored all interview requests. He wouldn't be happy about being trapped with a reporter.

She knew through Cody that all the major media outlets had offered him a pretty penny. Like more than she could ever earn in a year. More than the *Daily Reporter* could ever pay him. And he had walked away from the offers. Money wasn't a temptation for him. It should have surprised her about him, but it didn't.

"When I first got out of college I went to work for a paper in Fort Worth. A few years after that, I got a job at a paper in Austin. I've been living there ever since. I just came back to Sweet Hill a few weeks ago to help Nana after her knee surgery."

He tensed as expected. The air grew thicker. "You're a *reporter*?"

The way he said *reporter* . . . it was as though she'd just admitted to being a terrorist.

She nodded. "I'm a journalist, yes."

"Fucking vultures," he ground out.

She bristled. "Well. That's *nice*." She smoothed her hands down her thighs. She was accustomed to criticism. Years of bullying conditioned her for that, but for the most part her choice of career had been deemed acceptable if not impressive.

She had been the smart one. Her parents even called her that. At home she was the *smart one*. At school, Flabby Gabby.

She knocked it out of the park on her ACTs and SATs and got a full ride to Vanderbilt—and that's what she had wanted. To go *anywhere* that wasn't Sweet Hill. As far as Mom and Dad were concerned, she was robbed and should have been valedictorian. Their other two kids had good looks and charisma going for them. Gabriella had the brains. The expectation was always that she would have a lucrative career, but both her siblings outearned her. Her family expected better from her, but they weren't too disappointed. Mostly because Mom had been a huge fan of the show *Murphy Brown*, so there was that.

Friction crackled in the air between them. "Rather judgmental of you," she added.

"You're calling *me* judgmental?" He let loose a single bark of laughter. "That's funny considering all my life I've been judged and condemned. And you know who often led the charge?"

She arched an eyebrow. "Reporters?"

"You said it, sweetheart."

"And why do you feel like you've been wrongly judged? When did it start, Cruz?"

He was silent for a beat before bursting out with: "Are you fucking interviewing me right now?" Rage shook his voice.

"Um . . ." She winced. "Maybe." And that's when she faced the truth. She *wanted* to interview him. Somehow her opinion had changed since running into him in the hall. She wanted his story. She would tell it the right way. Maybe it was arrogant of her to think so, but who better to write the story of Cruz Walsh than someone who had been close to all the drama? No other journalist could claim that.

She wouldn't dick him over and twist his words or take them out of context, or spin an angle that would leave him blindsided. She'd get it right. She just had to convince him of that.

His weight rustled. "Incredible. Well. Good to

know. In the future, I'll keep my mouth shut around you."

"Oh, come on. Don't be like that. I promise to be nice. It won't hurt at all," she coaxed, reaching out to nudge his arm and her hand landed on his warm chest instead. *God*. The cotton of his shirt was so soft. She instantly wanted to nuzzle her face there and cuddle up against him. Her mouth dried. *Bad Gabriella*.

She started to pull her hand away but he caught it, holding it against him. His grip was strong and firm. No sweating palms on him. She usually ended up with guys with sweating palms.

The thud of his heartbeat filled her palm. Her heart constricted, the air trapped in her chest. Stuck in here with him and her overactive libido couldn't be good for her.

"You look at me and you see a story," he accused softly.

If he were only that to her, life would be so much simpler.

She saw more than that. She saw a guy she'd like to devour. She gulped down a breath. *Bad, bad Gabriella. Get it together.* She needed to quit thinking of him as her old crush . . . as her first kiss.

She should look at him and see just a story. She should have that focus and professionalism and . . .

Who was she kidding? With him, she had none of that.

"I'm not giving you an interview," he added, his voice hard with finality.

"Why did you do it?" she whispered. She couldn't help herself. She'd always wanted to know . . . wanted to understand what was in his head all those years ago. "Why did you confess to a crime you didn't commit?" That part had never come to light. Oh, she was certain the police knew. It had to be material to his release and to the subsequent arrest of Shelley Rae's true killer. Whatever the reason, it had been kept under wraps from the public.

"I'm not going to talk about anything relating to your cousin or my time in prison or my release . . . so you can just put your conniving little mind to rest."

"Conniving?"

"You're a journalist. Conniving seems about right."

They fell into silence for a while. There was only the hum of the AC. At least the air hadn't been shut off for the weekend. It would get sweltering in this closet.

"I never thought you did it," she volunteered.

"Really?" He sounded skeptical. "Well, you certainly were in the minor—" He stopped abruptly.

"Is that how you felt? That everyone believed your confession? What about your family? They couldn't have—"

"Enough," he bit out. "If you can't stop talking about things I don't want to discuss, then we won't talk at all."

Well, that was that.

Did she think she possessed some magic touch and that she could get him to open up? She had pushed too hard. He had shut down completely. She was no one to him. A girl he couldn't even remember from high school. She was no one to him then and no one to him now. That wouldn't change.

SIX

*H*E LIED.

He remembered her. Fully. Totally. He'd let her think he had only a dim recollection of her, but Gabriella Rossi had been the star of more than one wet dream in his adolescence. Even after his adolescence. He'd inserted her face into more than one late-night fantasy while he was in prison. The nights had been long and lonely, and she had ended up there, in his head, just as she often had when he was a kid.

The thing was . . . he'd been achingly aware of her since ninth grade. When freshman year dawned and Gabriella walked into his health class, he'd sat up straighter in his chair, immediately recognizing that she had changed over the summer. All her baby fat had shifted and settled into all the right places as far as he was concerned. Places he wanted to touch and explore.

From that day on, he'd developed a kind of radar for Gabriella Rossi. The moment she drifted into his sphere, it was as though some kind of pheromone was released into the air and he became instantly hard. It was embarrassing, really. He always had to make sure he got to class before her. Seated at his desk, he could appreciate her arrival without any humiliating incidents. In other words, no one had to know he was sporting wood.

He had been equal opportunity back then when it came to girls. Meaning he liked all kinds. Short, tall. Blonde, dark. Bad girls. Good girls. Good girls especially. They liked to slum it with him. They'd go behind their parents' and boyfriends' backs for a taste of the forbidden. Such fucking clichés, but he was there, ready and willing to play their games.

Except Gabriella Rossi. She was *not* his type. She didn't fit the mold of any girl he fooled around with. No. In fact, she was the kind of girl he deliberately *never* fucked. She wasn't just a good girl. She was smart. Too smart for him, and he credited himself with having a fair amount of common sense. Street smarts, his mom insisted. He always managed to stay out of trouble. Well, until he went to prison, of course. But that had been his decision. Strange enough, but true.

His mom had always called him lucky. He never got busted like the rest of the men in his family—not even like Mom. She couldn't seem to stay out of trouble. Of course, that had a lot to do with the drugs and alcohol. He never put any of that shit in his body. No drugs and he rarely drank. Not after watching the way it destroyed Mom.

Still, he didn't come close to being as smart as Gabriella. She was in a league of her own in that department. She actually cared about what teachers were saying. She'd push her glasses up on her nose and listen with singular focus, asking questions that didn't occur to anyone else. She cared about the news. The environment. She would never give two shits about him.

And she didn't *do* guys. He watched for that with dread, figuring someday he'd see her on some prick's arm. Some loafer-wearing guy who went to the country club with his parents after church every Sunday. Surprisingly, that day never came.

She never went to parties either, but he always looked for her there anyway.

No, his study of her was limited to school. He would watch her like a hawk in whatever class they shared or in the halls. He studied all her soft curves like there was going to be a test. She had a nice, round ass. Big tits. And hips that stretched her jeans tight. He remembered thinking how he wanted to sink into all that softness. How she would take him, fit him and cushion him. Her softness to his hardness.

She chronically wore her baggy T-shirts and sweatshirts like armor, but he saw through that camouflage. When she stood up from her desk, leaning forward to hand in her homework to the kid in the desk in front of her, her shirt would ride up to her waistband and he'd get a view of that ass spread out in front of him like a feast.

His dick would turn rock hard, blood rushing between his legs. He'd have to adjust himself and lower a notebook down there to cover himself. Even sitting down, it would still be obvious for anyone who looked his way that a boner tented his jeans. Sure. He was a teenager back then. A stiff wind could give him a boner, but it was her. Rossi with her nonstop ass and mouthwatering rack.

Of course, he never spoke to her. She wasn't like other girls. She wouldn't even look him in the eyes. So he kept it to himself. He kept his hard cock and dirty thoughts to himself. To this day, no one knew he'd ever had a crush on the smartest girl at Sweet Hill.

But here he was. Gabriella Rossi was asleep,

draped against him with an ass and tits even sweeter than he remembered. For multiple days. He closed his eyes in misery.

How was he going to keep his hard cock to himself? And did he even want to? They weren't kids anymore. He was done pretending. This was who he was.

He gulped down a breath and tried to hold still. With her so close it was damn near impossible. His nightmares weren't as bad as this, and that was saying something since most of his nightmares consisted of him back in prison, stuck in his old cell. Or out on the yard, being surrounded by a group of guys who decided they wanted to get a workout by kicking his ass.

He took careful sips of air, trying not to think about the fact that he was in an enclosed space. Ever since he got out of prison, he avoided tight spaces. For seven years he had lived in a cell. In a box. Sure. He got outside every day . . . exposed to the brutal West Texas heat of the yard. Still, it had felt good to taste the sun on his skin.

But every night the door clanged shut and he was back in his cage. He could still hear the slam of loud steel reverberating in his head. He only had to close his eyes and he was back in there again.

He'd lived like that for so long, so this shouldn't

be such a struggle. How could he develop claustrophobia now? All this time later? Now that he was free? It was a weakness and he didn't do weaknesses. He had never been able to afford vulnerabilities, and yet somehow he had acquired this one.

The weight of Gabriella Rossi's head flopped onto his shoulder. She was passed out, dead to the world . . . and apparently she had decided to make a pillow out of him.

He turned, but couldn't make out her features in the dark. Of course, he remembered what she looked like. He'd gotten his fill of her face during their encounter in the hall and before it got so dark in this little closet.

She had a nice mouth. Wide and full. Plump. The kind of mouth that didn't need lipstick because it was already a dusky pink. Sitting here in the dark, with her body pressed against him, an image flashed through his mind. An image of Gabriella Rossi putting her mouth on him. Her tongue licking his head and—

Fuck. This wasn't the place to fantasize about her, but the image intensified until his breathing grew harsh. He envisioned himself doing wicked, dirty things to her. *With* her.

Things he would be more than glad to teach her if she didn't already know.

Fuck. This wasn't him. Corrupting nice women wasn't his game. A fine moral woman like her might not like to do the kinds of things he was envisioning, but that excited him even more. He could teach her to like it. Open her eyes to the delight of dirty sex. Train that mouth in the finer points of proper cock sucking.

Suddenly he felt too hot. The weight of her radiated heat against him. He gently pushed at her shoulder, hoping to dislodge her from him. She muttered in her sleep and only turned to snuggle deeper against him like he was some damn teddy bear. She burrowed in closer, her breath fanning hotly on his neck.

One of her legs curled up on his thigh, her knee brushing his cock. A hissed breath escaped him. Okay. Maybe he needed that. A knee in contact with his dick was one way to cool his ardor. His hand flew to protect himself while he shoved her leg off him.

He'd taken a hit in the junk before, but not by an unconscious woman. This unconscious woman, however, clung like a monkey. He'd have to wake her up fully if he wanted to disentangle her, and he really didn't want to do that. He didn't want to endure all her talking again. The woman talked nonstop . . . and she was a fucking reporter. Hell. Nothing he said was safe around her.

He let loose a sigh. He should try to sleep. He slouched a little lower against the wall and closed his eyes with resolve.

His movements, however, disrupted her.

With a soft little mewl, she stirred again, reset-tling herself even heavier against him, one hand looping around his arm like he was a lifeline.

He was pinned.

She was draped fully over him, her head shoved directly under his chin. Soft tits pressed into his chest. They were a nice size. More than a handful and his hands weren't small.

Damn it. What was he doing noticing her tits?

Being a man with a functioning libido. Those breasts would require two hands to cup. Of course he was going to notice them. He'd always noticed them.

At the image of tits overflowing in his hands, he went hard, the blood rushing to his dick.

This time the air hissing out from his teeth had nothing to do with pain. Or it did, but rather pain of a different sort. The pain of self-denial.

He needed to get his lust under control. He was going to be stuck with her for another forty-eight-plus hours and he didn't need to walk around with a full erection the whole time. Yeah. That wouldn't terrify her or anything.

He might have been in prison for seven years,

but he didn't walk around with a perpetual hard-on. He wasn't some randy kid anymore. He had better self-control.

Sure. He'd gotten laid a few times since he'd gotten out. He was a man, after all—and he'd been locked up a long time. But it was uncomplicated sex. No strings attached. It worked for him. He didn't need anything else.

A fresh-faced freckled good girl like Gabriella Rossi who said whatever popped into her head was not for him. She came with strings attached. Sex with her would be complicated as hell.

She started snoring then, jarring him from his thoughts.

Un-fucking-believable.

At least she wasn't loud. He remembered his old man's snore. He'd sounded like a freight train. Especially after one of his benders.

Her soft, slow snoring reminded him of when Malia was a toddler. Innocent and sweet. He snorted. Not descriptors he would apply to Gabriella Rossi. Their interaction tonight had been illuminating. She was the same and yet different. She asked way too many questions. Which was annoying as hell to a non-talker like him.

But he could endure it. He'd have to.

They were stuck with each other until Monday.

SEVEN

SHE WOKE WITH a start, disorientated in the darkness. Her bedroom was never this dark. Nana Betty kept her outside front porch lights on all night. She claimed it scared away the raccoons. Even with the house blinds drawn, a modicum of light crept into Gabriella's bedroom and saved her from total darkness.

Her hands groped at her sides, gripping fistfuls of fabric. It was somewhat scratchy and not entirely comfortable. Definitely not her sheets or her down comforter.

Her head, however, was cushioned against a much softer material. She released her grip on the rougher fabric and stroked the softer stuff beneath her with a contented sigh. She snuggled closer, her fingers smoothing over the soft cotton, splaying wide. She noted that something was firm and unyielding under the material. She inhaled, turning her nose into the fabric. It smelled good. Clean. Like laundry sheets. And there was something more underlying that aroma. Something without a name. *Masculinity.* A faint whiff of deodorant.

A body. God. She was draped over a body. She inhaled sharply. She definitely wasn't in her bed.

She frowned and assessed a bit more, her fingers gently drumming, as though she were playing an instrument.

A man's very built body.

Cruz's body.

This was a familiar dream.

Except it was no dream. This wasn't the boat-house and she wasn't eighteen. She was thirty and boring and stuck in a closet with Cruz. Where nothing would happen between them despite her overactive imagination.

She registered that and yet her hand was still moving, touching him, roaming over his chest in appreciation. She couldn't seem to stop herself. He didn't so much as stir.

It was wrong, she knew it. She should not be *petting* him in his sleep.

She propped herself up on one elbow and looked down at him, her vision acclimating to the gloom.

They may have started out leaning against the

wall, but they ended up on the floor, spread out like they were in a king-sized bed, the drop cloth rumpled under them.

Her hand rested directly over his heart. It thudded strong and even.

Giddy flutters erupted in her belly. She was touching Cruz. Not dreaming it. Not remembering. Actually doing.

She. Was. Touching. Cruz.

Her hand continued its exploration, drifting up his neck to his cheek. She remembered touching that cheek. The scrape of his beard tickled her palm.

She touched him but still he slept on like Sleeping Beauty. She forced down a snort of derision. She knew it was a silly comparison. This big burly scarred-up guy straight out of prison was no fairy-tale princess. He wouldn't appreciate the comparison . . . and he was not waiting for any kiss either. Especially from her.

Still, she hovered over him.

Sitting up on her knees, she leaned closer. It was a powerful sensation, floating above him, looking down at his bigger body spread beneath her, splayed like some kind of sacrificial offering.

His breathing was a light, slow rasp. Soft as a moth's wings. Her fingertips brushed his mouth before she returned to her senses.

She snatched her hand away from him and rubbed her fingertips together, still feeling his lips there, on her skin. Years might have passed but his mouth was as soft as she remembered. Her hand drifted to her lips as though she could transfer the sensation of his lips to her own in that way.

A flash of guilt washed over her. She shouldn't be doing this. It couldn't be good. She didn't need to be getting any ideas. She might long to dive into him like he was a vat of chocolate, but she couldn't. She had more restraint than that.

A deep, masculine chuckle welled up on the air beneath her. "How long have you been wanting to do that?"

She dropped her hand from her lips. "What? You're awake!" Heat slapped her cheeks. "How long have you been awake?"

"Since you woke up."

Her mouth worked to get words out, her outrage a dangerous fire in her belly. All that time he was awake? When she was rubbing her hands over him? What must he think of her? "You've been awake that long?"

"Hard to sleep when someone's hands are running all over my body."

Oh. God. She was going to be sick. She had to get away from him. She scurried back, pushing off the ground with her hands and rising to her feet. "I did not—"

"Come on. You don't have to lie." He rose to his feet, his movements unhurried, leisurely even.

She wished he had stayed on the ground. Now he loomed over her. She was forced to glare up at him. "You should have let me know you were awake!"

"And interrupt your exploration of my body? But I was so interested to see what you would do next."

"I wasn't exploring your body!"

One corner of his mouth twitched, and that was when she noticed that the darkness was fading into dawn. The air wasn't quite so dense now. She could make out his features in the smoky blue, and she could see well enough to detect his amusement.

"No? What would you call it?"

Her mind leapt feverishly to an explanation. "I just woke up. It was dark. I was merely checking for . . . signs of life." Yes, those words just came out of her mouth.

"You thought I might be dead?" He was definitely amused . . . and she was definitely embarrassed. "That's a good one."

She shrugged defensively. "You never know."

"So you've heard of a lot of men my age who die in their sleep?"

"It happens." Okay, maybe it wasn't the best explanation. He was a thirty-year-old man in the prime of his life. A perfect male specimen, as her hands had been compelled to verify.

"You're being ridiculous. What's wrong? Too embarrassed to admit you were copping a feel while I was asleep?"

"I was not!" Okay. Maybe she was doing that . . . and hearing him say it in those terms only made her feel all the more embarrassed.

"How long have you been wanting to kiss me?" he asked mildly, sounding almost bored.

Oh! Shaking her head, she made a sound of disgust. "Arrogant, much?"

It was tempting to fling the truth at him—the truth that they had *already* kissed. It would feel good to catch him off guard and watch him absorb that fact.

She couldn't do it, of course. After the satisfaction of shocking him wore off, she'd be left with the awkwardness of him knowing she was the idiot who had kissed him in the boathouse while he thought she was someone else.

"You were stroking my lips," he reminded.

"I was checking to see if you were breathing."

He ignored her absurd defense and continued, "Is it something you've always thought about?

Left over from high school? Or is it something you felt like doing all of a sudden? Thought you might like a taste of the bad boy who's been in prison? Something you can tell the girls about in your book club?"

"Oh! You . . . j-jerk!" She shoved him hard in the chest and charged past him as though she had somewhere to go. Like there was anywhere to go. Like she could escape him.

He snatched hold of her arm and whirled her around, sending her colliding into his chest.

"Oh!" Her hands came up to his chest, palms flattening on the very body she had only moments ago felt at her leisure. Now it felt different. Now he was awake. Alert . . . his eyes as sharp as a hawk's gaze on her. Now his heart pounded swift and hard beneath her touch.

She lifted her gaze to his even as she felt her outrage ebb into something else. Something visceral. Something that throbbed deep in the half-dark between them.

He cradled her there, against him, one arm slipping around her waist to keep her close. "Might as well do it," he replied, his voice a low rumble between them.

She gulped. "It?"

He nodded once, the motion curt. "Since you're

so curious, why not?" His face inched closer. "We're stuck in here, after all. It would give us something to do."

Something to do? Well, wasn't that flattering?

She sucked in an indignant gust of air. "I don't—"

His mouth smothered the rest of her words. She blew out a startled breath and he took that inside himself, drinking in her air, his tongue sweeping inside her mouth.

She didn't react. She was too stunned.

He crouched in one quick motion, wrapping an arm around her waist and lifting her off her feet so that their fused mouths were level.

He coaxed and nibbled at her lips. It worked. She couldn't resist.

She could never resist him. Not in her dreams. Not in reality.

Apparently not ever.

She would worry about the implications of that later. For now, she wrapped an arm around his shoulders, hanging on to him like he was the only thing keeping her from flying away.

She opened her mouth to him and he deepened the kiss. This wasn't just a kiss. It was more than that. This was sex with lips. He ravished her mouth. Kissed her with lips and tongue and faintly scraping teeth.

Their bodies were moving. He guided them. He had that ease about him. Even as her world flew off its axis, he was in control.

She didn't open her eyes to look where they were going in the small space. She put her trust in him . . . surrendering, reveling in his tongue in her mouth, in the strong fingers diving into her hair.

He backed them against a wall, the edges of shelves digging into her body, but that small discomfort didn't make her want to stop. No. The kiss went on and on. It was dizzying. Her hands fluttered all around them, unsure where to touch, where to land.

He paused every now and then to look down at her. It was disconcerting . . . the way he would look at her—peering at her in the steadily increasing light with his dark, fathomless eyes. As though he wasn't certain of her. As though she was some puzzle with pieces missing.

At one point, she demanded in a hushed voice, "What? What is it?" Why was he looking at her that way?

He gave a small, distracted shake of his head and reclaimed her lips in a searing kiss. His mouth was hot and aggressive. She had never been kissed so fiercely. Not even before by him. Oh, that kiss had been thorough. She had felt it everywhere, in every nerve ending all the way to her toes. But this? Cruz all grown up—Cruz the *man*—was more than she had ever imagined.

"Is this what you wanted?" He pushed his hips against her and she moaned, shifting slightly so that the juncture of her thighs lined up more accurately with his. Yeah. The man was more aggressive. He was more . . . *more.*

The rasp of his voice continued: "Admit it. You weren't checking for signs of life."

Was he still referring to that stupid story she made up? "Shut up," she snapped and tugged his mouth back to hers, ready for his seeking tongue.

God. It had been too long. Forever, really, since it had been like this. Since it felt like this. Since she ached for it.

Since never.

Or at least since him.

Somehow they ended up on the ground, tangled up in the drop cloth. It was a nuisance. Her shoe caught in the fabric, preventing her from sliding her knee between his thighs where it wanted to go. She tried to kick her foot free and it somehow only made it worse, catching and bending her knee at an odd angle. "Argh!" Great. Other women did this thing all the time without pulling a muscle or straining themselves. She was hopeless. Desperate for him, but hopeless.

He broke away for a second and bent down to free her with a quick yank of the drop cloth.

"Oh," she breathed. "Thank y—" He cut her off, coming back up and seizing her lips again as though they were the answer to life. She'd never felt that way. No man ever made her feel that way. With other guys, there had always been that sense that she was dispensable. They could take a good baseball game, a hotter girl, or a juicy cheeseburger over her.

She touched his face and that action struck a familiar chord. That time in the boathouse when she had held his face while they kissed. As she did then, she slid both hands along his cheeks, cupping his face, reveling in the sensation of his skin, the bristly scratch of his incoming beard against her palms.

His lips slowed until they went motionless against hers. He pulled back and looked down at her in that strange, impossible-to-read way again.

The air around them thickened and stilled. Tiny dust motes hung suspended in beams of light trickling in from the window, as if they too were waiting for something. "Cruz?" she prompted.

She leaned up and feathered several kisses against his lips, still holding his face, her fingers stroking his cheeks, trying to coax him back to passion.

It didn't work. What she was doing didn't work. He wasn't enticed.

His dark eyes pinned her to the spot, burning with heat, and yet she felt cold. So cold. As though someone had opened a window and let in a chilly draft.

"Cruz?" she whispered, her chest tightening with a fear that she had never felt before. She didn't know where the fear came from, but it was there, simmering within as he continued to stare at her in that strange way. "What is it?"

Recognition flared in his eyes. "It's *you*."

EIGHT

*S*HE WAS THE one.

The girl from the boathouse.

He'd given up on ever knowing her identity, ever knowing whose memory he clung to all these years. Fury warred with excitement. He didn't know what he wanted more: to shake her or kiss her. Both, he supposed.

He'd tried running after her when Natalie interrupted them in the boathouse, but Natalie had gotten in the way. Natalie, whom he wanted nothing to do with after one taste of his mystery girl.

By the time he'd gotten outside, there was no sign of her. Just all the other kids up the hill at the house, drinking and acting like general jackasses. Still, he had followed, diving into the mob of his fellow classmates. He'd ignored the friends who clapped him on the back and tried to talk to him . . . searching among the girls as though he would somehow know her at a glance.

Of course, he didn't spot her. Or if he did he didn't know it. He couldn't even remember if he had seen Gabriella Rossi among them.

He'd resigned himself to never knowing who she was, telling himself she would be one of the great mysteries of his life and that he had to move on. Still, as the years passed and he floated through life, she'd hovered on the fringes of his mind. He'd worked as many shifts as he could get and did the best he could to care for his sisters . . . often still wondering why the girl from the boathouse hadn't revealed herself to him. Why did she run away before he could see her face?

Was it because he was Cruz Walsh and not good enough for her? It seemed the most likely scenario. He wasn't good. He knew this because all his life everyone had been telling him that.

Then prison happened.

In there, fixating on an anonymous girl seemed senseless. Even dangerous. Prison was not a place to dream. So what if the kiss they shared, the tender way in which she had held his face, had touched something deep in his soul?

In prison, there was no hope. Wishes and wanting was for fools, so he did his best to suppress such things.

Except at night.

In the dark of his cell he would pull out all the good memories of the life he left behind on the outside. Invariably, the memory of the girl in the boathouse would find its way to him. Lying there with his hand tucked behind his head, he would stare blindly into the dark, recalling that night: her hands, her lips, her curves, the soft voice saying his name.

He never forgot.

When he'd been released from prison, he would look at women on the street and wonder if maybe one of them was the girl with the tender hands and sweet curves. Not that he was looking to get himself permanently attached even should he discover her. He wasn't the relationship type and he certainly wasn't looking to get married. He didn't even want a girlfriend because that came with expectations. Expectations led to marriage.

But now the mystery was solved. He'd found her.

Now he knew.

Now he knew the girl he had kissed, the one he never forgot, the one he had thought about during all the long nights in his cell.

Gabriella Rossi. Bri. From art class. From . . . the boathouse.

Her memory had both driven him mad and helped him survive in that cell.

She stared at him with wide eyes. Something like fear shined bright in them.

"I found you," he whispered, and her eyes just grew brighter.

He nodded, smiling slowly and with deep satisfaction.

Her lips had felt familiar but he hadn't truly realized he was again kissing his mystery girl until she held his face in her hands, until her fingertips stroked his cheeks in that way of hers. As though he were something precious to be cherished.

In that moment the past collided with the present. It had been the same in the boathouse. Because it was the same girl. For one fleeting moment, he felt like he was eighteen again and had just graduated from high school, ready to combust if he didn't get inside the girl wiggling against him.

And now she was here. Staring at him like she'd seen a ghost.

He'd let her slip away from him before. He wouldn't let that happen again.

He had not been able to forget her when he was locked up. How could he expect to now? The fact that they were locked in this closet together was a lucky circumstance. She wouldn't be running from him now.

Splotches of color broke out over her face. "I—I—"

"It's you," he repeated with total certainty.

She shook her head. "I don't understand what you mean. I—"

"It's you. From the boathouse." He watched her closely. Her breath fell faster. "And you do understand," he accused. "That's why you're so jittery. You remember, too."

"What are you talking about?" She laughed nervously.

"Graduation night. Natalie's boathouse. That was you in there. You were the girl I kissed . . ." He inhaled a breath and decided to use a little strategy to get her to admit he was right. "My friend, Dan, came in. You kissed him, too—"

"I did not!" Her body shot straight like a board. "I only kissed you!"

"Ah-ha!" He stabbed a finger in front of her face, smiling triumphantly. "You do remember."

Her eyes narrowed. "You tricked me."

"You were lying." He shrugged.

"I remember," she admitted grudgingly, the

brightness in her eyes no longer fear but anger. "I remember everything."

"So do I."

She snorted. "I find that hard to believe. It's been a long time."

"You were memorable." He lifted a wild lock of hair where it draped over her shoulder.

She didn't look as put together as she had last night, but he liked her this way. Hair wild. Dark and loose and tangled. Whatever makeup she had on last night had long since worn off and her freckles were in stark relief against her olive skin. He could stare at her face and see something different, something new, every time. He felt his heart, a wild drum in his chest. He swallowed past a suddenly dry throat. God. He hadn't felt this way since he was fifteen and fumbling in the dark with his first girl.

Even though the door was locked and they were trapped in here together, he had the irrational fear that she might disappear again. Go up in smoke.

"I thought about you a lot over the years." He might as well admit it at this point.

She went still. "You can't mean that." This time her voice didn't sound so angry. Rather, it sounded like a plea.

After high school he had gone straight to work. Grueling work. He had to in order to support himself and his sisters.

He worked landscaping at first, until he got hired on a construction crew. The pay was better than his landscaping gig, but it was grueling, back-breaking work beneath a brutal West Texas sun. For four years, he had worked in that punishing heat, his body young and strong enough to endure it. He remembered looking at the older men working alongside him. He'd taken in their bent backs and faces locked in grimaces of pain. That was his path. His bleak future. He knew it then. He didn't expect anything else.

He hadn't expected prison.

Following his thirty-year sentence, he certainly hadn't expected freedom.

He hadn't expected a day when he would be alone with Gabriella Rossi. He didn't think he'd ever see her again.

He met her gaze. "Why did you run that night?"

"I wasn't who you wanted. You were there for someone else. She showed up." She shrugged. "I figured I should go."

He shook his head. "You were scared. Just like you're scared now."

She made a scoffing sound. "No, I wasn't. No, I'm not. You thought I was Natalie—"

"When she walked in the door, and I realized it wasn't Natalie I was kissing, I didn't give a damn. I only wanted to know who *you* were. Because I wanted you."

Her throat worked. "It was just a kiss."

"It was more than that, and as I recall, we were both really into it."

She looked anywhere but at him right then. "I wasn't exactly experienced then."

He trailed a finger along the edge of her collar, not touching the sliver of skin peeping out of the V of her neckline. "And what about now? Are you experienced now?"

She cleared her throat. "I've lived a bit since then."

"Have you?" His finger stalled at her collar. Holding her gaze, he decided her definition of *living* probably didn't match up with his. Gabriella Rossi had *good girl* written all over her.

She nodded, her lips a tight, unsmiling line. "Of course, I have. I'm not a kid anymore."

"That's right," he agreed. "It has been twelve years . . . so we have a lot of catching up to do." He paused and took a steadying breath. He didn't need to fall on her like some overeager youth. He might feel like doing that, but he wanted to treat her with more finesse. He'd dreamed of this. He wanted it to be good. "I know who you are now, Gabriella Rossi. And I want this to happen."

That said, he tugged her closer again.

"Oh," she breathed, her eyes fixed on him as he inched closer to her even as he simultaneously pulled her in.

NINE

*H*E WAS GOING to kiss her again.

Only this time he knew she wasn't Natalie.

He knew everything.

Incredibly, he had never forgotten her, if she was to believe him, and why would he lie about such a thing? He not only remembered that night, he recognized how she kissed him. She couldn't have fathomed it.

The way he was looking at her now warned her he meant to do more than kiss her. He meant to do everything to her.

She trusted that he would stop if she told him to. He was not a *bad* man. She'd always known that, contrary to local opinion.

She just didn't trust herself . . . and that was the larger problem. She felt naked, exposed before him. Stripped of everything. The years between them didn't matter anymore. It's like they were eighteen again and ready to continue, to pick right back up where they left off. Without fear of consequences. Without fear of tomorrow. Like most teenagers, living carefree in the moment.

Except they weren't kids anymore.

She was thirty years old and very much concerned with all her tomorrows. As soon as Nana was well enough she would return to Austin and get her career on track. If she didn't start getting better stories—maybe a feature now and then—she'd get her resume out there. She knew sometimes you had to leave a job to find a better one.

She'd get her own place again. Find a nice man. Not partake in some . . . meaningless *tryst* with someone who couldn't offer anything more than a fling. That was *not* getting her life on track. He was only a further complication.

Easier said than done, of course.

His head descended. Her fingers curled into his shirt, digging, clinging, not pushing, not pulling. She watched his mouth, feeling dazed.

Who was she kidding? She couldn't deny herself this. She lifted her face to him.

Faint music registered. She frowned, her ears perking up to the sound.

The song, "You Make Me Feel Like Dancing,"

played from somewhere outside the closet. Disco? Really? The peppy beat and lyrics were incongruous to the moment.

She pressed a hand to his chest, putting a halt to his amorous intentions and pushing him away. "Wait. What is . . ."

She heard something else then. Not just the music. No. Squeaking wheels over tile. Right next to the closet door.

They weren't alone in the building!

It was Saturday, but someone was here. *Someone was here!* They were saved. Or rather, she was saved. Just in time from making a mistake.

She squeezed away from Cruz and launched to her feet. She tossed back her hair, grimly acknowledging that it must look like it did every morning—a tangled nest. Later she would mourn the fact that he saw her this way. Later when she was free and could reflect on the crazy Friday night she spent locked in a closet with Cruz Walsh.

Now, however, she had a closet to escape.

She lifted a hand and pounded on the door. "Hello!" Behind her, it sounded like Cruz muttered an obscenity. She couldn't be sure over the volume of her banging and shouting. She wanted to make sure she could be heard. "IS SOMEONE OUT THERE?"

The door opened.

A man stood there, wearing overalls. A cart was parked behind him where an old-school boom box circa 1990 played disco. She remembered the custodian from when she was in high school. She was pretty sure he wore the same overalls back then, too. She didn't know his name but the kids had dubbed him Squeaky because of the way his shoes squeaked over the tile.

"What are you doing in here?" he demanded, his eyes large behind the coke-bottle lenses of his glasses. "No one's supposed to be in here. The school is closed for the weekend."

She decided not to even bother defending them. After all, did he actually think they wanted to be locked in a cramped closet? Over the weekend? With no restroom or food?

"You're right, of course. No one should be here." She nodded and stepped around Squeaky out into the hall. "Sorry about that. I'll leave now."

Her name rumbled behind her. "Gabriella." There was a cautionary note to Cruz's voice, and she knew that he *knew*. He knew her plan was to put as much distance between them as she could.

She glanced back, taking him in before she bolted.

He stood on the other side of the custodian, still

stuck inside the closet. Squeaky looked back and forth between them, clearly indecisive. He settled on facing Cruz and demanding, "You there. What's your name?" The man narrowed his eyes as he studied Cruz. "You're familiar. I've seen you before." After a moment, he shook his head as though that was of no account. "I'm turning you both in. You shouldn't be here."

Cruz blinked at the man, clearly caught off guard. Of course, the custodian had seen him before. All over TV and social media.

She felt the totally inappropriate urge to laugh. *Turn them in?* Like they were still in high school. A couple of kids caught making out in a closet.

"Shouldn't you be asking if we're okay? We were locked in here overnight." She motioned to the door. "That's a hazard. What if we were students? What if I had a health condition? This school could face one hell of a lawsuit."

The custodian blanched and started to stammer.

She continued, "I'm sure you're going to want to fix this and change out the doorknob for one that doesn't lock."

"So sorry, ma'am." He bobbed his head, looking back and forth between them both.

Satisfied that he had ceased his ridiculous threats, she turned and marched away, walking briskly and hoping to put as much distance between her and Cruz as possible. It stung knowing he knew the truth. He knew how pathetic she had been. That she had used anonymity to kiss him.

She didn't need to lose any more of her pride. She just needed to put some space between her and Cruz Walsh. Distance to lick her wounds. Eventually the embarrassment wouldn't feel so acute.

Once she was alone in her bedroom, she could reflect on exactly how the past and present had collided . . . and how to make certain it didn't happen again.

That shouldn't be too difficult. They wouldn't come into contact again . . . as long as she avoided events at the high school. She winced. Yeah. So she had a niece and nephew who attended Sweet Hill High alongside his sister. That didn't mean she would have to talk to him at those events.

She had not forgotten the layout of the school. It was imprinted in her mind. She knew the quick getaways. She'd mastered those routes. Never knew when you needed to get away from a bully.

She walked swiftly, exiting the back of the building. It slammed loudly after her. She blinked against the sudden sunshine.

Ten seconds later she heard the door open and slam again.

She whirled around. Cruz stood there in the full morning light, looking not in the least rumpled from spending a restless night on the hard floor. No, that dark shadow of scruff on his face only made him look sexier. He slipped one hand into his front jeans pocket as he stared at her, early morning cicadas a loud purr on the air.

"Bri," he said, and she tensed. No one called her that anymore and the fact that he did smacked of a familiarity that both warmed and alarmed her. He lowered his hand from his pocket. "Where are you going?"

It seemed a loaded question. Innocent on the surface but so much more was being said with his dark eyes . . . in the way his chest lifted deeply on a breath. Her gaze dropped to the hands hanging at his sides. His long fingers twitched as though itching to make a move.

"Home." She motioned behind her.

"Do you need a ride?"

She shook her head vehemently. "I can walk." It struck her as funny then. What a strange turn of events. Here she was standing outside her former high school and Cruz Walsh was asking if she needed a ride home. She'd had this fantasy on repeat in her mind between the ages of fifteen and eighteen. "I'm not far."

"Okay then." Still, he hesitated.

And so did she. As though she were waiting for something, and that was just wrong of her. There was nothing more to say. Nothing more to do.

She finally moved. Turning, she started walking. She looked over her shoulder several times to assure herself that Cruz wasn't following. No sight of him. He wasn't following her. She was free.

She sighed again even as her chest twisted in discomfort.

She didn't dare examine the sensation. It couldn't possibly be disappointment. As far as she was concerned, the custodian had arrived at just the right time. Who knew what would have happened if they hadn't been interrupted?

Okay. She had a pretty good idea of what would have happened. She would have been reckless and irresponsible. She would have let things happen that had only happened in her fantasies.

And she would have regretted it as soon as it was over.

Lucky for her, Nana only lived four blocks from the high school. Keeping a fast pace, she took the winding sidewalk that roped behind the school, recalling the years before she could drive. She had used this sidewalk to bike to Nana's house after school freshman and sophomore year. She spent more time hanging out at Nana's than she did at her own house. Mom and Dad didn't seem to mind.

Once Tess graduated from high school, Gabriella was the only one left at home, and her mom and dad didn't make too much effort anymore. Mom quit cooking altogether. She joined a knitting club, and Dad spent every spare moment he had working on his trains or golfing. Nana was always happy to have her. Happy to bake cookies and watch TV together, asking about her day as though Gabriella's life was important to her.

Unlucky for Gabriella, however . . . she couldn't get into her garage apartment without her key. Which meant she had to knock on Nana's front door at eight o'clock in the morning looking like she had been rolling around in bed all night with someone. A fact that wasn't too far off from the truth.

She knocked three times and sent a quick glance over her shoulder to make certain Cruz still hadn't followed. She knew she was being paranoid at this point. Once he got out of that closet, she was sure he just got in his car and went home.

She could hear the television through the door. Nana's hearing wasn't great and she refused to wear a hearing aid, so that meant the TV volume was set to eardrum-shattering decibels at all times

of the day—because Nana never turned the TV
off. The only time it was off was when Nana went
to bed. She said she couldn't stomach an empty
house. Ever since her children left and her husband died, the place was too quiet. When Gabriella
returned home, Nana asked her to move in to the
house with her. She'd declined. She wouldn't have
functioning hearing if she lived in Nana's house full-
time. Instead she had moved into the garage apartment. Still close enough to be helpful, but far
enough away that her ears were spared.

Standing on the front porch, she knocked again
until she could hear the steady thump of Nana's
walker accompanied by Coco's high-pitched yips.
"I'm coming!" she shouted. "Who is it?"

"Nana, it's me! Gabriella!"

There was a scrabbling of the lock and then the
door swung open. Nana peered out at her as Coco
continued his infernal yips. The fifteen-pound
mutant Chihuahua didn't trust anyone except Nana.
"Where've you been? I thought you were abducted
and sold into some sex trafficking ring."

Well, at least someone had worried about her
disappearance. "No, Nana. I'm fine. And you really
watch too much *Dateline*."

"It's a good show! And I told your sister to call
the police, but she said you'd turn up."

As much as she hated to feel gratitude toward her sister, she was thankful she had stopped Nana from calling the police. Of course, if she was face-down in a ditch somewhere, the sentiment would be different.

"I got locked in the school overnight."

Nana's eyes widened. "You mean you spent the night in the school?"

She nodded. "The custodian let me out this morning. Do you still have my purse?"

"Yes. It's on the kitchen table." Nana turned and clattered down the hall to the kitchen.

Gabriella followed her, sticking her tongue out at Coco when Nana's back was turned. The dog narrowed its eyes and intensified its growls.

"Coco, behave or I'll have Gabby give you a bath. You're due for one."

Gabriella immediately retracted her tongue and the little beast ceased its growling. Both of them apparently understood the threat and neither one relished it. Before joining Nana in the kitchen, she ducked into the hall bath. It had been a while since she visited the restroom. Or ate for that matter. Her stomach grumbled as she finished her business and washed her hands.

"Did you eat breakfast already, Nana?" she asked as she joined her again. "Want me to make you something?" She poked her head into the fridge and grabbed some grapes from a bowl. She'd washed them and put them in a bowl for Nana a couple days ago. Otherwise, the contents of the refrigerator were getting low. She'd have to make a store run after her shift today.

"I ate some oatmeal."

Shutting the fridge, she tossed a couple grapes into her mouth, already imagining the frothy latte she planned on making herself at work. One of the perks of working at a coffee shop.

She picked up her purse from the table. "Do you need anything right now? I'm going to shower and get ready for my shift. How about I make you dinner tonight? I'll go by the store and get groceries."

"It's Saturday night. Sure you don't have a date?" Nana let out a groan as she eased down into a kitchen chair.

Immediately her mind tracked back to Cruz. He was hardly bring-boy-home-to-mom material, but he was the first guy to pop into her mind at the mention of *date*. She supposed it was natural to think about him since they had been making out like two adolescents no more than an hour ago. Any other day she wouldn't instantly think about him. In a few days, she wouldn't think about him at all.

"No date." She gave her grandmother an indulgent look. She was always prying into Gabriella's love life—or lack of love life. "You just want me to marry someone here so I don't move back to Austin."

"Plenty of nice fellas here in Sweet Hill." She nodded.

"And in Austin. *If* I want a fella at all, Austin is a much larger city. Stands to reason my odds would be better there."

"Too far away from Sweet Hill though."

Which was what Gabriella liked about it. Not that she would tell her grandmother that. She didn't want to hurt her feelings. Nana, as far as she was concerned, was the best thing about Sweet Hill.

And Cruz Walsh.

She shoved that treacherous voice aside. He was *not* one of the best things about Sweet Hill. He was not a *thing* at all. Not to her, he wasn't. "How about tacos for dinner?"

Nana nodded. "The crunchy kind."

"Okay. Crunchy tacos, it is. I'll stop off at the store."

"Don't forget the sour cream. And no hot sauce unless it's just for you." She rubbed at the center of her chest. "It repeats on me."

"Yes, Nana." She swung her purse over her shoulder and backed out of the kitchen, sidestepping

Coco as he growled at her ankles. "Call me if you need anything."

Her grandmother flapped a hand in the air. "Go on. See you tonight. Unless you get a date! Get a date," she shouted, her voice trailing after Gabriella.

Rolling her eyes, she hurried outside, darting across the driveway to the garage. She took the side staircase up to her apartment. Digging out her key, she unlocked the door and fell into her own private little sanctuary with a sigh of relief.

It was a simple apartment, on the small side, but it was home. It was a place where she could escape from the world. After the last twenty-four hours, she especially needed that.

She locked the door to her apartment, breathing fully, perhaps for the first time since being trapped in the closet with Cruz. She leaned against the door and took several more deep breaths, filling her lungs and telling herself she was being silly. There were no monsters or bogeyman after her. She winced. No. Just the ghosts from her past. Not the actual embodiment of her past. She'd left him behind. He wasn't after her. She didn't need to feel like she had to keep looking over her shoulder.

She felt safe here. Although that didn't stop her from moving to the living room window to peek out the blinds. Nana Betty's front yard stared back at her in the brightening day. Nana came into view, holding a watering can for the azaleas lining her walk. Coco trotted alongside her, eyeing the horizon for squirrels or other equally malevolent vermin.

Turning away from the window, she started stripping off her clothes, letting them hit the floor where they fell. She'd pick them up later. Right now she just wanted the hot spray of water on her skin. Maybe it would do more than wash away the grime.

Maybe it would wash away the last twenty-four hours, too.

TEN

LEAVING THIS PARTICULAR building behind with an aching cock wasn't standard for him. When he had attended high school, he'd never suffered from lack of sex. He had been an adolescent living with zero parental involvement and girls liked him. They wanted to be with him.

He'd spent his fair share of time making out behind the bleachers. In the theater box. In the boys' bathroom. In the *girls'* bathroom. In the dugout. Yeah, even in closets. Squeaky had caught him before, too. That's probably why the old man recognized him all these years later.

If there was a willing girl, Cruz was on her like a bee on honey. It didn't matter when or where. He'd find a place for them to go. The memory made him wince. He wasn't proud to have been such a manwhore back then. It's just the way things had been.

His home life had sucked. The only reason he stayed and didn't run away was his sisters. He couldn't leave them. Not even when things got bad. And life with Mom and her countless boyfriends all looking to beat the shit out of him in some perceived rite of fatherly devotion was pretty bad.

He'd searched for something more outside their cramped home. Sex had fulfilled that need. Girls. They gave him something to feel besides anger, resentment and the ache of poverty. A few of his girlfriends would even bake him cookies and cakes, claiming he could use a little more meat on his bones. He would bring the food home to share with Piper and Malia, making sure they had something to eat, too.

That night in the boathouse hadn't been the first time he visited Natalie. He'd met her there a few times for feverish couplings. Once she even snuck out during her grandmother's eightieth birthday party to meet him. He had no misconceptions about what they had been about. They'd used each other for empty, meaningless sex, for brief physical gratification.

He pushed away the bitter memories of those years.

He didn't want to be that kid again and he hated feeling like him now, horny and needy for sex.

But you're not that same kid anymore.

Girls weren't his drug of choice. These days he didn't need a crutch like that. He didn't need to numb himself. Prison had taught him to endure.

Now he rarely felt anything at all.

Except Gabriella Rossi made him feel.

Fuck. It was problematic considering who she was, who he was . . . but it couldn't be ignored. Piper had accused him of being an icicle more than once since he'd been released.

Well, he didn't feel like an icicle with Gabriella pressed up against him. No, he felt like a flame.

Even though she persuaded the custodian to let him go without calling the authorities, Cruz planned to call the authorities himself. Specifically, his brother-in-law, the sheriff of Sweet Hill.

As he didn't own a cell phone, he had to drive across town to his house, a turn-of-the-century bungalow with an oversized front porch. He'd bought the place a couple months ago. It needed a lot of repairs, starting with a new roof, but he could do it. Before prison he worked in construction. He'd been on roofing crews, drywall, masonry. You name it.

He enjoyed working with his hands and being out of doors. Freedom tasted especially good after years in a cage. The sun beating down on him as he worked on something that belonged to him was never a dream of his. He knew better than to dream big.

But the settlement granted to him by the city for his wrongful imprisonment had changed that. He was free. He owned a house . . . something no one could take away. He had his own walls and roof and a front door he could open and close, letting the world in and shutting it out whenever he wanted.

When he turned off the highway, it took him five minutes to reach the house. It sat on twenty acres. He felt a sense of peace every time he parked in the driveway, but today that peace eluded him. His skin buzzed and sparked. He felt as though he had been jerked awake from a decade-long sleep.

She may have run away, but every instinct in him demanded he give chase. Chase her and catch her and pin her with his body . . .

It was fucked up. He knew it. Since prison, women had ranked low on his priority list. Suddenly, however, she was at the top of the list.

Unlocking his front door, he heard a train whistle in the distance. The tracks coiled between his house and the trailer park where he grew up. Back then, he remembered listening to that whistle as he lay awake at night. He imagined himself on a train.

Imagined all the places it would take him far from Sweet Hill.

And yet here he was.

The cage door had been flung open, and he hadn't left. He felt needed here. His sisters were here and so was a whole new generation of kids growing up on the wrong side of the tracks. Kids like him. Poor. Scorned. Searching for something. He knew what that felt like.

He might have the money to start over somewhere else, but he couldn't walk away.

Snatching up the cordless phone from where it sat on the counter, he dialed—and wondered if maybe he did need to get a cell phone, after all.

His sister answered on the third ring.

He got right to the point. "Piper, is Hale there?"

"Cruz, what's wrong?"

He didn't want her to know where he spent the night . . . or with whom. It might give her ideas, and she already had ideas enough. She was determined to see him settled with a nice girl and he knew she would think Gabriella Rossi qualified as that, even if she was related to the woman he went to prison for killing.

"Nothing. I just need to speak with Hale."

He felt her hesitation in the beat of silence. He'd never called Hale out of the blue and asked to speak with him. "Okay." She pulled the phone away and he heard her muffled voice call for Hale.

Moments later, Hale was on the line. "Hey there, Cruz. What can I do for you?"

He didn't hate the guy. If his sister had to be with anyone, he figured she could do a lot worse than Hale Walters. He was decent even if he was a lawman. He would take care of her. Not that Piper needed a man to take care of her. She'd managed the majority of the time he was in prison on her own, taking care of both herself and Malia. Knowing his sister was with a man that *could* care for her mattered though.

Still. It wasn't easy knowing that his little sister was married to the sheriff of Sweet Hill. The guy was the town's golden boy. Former homecoming king and quarterback star. He was a walking cliché. A cliché who shared a bed with his baby sister now. It made him want to punch something when he thought about it—which was why he tried not to think about it.

"I need the address of someone," he explained.

A pause met his declaration. He'd never asked Hale for anything before. And now here he was, asking for something that was probably illegal.

To his credit, Hale didn't automatically say no. "Whose address do you need?"

This time, it was his turn to pause. Saying her

name out loud would make it real. It would mean he really was going after her like some bloodhound. "Gabriella Rossi."

"Cruz," he started in a warning voice. Of course, he knew the Rossi family. Her brother was the high school principal. Her sister had billboards all over town. Her cousin . . . well. They both knew who she was . . . who she *had* been.

"Just give me her address, Hale. I'm not going to cause any trouble."

His brother-in-law sighed. "Should I even ask why you want her address?"

"Because I want it."

Another sigh. "That's what I thought," he said as though Cruz had stated the words he had been thinking. *Because I want her.*

"Look. I don't mean her any harm."

"I know that. Just be careful, Cruz. She's . . ." His voice faded away. Cruz could almost imagine Piper staring at her husband, worry knitting her forehead as she tried to figure out what they were talking about and whether Cruz was going to get himself into any trouble. He might have been exonerated, but that didn't stop her from worrying.

"I know who she is, Hale," he reassured him.

He knew. And he still wanted her.

GABRIELLA WAS JUMPY all through her shift, looking up every time the door chimed and a customer entered. One of the other baristas dropped a glass mug halfway through her shift and Gabriella actually yelped and jumped. She didn't know what she expected. It wasn't as though Cruz Walsh would walk through the door. He'd never done so before. This wasn't exactly the type of place he frequented. Five-dollar coffees weren't for everyone and she doubted they were for him. He'd been locked up for years without such luxuries. She doubted he even indulged in those types of frivolities before he had been locked up. She knew he'd worked in construction. With only a high school diploma, he couldn't have been making very much money.

"Skittish tonight, aren't you?" Jabal asked as she bent to clean up the mess she made. Bianca, the manager, glared at her as she retrieved a chocolate croissant from behind the glass for a drive-through customer and then turned to glare at Gabriella as if she were somehow complicit in the mishap. She'd been ten minutes late today and Bianca was still annoyed with her for that.

She made a point of looking industrious and forced a smile for Jabal. "Not really."

"Anything wrong?"

She shook her head and rubbed at her forehead. "Just tired. Didn't sleep well last night." *Because she slept on a hard floor in a closet . . . with Cruz.*

At least her shift was almost over. She'd eat dinner with Nana and go to bed early. Wake up new. Refreshed. With a plan to get out of town and on with her real life.

"Have a hot date?"

She flinched. Was Jabal reading her mind?

"Um. Not exactly."

"Well, you gotta get your rest, girl. You're thirty now. Use moisturizer."

"Gee, thanks."

The door chimed. She looked up and spotted Mr. Brown entering the café.

"Mr. B!" Jabal exclaimed. "You want your usual?" She moved to the extensive tea collection.

"Yes, Earl Grey tea, please."

Jabal selected a tea bag while Gabriella moved to the cash register. "How are you doing today, Mr. Brown? Any exciting news in town?" Mr. Brown owned the local paper. Gabriella actually worked for him for two summers. He wrote her an excellent college recommendation.

"Oh, busy with lots to cover! The county fair is fast approaching." He leaned an elbow on the counter. "I could always use someone like you, Gabriella."

"Oh, Mr. Brown." She forced a smile. He had made the offer before. He only had a few part-time staffers. He practically ran the town's sole newspaper by himself. He'd offered her a full-time copy editor position, but working at the local paper and covering news like the country fair was not her idea of serious reporting. "You know I'm only here temporarily."

Jabal handed him his steaming cup of tea. He held it aloft in salute. "One can hope. You were my favorite protégé, Gabby."

"I'm the only high school kid who actually went into the business, Mr. Brown. Of course, I am." Out of the corner of her eye, she caught Bianca glaring at her again. In Bianca's opinion, there was being friendly to customers and then there was socializing.

"My door is always open, Gabby."

"Thanks, Mr. Brown." He waved and exited the café just as a group of noisy teens entered.

Gabriella spent her remaining shift taking complicated orders from teenagers and then cleaning the bathrooms—Bianca relished assigning her that task.

"See you later," she said to Jabal as she hung up her apron in the back and grabbed her purse.

"So let me just get this straight." Jabal hung up her own apron. "You *could* work for that nice Mr. Brown, but you'd rather work here part-time taking drink orders from entitled little brats and cleaning bathrooms?"

She shook her head. "It's complicated." She couldn't explain it. Taking the job with Mr. Brown would mean she was accepting a life here. In Sweet Hill. That she was okay being Flabby Gabby for the rest of her life. It meant no Austin. No career as a reporter working for a serious newspaper. No redemption. No becoming the shining star she told herself she would be one day.

"Isn't it always?" Jabal released an exaggerated sigh. "Complicated. Except complicated for me involves guys."

"Guys are not my problem." Unless one counted the *lack* of guys. That had been her problem for some time. Finding a good guy. Getting a good guy to stick around. That was not her strong suit.

"Girl, you just need to get laid." The back door banged shut after them as they headed into the employee parking lot. "You even gotten any since you moved back here?"

Laid? In Sweet Hill. "Who would I sleep with, Jabal?"

"Ain't no shortage of men here."

God. She sounded like Nana.

Immediately, Cruz filled her mind. Larger than life. His lips. His taste. His muscled body. His hands so strong and sure everywhere they touched. She gulped down a breath and spit out the lie, "No men I want."

Jabal snorted. "I sure don't have a problem finding men I want here."

Gabriella fished her keys out of her bag with a laugh. "Yeah. Aren't you juggling like . . . four?"

"Three," she corrected indignantly as she stopped between their cars.

"Well, I've never been that . . ." She searched for the word. "Magnetic," she supplied. Understatement.

"Girl, you got it." Jabal gestured at her in one sweep of her fingers. "You just gotta own it. Work that shit." She fluttered her fingers in the general area of Gabriella's significant chest.

Shaking her head, Gabriella opened the door to her car. "See you later."

She made the short drive to the store and grabbed everything she needed for tacos, making a point not to forget the sour cream. Nana was watching *Wheel of Fortune* when she came in with the bags. Coco tore into the room, nails scrabbling on the floor as he barked his head off over the din of the show's applause.

"That you, Gabriella?"

"Yes, Nana. I'm starting dinner," she called as she pulled out a frying pan from the cabinet and got it heating on the stove. She tore into a package of ground beef and plopped it into the pan, breaking it up with a spatula and sprinkling in the taco seasoning.

While it cooked, she got the rest of dinner going. She slid the taco shells into the oven to brown as the meat sizzled and then busied herself dicing tomatoes and peppers. Nana called out her guesses to the TV as she worked.

The doorbell chimed.

"Gabriella!"

"I'll get it." Wiping her hands on a dish towel, she cut across the living room toward the front door, Coco fast on her heels, ready to light into someone besides Gabriella.

Hoping it wasn't one of her family members—who would undoubtedly grill her about her disappearance last night—she opened the door, braced for whatever stood on the other side.

And she still wasn't prepared.

Not for the sight of Cruz, limned in the day's fading light, one big hand propped against the doorframe, his dark eyes fixed on her with a searing intensity that made her chest tighten.

Not for the way her breath froze within her tightening chest.

Not for the way her body reacted, coming alive

like someone flipped a switch. *Her* switch. Cruz Walsh could flip her switch simply by entering her sphere.

His hand on the doorframe put him much too close to her. The position also did delicious things to his T-shirt, pulling it snugly against his chest, shoulders and biceps. She sucked in a breath and that was a mistake. She got a whiff of him. Cruz pheromones assaulted her nose and made her knees go weak.

Expelling that breath, she stepped outside, pushing him back on the porch even if that meant she had to brush up against him. She shut the door on a growling Coco and then took several steps back from his bigger body. Several safe steps back.

"What are you doing here?" she demanded, crossing her arms over her chest and sliding a look between the living room blinds into the house. Nana still sat in her chair watching *Wheel of Fortune*.

"I wanted to see you. We left things unfinished."

Incredible as it seemed, he had one thing on his mind when it came to her. And he didn't waste any time reminding her what that *thing* was.

He came at her like a train, backing her up against the wall. "You thought I was gonna forget? We started something years ago." His body pushed hers up against the wall, mashing her breasts into his chest. God. Her breasts felt even heavier. Aching. "You think I'm gonna let another twelve years go by?"

God, I hope not.

As soon as the rebellious thought entered her mind, she mentally kicked herself. Hard. No, no, no.

"Gabriella!" Nana bellowed from inside.

She pushed frantically against him. "Stop. I have to go. *You* have to go!"

He eased away, but only slightly. His hand splayed against the wall near her head, blocking her escape. A faint smile played about his lips. "Want me to come back later? It's been a while since I snuck into a girl's bedroom, but I'm sure I can—"

"I don't live here," she blurted and pointed over his shoulder to the garage apartment. "That's my place." The instant she admitted that, she regretted it. It seemed almost like an invitation. His smile went from faint to definitely there on his face. "But don't do that. Don't come over." She definitely didn't need to be alone with him in her apartment with a bed in proximity. Heaven help her, she wasn't strong-willed enough for that.

"Gabriella!" Nana shouted from inside. "Is something burning?"

"Shit! Dinner." She shoved past him.

He snatched her hand before she could dive

inside. "I'll see you again, Gabriella." His dark eyes roamed her face as though memorizing every feature. She felt his gaze like a caress. His words sank right into the marrow of her bones. She stared at him helplessly, both delighted by and dreading the prospect.

"Gabriella! Who are you talking to?" Nana's walker started thudding for the front door. Gabriella's head whipped in that direction, panicked that Nana would emerge to see Cruz standing on her doorstep. She choked back her dismay and looked back at Cruz, ready to plead with him to leave, but he was already gone. A retreating figure down the front walk.

She released a deflated breath.

"Gabby!" Nana stepped out onto the porch and stared at her crossly. "I'd like dinner."

She sent one final lingering look down the front walk. Cruz was gone, but she could still see his dark eyes in her mind. Hear his stark promise to return.

"I'm coming, Nana."

ELEVEN

SHE WAS MOST definitely a coward. She lingered at Nana's, eating dinner . . . and then offered to make brownies. It took a good hour to prep and bake, but Nana loved her sweets and Gabriella was stalling, after all.

Nana had a serious sweet tooth and since her doctor actually wanted her to gain a little weight, there was no guilt in the indulgence. At least for Nana. Gabriella indulged, very much aware that she shouldn't. Tess would say something snarky if she were present. Gabriella had long accepted she would never be a size four. She wouldn't even be a size ten. Those aspirations had long since fled. Right about the time she gave up on the idea of a guy being able to get her off as well as she could get herself off, she gave up on the idea of ever having a bikini body.

To be honest, Gabriella probably would never eat brownies in front of her sister to simply avoid the snark. The pleasure wasn't worth it.

But Tess wasn't here. And the last twenty-four hours had been a bit much. She deserved brownies. Thinking about Cruz and the way her body burned from lack of fulfillment . . . well, she deserved ALL the brownies for the willpower it took to walk away from him.

Okay, so she ran away. It was her only choice in that moment. Her libido was running rampant and she did not want to get more entangled with her old life in Sweet Hill than necessary.

Turning him away from Nana's house had been her only choice, too. He was only coming around for one thing. Curiosity. Some compulsion to finish what they started all those years ago. Once—*if*— she gave in he would disappear. It would be the last she ever saw of him.

With brownies in hand, she and Nana settled in to watch television together. She got up several times and peeked out the front window, assuring herself there was no sight of Cruz. She didn't know what vehicle he drove, but there was no car parked along the curb.

"What's wrong? You looking for someone? Got a man coming over?" Nana waggled her bushy eyebrows as she shoved another bite of brownie into her mouth. She was on her second brownie now.

"No, Nana." Her grandmother really was far too perceptive. Old age may have robbed her of good bones and dexterity, but it had not robbed her of her mind.

Thirty minutes later, Nana announced she was ready for bed. She pushed up from her recliner, reaching for her nearby walker. "You're welcome to stay and finish the movie but I'm tuckered out. I have bridge tomorrow and I need my rest to stay sharp."

Gabriella glanced rather desperately at the television set. "Don't you want to see the end?"

She batted a hand. "I've seen *Terminator* a dozen times. The sexy part is over anyway." She headed for her bedroom. "I'll see you tomorrow."

Gabriella got up from the couch. Like Nana, she had seen the movie before. She let Coco out back to potty. That took another half hour. The dog had to sniff *everything*.

She tidied up inside, took out the trash, and finished the last of the dishes. She checked on Nana one final time. Her grandmother was already fast asleep, tucked in beneath one of her handmade quilts.

Coco, a plump furball at the foot of the bed,

lifted his head and growled at Gabriella as though she posed a threat. As though Gabriella had not fed the little beast tonight and just taken him out to the bathroom.

She turned and headed back down the hallway, her feet creaking over the wood floor. The routine was much like every night. At least since she returned to Sweet Hill. Taking care of Nana was the reason she came home, after all. Nana was recovering well. Soon she wouldn't need the walker at all. Soon Gabriella could go back to Austin.

She walked through the house and shut off all the lights, double-checking that Nana's walker was close by the bed and Nana's phone was on her nightstand in case she should need it in the middle of the night to call Gabriella.

She wasn't stalling. She released a heavy breath. Not at all. These were things she had to do. It had nothing to do with avoiding her apartment. Definitely not avoiding *him* because *he* was gone. Back to wherever he lived. He wouldn't come back tonight. It was late. Too late for him to come by her place. He had to be exhausted after their uncomfortable night in the closet.

She worked to convince herself of this as she locked up Nana's house and crossed the lawn. She placed one foot on the bottom step. The wood groaned beneath her weight as she climbed to the top slowly. Nana really needed to get someone out here to replace a few of the boards. They were beyond weathered. Gabriella feared that one day her foot was going to punch straight through one of them.

She suddenly felt the effects of little sleep and a long day. Forcing a smile and cheerful conversation took a toll. Especially on a classic introvert like her.

He'd said he'd see her again. Guess he didn't mean tonight. She quickly tried to ignore her stab of disappointment. She had no business feeling that way.

She yawned as she entered her apartment and quickly stripped off her clothes, changing into a well-worn T-shirt and shorts. She had a shift tomorrow afternoon, but she needed to get up early for Nana's physical therapy appointment. Nana liked her there when the therapist worked on her. Gabriella suspected it was because the therapist was easier on her when Gabriella was present. Rhonda was a chatty sort and she often got caught up talking to Gabriella.

Finished brushing her hair and teeth, she dropped into her bed and pulled her pillow close to hug. It was a body pillow. Easily five feet in length. She'd always had it. Her college roommate had teased her and accused the pillow of being her boyfriend.

She'd laughed off the cheerful accusation back then with: "That's right. Who needs a boyfriend when I have my pillow?"

Except as she drifted to sleep, she couldn't help thinking that the pillow was a poor substitute for a firm, male and very alive body. A body like Cruz Walsh's.

HE WENT TO bed alone. Alone with thoughts of Gabriella. *Bri.*

As much as he promised he would be seeing her again, he wasn't going to hang around late into the night hoping for a glimpse of her like some kind of stalker. He could almost hear Radiohead singing "Creep" in his head. He might have spent years in prison with dangerous men, but he wasn't a menace and he had no intention of making her feel uncomfortable.

He tucked his hands behind his head and listened to the faint drone of cicadas outside his window. He'd bought this house to have something of his own. Space. Only in this moment he felt a little too much space. A little too much solitude. He had never brought a woman back to his place. Not in the six months he had been living here. There was something sacred about this house, a place of his own. He wanted to keep it to himself. Safe and untouched. His alone. And yet he didn't think he would mind having her here.

His smile slipped. Except she was a fucking reporter. He'd rather she be a lawyer . . . or a guard at the prison. Hell, the fucking warden. All professions for which he held no fondness. The media had hounded him since his release. They even had nerve enough to harass his sisters and Hale. Bloodsucking parasites.

She hadn't even hidden the fact that she wanted a story from him. *His* story. The truth. Damn if he'd ever divulge that to her of all people. That meant he'd have to let her know exactly what kind of person her cousin had been. He'd made a point to not share that with anyone. Shelley Rae's family had been through enough. She was dead. She had been dealt the worst of all punishments. No reason to make them suffer any more for the deeds that led to her death.

But Gabriella looked good tonight. Better than memory served. The years had been kind to her. She wasn't hiding her curves anymore in baggy sweatshirts. The fabric of her blouse draped lovingly over her well-endowed chest.

Her freckles were still there, even more of them than before, but not a line or wrinkle marred her face.

He shifted restlessly on the bed. His dick was hard, pulsing with hunger. Before he could consider what he was doing—or why he shouldn't—he wrapped a hand around himself, stroking the tight, warm skin, building friction.

He tilted his head back and pumped his dick, working it almost savagely from the base to the head, desperate for release . . . for something to take the edge off so he could stop thinking about the girl he'd craved since his voice first changed its pitch.

His eyes drifted shut and the image that rose in his mind was of Bri sitting before him in high school, leaning forward and showing off her ass in too-tight jeans—and of Bri draped over him last night, her breasts pressed against his arm as she slept.

He envisioned stripping her out of her clothes and parting her thighs, wrapping a fist around her hair and gripping the curve of her hip as he sank inside her.

He saw all of that perfectly, clearly, achingly as he fisted himself hard. His breathing grew ragged and his balls drew up tight.

Thinking about her wasn't hurting anything, he rationalized. It was simply an image that got him off. That was all. That was it.

He closed his eyes, feeling a flash of frustration. He didn't want the image of her though. He wanted *her*. The sound of her voice. The solidness of her body under him. The roam of her hands on his skin. *His* hands on her soft skin. He visualized his fingers digging into tender flesh as he worked himself inside her. In his mind he was spreading her thighs wide and driving the swollen length of him into her.

He came with a head-tossing groan. His spine arched on the bed as he shot out over himself, rattled in the aftermath of his orgasm.

That shouldn't have felt so good. Just the thought of Bri had him jacking off to the best release he'd had in memory. It shattered him. Masturbating should not be better than the reality of a genuine flesh-and-blood woman, and yet it had been. Maybe he was tired of empty sex . . . maybe he wanted something else. Maybe that's why nothing and no one seemed to satisfy him lately.

Dropping back down on the bed, he stared into the dark of his room, his heavy breaths slowing as he wondered what the hell that meant for him. Did it mean he wanted more than sex with Bri?

Groaning, he quickly rose from the bed and

cleaned himself off. That finished, he strolled naked out onto his porch and breathed in the clean air, his bare feet flexing on the wood planks underneath him.

In the vast distance, a coyote cried out until one of its pack mates answered the call.

TWELVE

"*G*'NIGHT, NANA!" SHE called out from where she hovered in the front door, ready to lock up for the night. "See you in the morning."

Her parents had taken Nana out to dinner tonight to her favorite Tex-Mex restaurant, and she was already in bed by the time Gabriella got off work and stopped in to check on her.

Coco growled at her, indifferent to the fact that Gabriella just let the little beast out to potty. She stuck her tongue out at the Chihuahua. The dog went wild, yipping and hopping, his considerable belly bumping the ground.

Nana shouted from her bed where she watched television, "Coco, come."

With a final sniff for Gabriella, the dog trotted off, obeying his master's bidding.

Locking the door, she turned down the walk

and cut across the grass toward the garage. Nana must have run the sprinkler. The lawn squished under her shoes.

Cicadas chirped on the night. A slight evening breeze lifted her hair off her shoulders. It was the kind of evening for barbecues and sitting on a porch swing. Sitting on a veranda with someone you love beside you . . . hands locked and fingers laced together as you watched the world float past. She sighed and rubbed the back of her neck, wondering why she was being so maudlin. Aside from high school, when she would daydream— and nightdream—about Cruz Walsh, she wasn't the kind of person that longed for a relationship. Either she met someone or she didn't. She didn't need a man in order to feel complete, but for some reason tonight she felt . . . lonely.

And she couldn't help wondering if she would be feeling this way if she hadn't come face-to-face with Cruz Walsh this week. He'd brought back a rush of emotion. She felt alive . . . awake in a way she had only ever felt when he kissed her in the boathouse.

She had convinced herself that those brief moments in the boathouse had somehow been inflated in her memory. That it couldn't have been as good or as sweet or as special as she remembered.

She'd been wrong.

It was all that and more. Somehow she had forgotten the want . . . the way her body could ache, the way blood could turn to lava in her veins, reducing her to a puddle.

He brought back all the longing and now it was worse because she was no longer some unsure virgin. She knew what she wanted. She knew what she had been missing . . . and she felt certain he could take care of all her achy parts.

Also, there were no longer any secrets between them. They were adults. There was freedom for them to do what they wanted. At least in regards to each other. They were no longer teens that had to resort to clandestine, hasty couplings.

If not for her conscience, she could take him up on his offer of a fling. They could take all the time in the world with each other.

She released a sigh. Maybe she should have gone out with Jabal tonight. Then at least she wouldn't be thinking about Cruz.

Jabal actually tried to convince her to go out for drinks to a nearby bar.

"Come on. It's new. You've got to check it out. They have the hottest bartender working there. And the clientele is pretty decent. Can't tell you how many decent hookups I've scored there."

Gabriella had declined. Jabal was younger, still up for all-nighters and random hookups. Gabriella was past all that. She preferred her yoga pants, takeout and a Netflix marathon on a Friday night.

She started up the steps, already thinking about relaxing in a hot tub with a book.

She was halfway up when she heard a voice on the night.

"I was starting to wonder if you were ever going to come home. It's getting late," he announced.

Her head snapped up. He sat on the top step, his elbows relaxed on his knees. His dark eyes pinned her to the spot. She froze, one hand gripping the railing. Elation filled her at the sight of him before she could suppress it.

It took her a moment to find her voice—it was trapped somewhere in her throat like a fluttering bird. "What are you doing here?"

"Waiting for you."

She glanced around, searching for what she didn't know. She faced him again. "Have you been here long?"

"Not too long. I mean, I haven't been sitting here all day." His lips quirked. "I went to work. Are you unhappy to see me, Rossi?" He cocked his head, his gaze narrowing thoughtfully on her. "I think you're angry because you *are* happy to see me."

Her face heated at how accurately he pegged the situation. "What? No! I'm not happy . . . I'm not *anything*." His expression turned faintly smug. As though she had just confirmed it. "You can't know what's going on in my mind, so don't act like you do."

She lifted her chin and continued, "I just didn't expect you."

"I said I'd be seeing you again."

"Yes, and I wanted to see you. For that interview," she lied rather desperately.

His face went cold. "I didn't agree to an interview."

She looked up and down the street. "Where's your car?"

"You seemed concerned about your grandmother knowing I was here." He paused with a light shrug. "I can understand how your family might react to me hanging around you." Another pause. He wasn't saying it, but she knew they were both thinking about Shelley Rae. And he was right. Her family would not take it well. "I parked out of sight. Around the corner."

Was he actually looking out for her? She didn't think he cared for himself one way or another. He was still living in a town where half the residents treated him like a guilty man.

So he was considerate. She squared her shoulders and tried not to let that go to her head. She lifted her foot and started up the steps, her hand skimming the wood railing to her right, heedless of the fact that she was probably going to get a splinter.

"Shouldn't you be avoiding *me*? I'm the press, after all." She stopped before him. His knees were close. Just inches from her.

"I'm not worried. What we're going to do doesn't involve a lot of talking. At least not the kind of words you can put in print. Pretty sure the censors wouldn't allow that."

She sucked in a breath, her face catching fire. "That confident, are you?"

His gaze held hers and her face grew even hotter. Damn it. Why couldn't she be cool and unaffected?

Because this is Cruz Walsh. Your fantasy come to life.

Shoving that annoying know-it-all voice aside, she stepped around him onto the porch, moving toward her front door, determined to be strong enough to resist the fantasy rising to his feet behind her.

Fantasies weren't supposed to come true. They were supposed to stay well and properly in her head, ready to be pulled out on lonely nights. It would throw her world off-kilter if he were to seriously *like* her. If fantasy became reality.

But no no no. This wasn't about liking. Believable or not, it was about sex. It was only physical. Only about fucking . . . or the *prospect* of fucking.

She inserted her key into the lock and sent him a look over her shoulder. It was a strange thing. She'd never been with a man, Cody included, that wasn't a boyfriend. And she'd never had a boyfriend who didn't *like* her first. They fell for her personality. The physical stuff was secondary. They never uttered naughty or suggestive things to her. They had sex (usually scheduled and in the dark) but they never *fucked*. What they had were mutual interests. It was largely cerebral.

Looking back at Cruz with his hooded eyes and sensual mouth, she knew he fucked. That's the kind of man he was and damn if all her girl parts didn't quiver and throb and whisper in need.

She whipped her head around and faced forward again with a shaky breath.

At times, she wasn't even convinced her boyfriends had found her that attractive. It was what was on the inside that mattered to them . . . and don't get her wrong. That's how it should be. Personality and compatibility and the soul within mattered.

But with Cruz hovering at her back, his warm

breath on her neck . . . she felt desired. Wanted in a way she had never felt before.

She fought to control her breathing as she pushed open her door. Then she just stood there, not yet taking a step to cross the threshold. It's what she should do. Step over the threshold and shut the door on him with a firm good-night.

Should do.

But it would be so easy to turn and invite him inside. So easy to let him inside in *every* sense.

Desire warred with her sense of responsibility and good judgment She wasn't an adolescent. She couldn't let her libido rule her. She needed to be responsible.

Her fingers flexed in the doorframe, clenching into the wood, the pressure threatening to split her nails.

Still, she didn't move. Didn't close the door.

She opened her mouth to speak without turning around. "There has to be some other woman who would be delighted if you showed up at her front door."

He chuckled, rustling her hair. "Are you trying to talk me out of liking you?"

Liking her?

"That's not what *this* is."

"Oh?" His arms appeared on either side of her, each hand propping on the doorframe directly below her own hands. "What is *this* then?"

"To you? Some game—"

"No. I don't play games," he quickly rebutted.

"I mean, it's just . . ." She swallowed miserably. "You only want to sleep with me."

"That's not untrue," he agreed. "And you know what else is true?" Still beyond speech, she shook her head. "You want to sleep with me, too."

God. She did.

Immediately her mind raced, rationalizing it, lying to herself . . . telling herself it wasn't too big a deal to sleep with her high school crush.

Immediately she saw them tangled up together in the sheets of her bed. She had nice sheets. A zillion thread count and a plush down-filled comforter. It was her weakness. An indulgence she couldn't resist. Good quality bedding that they could wreck.

His gravelly voice continued, "But I take exception to the word *only*. There won't be anything *only* about it. What I want to do to you will take hours. Maybe days. It's the kind of thing that could span weeks. Maybe longer."

She choked back a gasp. A long-term affair? How could he promise that? He was bullshitting her.

She should step inside. Slam the door in his face.

"Amateurs *only* sleep together," he added. "Or people who can take it or leave it. They care more about what's on their DVR. For them, sex is not essential." He paused a beat.

She tensed, unable to draw her next breath, all of her pulsing and humming with desire. God. His words alone did this to her. Imagine what he could do with his mouth and hand and cock.

"So you have to realize that I'm going to ruin you for any other man. When we fuck, Rossi, it's going to feel like the thing you need most in your life. Forget about food and water. Me. Between your legs. You're going to need it like air to survive. It will never be as good with anyone else."

A tiny little whimper escaped her. *Who says shit like that?*

And the terrible thing was . . . she believed him. Every. Single. Word. She felt like she was already on the verge of combusting. Her pussy contracted, squeezing in need.

He gently swept her hair off her back and onto her shoulder.

Then she could feel his soft breath as he brought his face closer. Close enough to brush his lips to the nape of her neck. Shivers broke out over her skin. She bit her lip to keep from crying out until she tasted a coppery wash of blood over her teeth. Her fingers clung harder to the doorframe, hanging on. She feared if she let go she would drop and melt into a puddle at his feet.

He followed that tiny kiss with a long and lingering one at the very top of her spine, eventually opening his mouth over her skin. She dropped her head with a whimper as his tongue trailed hotly on her goose-bumped flesh.

He came in closer, crowding her until his chest was flush with her back. She stayed where she was, square in the middle of her doorway, arms splayed out at her sides.

His entire body was aligned with hers, every hard ridge of him palpable . . . solid and substantial behind her. Against her.

Their clothing was nothing, just a thin barrier. The heat of their two bodies fused together. His dick bulged against the small of her back and she wanted to wiggle against that part of him, turn and fit his hardness directly against her core.

It had been too long. So long. Twelve years too long, in fact. How was she supposed to resist?

She throbbed, physically aching to have him there, filling her.

He continued to kiss the back of her neck. Who ever knew that was such an erogenous zone? It was totally new for her. No one had kissed her there before. Everything with him was new.

His fingers played with the hem of her shirt, teasing at her waist and then sliding around, his broad palm gliding over her stomach.

She tensed, sucking in a breath and her stomach at the same time. She didn't like to be touched in that area. She was too self-conscious by far. Sex had always been something she did in the dark, and she had always steered her boyfriend's hands away from her midsection.

"What's wrong?" he husked against her neck, clearly sensing her tension.

She shook her head and tried to relax and accept his touch and not be weird about it.

His hands weren't long for her stomach anyway. They slid up to cup both her breasts. He gently squeezed the heavy mounds and she moaned, dropping her head back against his chest, all self-consciousness fleeing as sensations flooded her.

Something that sounded suspiciously like a groan rumbled out of his chest and it only got her hotter to know that he was affected, too. That *she* turned him on.

"God, I've dreamed of these."

Since yesterday? It seemed a strange thing for

him to say, but she shook off the curious thought as a rush of wetness flooded her panties. If this was what his hands on her breasts felt like . . . what else was in store for her if she really cast her inhibitions aside and invited him inside her place?

His mouth landed on the side of her neck, feasting with tongue and teeth as his hands massaged her sensitive breasts. His touch grew firmer, rougher, until he yanked the demi cups down. *Finally!*

Her boobs spilled free and then his hands were on her, still under her shirt but on her naked breasts. Wild whimpers escaped her as his work-roughened palms abraded her flesh. His fingers played with her nipples, his touch growing firmer the louder her moans grew. Her head rolled side to side on his chest as the moisture gathered between her legs. Never had a man played and maneuvered her so expertly, using her reactions to guide his next action.

She came in a blinding-white rush. Hard and fast. Chest thrust out brazenly into his hands. His fingers clamped down on her nipples, pinching and twisting the distended tips as she rode out her climax, barreling from one directly into the next one. It was a never-ending orgasm.

"Fuck," he growled, grinding into her from behind. "That made you come? You're so hot for it." He panted into her ear. "I want you to come apart like that with me balls-deep inside you."

She nodded jerkily.

Broken, shattered sounds escaped her, but no words. She was beyond that. But it was enough. Consent given and he knew it. Their time had come.

THIRTEEN

*H*E WRAPPED ONE arm around her waist and lifted her from the doorway like she weighed nothing at all. She gave a little yelp, her hands flying to his taut forearm locked around her.

They didn't make it very far.

Two strides and the door slammed behind them, and he spun her in his arms and kissed her. Somehow her feet were off the ground, toes dangling above the carpet. She knew rationally, cogently, that he was holding her, lifting her clear off her feet. And yet her lifelong neurosis prevented her from accepting that any man could be carrying her and not spraining his back.

Their open mouths collided, tongues diving and licking and tangling. Her arms looped around his neck. They backed into a wall rather forcefully.

Picture frames rattled dangerously, but she didn't care. Didn't stop to look. The pictures could have shattered to the ground in a million pieces and she would have kept kissing this man. Cruz Walsh. *Cruz. Cruz. Cruz.*

Hell. A bomb could go off and she wouldn't stop.

She could be dead and she would return to life to kiss this man . . . to have him.

"You taste like chocolate," he muttered against her mouth. His hands dropped to the waistband of her leggings and she tensed. This was happening. Cruz was about to strip off her clothes and have sex with her and she was okay with that. More than okay. She was an eager participant . . . and her living room was fully lit.

"The lights," she muttered into their kiss, her hands tightening where they braced on his shoulders.

His fingers curled inside her waistband and started to push her pants down her hips. Her heart skipped in panic.

"The lights," she repeated, her voice clearer, more insistent.

He lifted his head, his dark eyes gleaming and glazed with a certain lack of focus. "What about them?"

"Off. Turn them *off.*"

He frowned, growling, "I want to see every fucking inch of you." He held her gaze, his jaw locking stubbornly. He was ready to battle for this.

Her pulse skittered at her throat with both delight and fear. No man had seen every fucking inch of her in full light. Up until now she had been pretty sure that no man ever would, but here he was, demanding it with his velvety dark eyes.

"Please," he added.

It was the *please* that undid her, unraveled the last of her resistance.

He dipped his head then and kissed her throat, that amazing mouth of his nibbling and sucking at her pulse point until she was squirming and gasping.

"I want to see your skin against mine . . . I want to watch as my hands roam all over your bare skin."

God, yes. So did she.

"Don't you want to see me naked, too?" he murmured against her skin.

God, YES.

His deep voice went on. "Don't you want to watch my cock moving in and out of you?"

Oh. My. God. He was sin. Unadulterated sin. She nodded jerkily, feeling like one of those bobblehead dolls.

"Then we both have to be naked with the lights on for that to happen."

She grasped his face and brought his lips back to hers, kissing him eagerly. Suddenly they were sliding down the wall and then she was on the floor under him. With anyone else the entire action would have been graceless and awkward but there wasn't anything bumbling about Cruz. It was impossible for him to be physically awkward. He was all animal grace and fluidity.

He broke their kiss and leaned back to sweep off her leggings in one swift motion, tossing them over his shoulder. He came back over her, his mouth robbing any protest she might have waged. Not that she was protesting. She had given up all notion of that.

His fingers played with the sides of her panties at her hips, alerting her to the fact that he had not stripped those off along with her leggings. She wasn't totally naked under him, at least. Of course, she couldn't precisely remember what panties she was wearing today, so there was that worry. *Please, don't let them be my time-to-do-the-laundry granny panties.*

His mouth was addictive though, pushing away all cognizant thought, and she soon forgot about her panties worry. His hands drifted from her hips, trailing down to her crotch and running along the seam of her.

"God, you're soaking," he rasped against her mouth as he ran a finger up and down her lips.

Her face flushed with embarrassment. "Sorry—"

He lifted his face to look down at her, his dark eyes snapping heat. "Never apologize. I love that you want it. That you're this hot for it."

Then she watched him as he made his way down her body and buried his face between her legs.

"OhGodOhGodOhGod." Her hands flew to his hair, spearing through the strands as she arched her spine off the ground. He feasted on her through the thin barrier of her panties, nibbling and licking and nuzzling until he found the little pearl nestled at the top of her folds. He attacked it, trying to get to it through the fabric. The barrier of her panties was drenched now, slippery between them, and that somehow increased the sensations.

Shrieking, she tightened her hold on his hair as she felt the stabbing pressure of his tongue and sharp little nips of his teeth. She squirmed, desperate for him to push her panties aside, desperate to feel the abrasion of his tongue, the satisfying graze of his teeth directly on her.

His hands gripped hold of her thighs, spreading her wider for him. His fingers burned twin imprints into her yielding flesh as he settled deeper between her legs with a contented sigh, as though he were settling in for the long haul, prepared to gorge on her for hours—just as he had promised.

She started to shake the instant he started toying with the edge of her panties—toying with *her*—even as he continued to nuzzle her through her panties, whispering naughty words into her wet crotch. "So hot . . . so sweet . . . your pussy tastes like candy, Rossi . . . I can't wait to slide my cock inside . . ."

It was the filthiest, most erotic thing she had ever done. It dimly registered that with any other man she would be embarrassed in this scenario, but not with him. Actually, the dirtier he talked, the wetter she got. With him it felt perfect and natural. Like she had been waiting for this her entire adult life.

Then suddenly his fingers hooked inside the elastic edge and tugged her panties aside, baring her to the room, to the air, to his gaze . . . his *mouth*. "Ahh," he sighed. "There's my pretty pussy."

Fire burned through her as he latched onto her, tasting her with a muffled groan that made her sink deeper into the ground. Her legs fell wider apart, limp appendages. She was totally boneless as his tongue lapped at her, working her like she was some delectable treat. It was too much. Incoherent words choked from her lips.

His voice vibrated against her flesh. "You taste better than I ever imagined . . . and you're such a pretty pink. I can't believe you wanted to hide this from me." He gave her pussy lips a gentle slap that made sensation zing directly to her clit. She arched and cried out, whimpering as he followed the little slap with several savoring licks.

"Again," she begged.

He paused. "What? This?" He gave her another light slap, this time directly making contact with her clit.

"Yes!" She had no idea she would react to such a thing . . . *want* more of it. Want it firmer. *Harder.* Her desire tightened, coiling in her core as her clit tingled from the contact.

He growled in satisfaction and lowered his head. "I know what you want." To prove it, he pulled her clit between his lips, flaying it with his tongue.

"Yes!" Her fingers clenched in his hair, but he didn't make a sound of protest, simply lashed her clit faster, harder. She shook from head to toe.

"There you go. Come for me, Rossi," he continued, speaking against her aching bud of flesh.

She curled her toes and drew her wobbly knees up, looking down at him where he was wedged between her thighs. It was wicked and indecent and lewd and she couldn't remember ever being in

such a position—on the floor beneath glaring fluo-
rescent lights that did all manner of unkind things
to her body. But here she was. Exposed. And she
didn't care.

He gazed up at her, his dark eyes languid,
drugged. Drugged from the effects of her . . . it was
hard to fathom.

Still watching her, he bent back down to lick her
long and slow, relishing her as his thumb landed
unerringly on her hungry clit, pressing down on it
hard and rolling it until she was done. Shattered.
Her body broke.

The tension tightening every muscle snapped.

She flew apart into a million particles into the
stratosphere.

He was right. She was ruined. He had just destroyed her. Without even having sex yet. She knew
she could never have anything close to this with
another man.

She fell back down to the ground, gasping and
panting as though she had run a marathon. She
couldn't stop shaking. Couldn't catch her breath.
Tears leaked out from the corners of her eyes. She
turned her face away and swallowed, fighting for
speech.

Now the embarrassment came. Embarrassment
over her intense reaction. Her unprecedented reac-

tion. Maybe he did this to every woman he was with, but it felt wholly singular to her. Biblical in proportion. The experience rattling and soul-touching.

Rationally, she knew it had to be her getting caught up in the best orgasm of her life. She had orgasm brain. That was it. Pure and simple. She was dead of it.

Dead of orgasm.

Her heart pounded in her ears. A loud, steady thumping. She pressed a hand over her heart, attempting to inject herself with a level of calm.

It didn't help.

The pounding just seemed to grow louder.

Loud enough that he could probably hear it, too.

She frowned. Loud enough that it wasn't just in her head?

Loud enough that it actually existed.

Oh God. It wasn't only in her head. It was real. A very REAL pounding. She blinked and gave her head a small shake as though returning to her senses and shaking off the orgasm cloud.

Someone was knocking at her door. The front door right beside where they were tangled up on the carpet in a messy pile of limbs . . . she half naked and he, sadly, not. Her frown deepened and she paused at that realization. She suddenly felt very cheated. How could she have just had the best orgasm—correction, *two* orgasms—at the expert hands of Cruz Walsh and she didn't get to see him out of his clothes? It was vastly wrong.

But back to the point she couldn't ignore right now . . . someone was at her door.

Someone was pounding at her door just as she was two seconds from having sex with Cruz. Sex with Cruz seemed like a non-thing now. She lurched into a sitting position, bringing her legs together and arranging her panties back into place.

It wasn't going to happen. Definitely not now. Apparently she had company. She couldn't imagine who was at her door at this hour, but she wasn't about to ignore the knocking. There could be an issue with Nana Betty.

She reached for her leggings. They were inside out. With a curse, she struggled to set them to rights, stabbing her feet into the leg holes and then hopping like a mad woman. He was slow to get to his feet, and then she noticed why.

A giant erection swelled the front of his jeans. She felt her eyes widen . . . for multiple reasons.

Firstly, his size was impressive . . . and intimidating. He was big. As in is-that-thing-real-or-is-there-a-sock-stuffed-in-there big. Secondly, he actually wore a pained grimace. He actually appeared to be in pain.

That was some consolation. She didn't think any man had ever wanted her so badly . . . or ever *would*. She didn't consider herself the kind of woman to inspire such arousal. And the fact that they couldn't do anything about it right now made her want to weep.

"Are you . . . okay?" she asked in a voice she hardly recognized as her own. It was breathless and soft . . . and frankly . . . it sounded a little Jessica Rabbit. It had that I've-been-well-pleasured quality to it.

His big hand lowered to himself and, still grimacing, he adjusted his engorged member. "I'll survive. Self-denial is character building. Isn't that what people say?"

She simply stared at him, stunned that he could feel any degree of anguish over not having her. As though she were some . . . *prize*.

"Aunt Gabby! I know you're in there."

She jerked out of her thoughts. "Oh my God. It's my nephew."

Cruz sighed. "So this definitely isn't happening. Is that what you're telling me?"

Pleasure suffused her to hear the longing in his voice. Longing for *her*.

It hadn't gone away simply because they stopped touching each other. She gazed into his dark eyes and felt herself melting all over again. God, she wanted to attack him. Throw herself at him. She wanted to unzip his jeans and free that cock of his she'd been ogling.

"Aunt Gabby!"

Shaking her head, she rushed to the door and looked through the peephole, confirming that it was, in fact, her nephew standing on the other side of the door, looking decidedly impatient. She spun back around, her hand going to her throat in dramatic fashion. "He can't see you," she whispered shrilly.

"Aunt Gabby? My dad sent me over to check on you and Nana."

She frowned. Anthony had never sent Trent to check on her before. Why, tonight, did he suddenly decide to do this? Was there some kind of internal big brother alert that warned him his little sister might be getting some action and he must impede?

Almost in answer to her thoughts, he added, "He was worried after you disappeared at Dakota's ceremony and then you didn't call him."

Oh. Yeah. She winced. She never answered her brother's earlier texts asking her to call him. She got caught up in work and then Nana and then Cruz. Her gaze skimmed over his impressive body. Obviously, Cruz.

Plus, she didn't love conversations with her

brother. It always felt a bit like she was talking to her father—if her father had ever been the type to go all fatherly and judgmental on her. But he wasn't that type. He pretty much kept to his hobbies and let her live her life. She wished her brother would do the same and not try to parent her.

"You have to go," she mouthed and then winced as her mind tracked over the layout of this apartment. "But there's no back door."

He nodded. "Yeah. That's a problem."

"You'll have to climb out a back window."

He snorted. "It's been years since I had to do that. Sorry, but I'm past the age where I climb out of windows." He stepped around her, lifting a hand for the door knob.

Her mind raced ahead, envisioning him stepping outside and coming face-to-face with her nephew . . . and how then her nephew would carry tales to the family. Soon they would all know Cruz Walsh had been in her apartment late at night. She couldn't even pretend it had been innocent. That would have been a lie and she was a terrible liar. Her siblings could always see right through her. Plus, he was Cruz Walsh. One look at him and a person didn't think *innocent*. Clearly.

She grabbed his arm, desperate to get him to stop. "You can't—"

He whirled around and snatched her up in his arms, lifting her off her feet and planting his mouth on hers in a searing kiss that tasted faintly earthy and she knew it was herself she was tasting on him. She knew and didn't care because it was his mouth on her. His hands. His body hard against her softness.

She should be resisting. *Hello.* Her nephew was two feet away on the other side of the door. Unfortunately, she couldn't resist. She just wasn't that strong. Or smart, apparently. She dove right back into the kiss, circling her arms around his neck and clinging to him like a vine.

It was Cruz who ended it. Who broke away with a ragged breath. He held on to her face, his big hands burning twin imprints into her cheeks. His gaze crawled over her face. He was all intensity as he uttered, "I'll be seeing you again."

Excitement thrummed through her veins, followed swiftly by panic. She shouldn't want that so very badly. She liked him too much. Always had. She could fall hard for him and nothing could ever come of it. She should stop it now before the eventual heartbreak. "Really, no."

His dark eyes seemed to grow even darker. "This isn't finished between us."

"We can't—" She stopped, unsure any longer

why they couldn't. What was her resistance? She had put to bed the idea of interviewing him. There was no professional conflict.

"Why not?" he prompted.

She frowned, still reluctant to agree to this . . . whatever *it* was.

A fling.

His voice dropped to a velvet pitch. Almost as though he could read her internal battle, he drawled in a voice that she felt like a caress, "The next time we meet, it's going to be to fuck."

She gasped and, admittedly, felt a small thrill. He was bold and primal and visceral and she wanted to wrap herself in all of that, snuggle into it like a warm blanket. Into *him*. He made her feel feminine and wanted in a way she had never felt before.

Apparently done talking, he turned and opened the front door.

Trent almost fell forward into the small entrance hall, but he caught himself. His gaze landed on Cruz and then his eyes nearly doubled in size on his face. "Ahhh. Sorry. I didn't know you had company, Aunt Gabby. I was just coming home from a party and Dad asked me to stop by."

Cruz gave him a brisk nod of greeting and then walked out the door, leaving them both standing there in the doorway to her apartment looking after him. Gawking after him, really. And it was a fine sight indeed. She couldn't help from watching the way his jeans hugged his ass nicely.

"Isn't that the guy from the news? The one who . . ." Trent's voice deliberately faded. Shelley Rae's name wasn't discussed freely within the family. He knew that. He'd been trained about that from an early age. She was a subject to be avoided. Clearly, their family didn't do grief or complicated subjects well.

"Yes," she supplied.

Her nephew glanced at her. "Cruz Walsh?" he asked, as though needing absolute confirmation.

She nodded once, feeling suddenly very grim, already imagining him reporting this information back to his dad. "Yes."

"The one who went to prison for murdering Shelley Rae?" Okay. So Trent was more at ease stating the facts than the rest of them. Must be a generational thing. Good for him.

"Yes, Trent. But he was exonerated, remember?" She winced at her defensive tone. "But yeah, it's him."

"He was in your house . . ."

She nodded with a sigh. Clearly this was something her nephew was grappling with. She couldn't fault him, she supposed. She was still grappling with it, too.

He continued, "And you look . . ."

He looked her up and down in a thorough inspection. She tried not to fidget. She was fully dressed. He could have no idea what just transpired in the very spot they were standing. Plus, she was his aunt. In his mind, she was old and boring and past the age for sexy times.

His silence stretched, making her more uncomfortable. "I look like what?" she asked.

His survey seemed to linger on her wrinkled blouse. Her hand crept up self-consciously to smooth over the fabric.

"You look like you've been making out," he finished.

Heat flamed her face. How could he know that? Her nephew was young. What did he know about such things? She could still remember when she changed his diapers. Five years ago, he was still watching cartoons.

Trent is now the same age she was when Cruz rocked her world in the boathouse.

The reminder didn't help. It didn't make her feel better. She was his aunt. An adult. She should be sensitive to his sensibilities. She didn't want to scar him with the image of her making out. Nor did she want him telling any of the family his theories about her and Cruz Walsh.

"Trent," she tsked, determined to convince him he was wrong. "Of course, I wasn't—"

"C'mon." His gaze flicked over her in amusement. "I know the signs. I mean, not that I blame you." He glanced back out in the direction where Cruz disappeared. "He's hot."

It was her turn to gawk. "Trent?" She was pretty sure guys didn't call other guys hot with the same appreciative inflection she just heard in her nephew's voice. At least not most hetero guys.

Trent looked back at her and shrugged. "Yeah. I'm gay."

She blinked. He said it so matter-of-factly. Like she should know. "I . . . did I somehow miss this information? I didn't know that—"

"Yeah, I haven't told the family yet. My sister knows. And you. Haven't told my parents yet. I was waiting until I leave in a few months for college." He smiled and shrugged nonchalantly. "But now you know I'm gay. Figure you can handle it."

"Well, yes. Of course. I'm glad you told me . . . are you sure you don't want to go ahead and tell your parents? Are you worried they won't be understanding?"

"Oh, I know they'll come around, but they're going to have an adjustment period. It could get difficult and I'd rather not be here when that happens. They can mourn the me they thought I would be while I'm away at school."

"They may not *mourn* at all," she pointed out. Her brother might be a hoverer and rule the family like some patriarch à la *The Godfather*, but he loved his kids. She knew he'd love them no matter what. "It may not even be a thing for them at all. Have a little faith. Tell them."

He arched an eyebrow. "When are you going to tell the family you're dating Cruz Walsh?"

Her face heated at his clever rejoinder. "We're not dating."

"Oh?" He made a knowing humming sound. "So you're just . . . friends?"

She squirmed and shifted on her feet. Even admitting to that didn't feel right.

"Friends with benefits?" Trent amended with a smirk.

"Oh, you brat! No!" She swatted his arm.

"I have eyes . . . and a nose. I could practically smell the sex pheromones in the air when I entered the apartment."

"Trent!" It was like she was seeing her nephew for the first time . . . and her biggest shock was that he had just uttered the word *sex* in her presence. She may never recover from that.

"C'mon. Clearly I interrupted something."

"Nothing," she insisted. "You interrupted nothing," she lied. "I'm hoping to get an interview out of him for my paper." God, she was going to hell for all the lies tripping off her tongue. What she had been doing with Cruz had nothing to do with work. "I would appreciate it if you didn't mention it to the family though. Given past history, they might not understand."

He lifted both eyebrows. "That's an understatement."

"Promise me?" she pressed.

"Of course." He nodded. "I'll report back to Dad that I interrupted you reading a book." He smirked. "The Bible."

"Nice." With a roll of her eyes she shoved him lightly toward the door. "Now get home and do some homework or something."

He pulled a face. "It's the weekend."

"It's Sunday. You should have something due tomorrow."

"Not really." His grin suddenly deepened.

"What?" she asked warily. "Why are you smiling like that?"

"Now we both know each other's secrets."

She blew out a breath and looked heavenward.

Except her secret needed to stay that way. Forever. It needed to stay hidden. Actually, no. Her secret needed to be expunged. It needed to *not* be a thing.

True. She was thirty, and she should definitely feel free to live her own life, but that didn't mean it was okay to have Cruz Walsh in her life. On the surface, it just seemed like a bad idea to be involved with anyone she couldn't introduce to her family. Not that he was proposing or anything. No, he was only about one thing when it came to her. Maybe she should just focus on that and go for it. A fling. Would it be so wrong?

Trent left and she locked the door after him. She waited, lingering in her kitchen for a few moments. She knew what she was doing. She had to be honest with herself at the very least. She knew she was waiting . . . *hoping* Cruz would come back. Ugh. She really was a sad, desperate creature. On one hand she told herself: *no, you can't have that*. Then, a moment later, she was sidling close and purring against him like a cat.

"Screw it." She moved into the kitchen and raided her pantry. She snatched a few Oreos, dropped them on a plate and then poured herself a glass of milk. Oreos seemed like a fine post-orgasm snack. She headed into her bedroom and settled on her bed. Flipping channels, she found a rerun of *Golden Girls* and settled back with a contented sigh.

It was a crazy weekend. She got locked in a closet with her high school crush.

And they made out like they were hormonal teens.

These things happened. It didn't change her goals. She was still heading back to Austin the first chance she got and putting Sweet Hill far behind her.

FOURTEEN

*N*EVER IN HIS life had he been so glad and so sure of the decision to open a gym. He had a place to go. A place to release all his pent-up sexual frustration. A place that was his own. He'd had few to none of those things in his life.

As soon as he left Gabriella's apartment, he made a beeline for the building. He was a man accustomed to self-deprivation. He spent seven years in prison. Of course, he was used to it, but he physically hurt leaving her. He ached. He could still taste her on his lips and tongue, still feel the satin of her skin against his hands.

Her body was better than all his imaginings. Soft and yielding. Wide-hipped. Plump thighs and breasts that overflowed in his hands. His slightest squeeze could make her go wild, wiggling and whimpering in need.

He debated turning his car around and parking in front of her place again, waiting for her nephew to leave. But that felt too much like stalking. And he wasn't a criminal. Even if the majority of the population would disagree with him.

He had his boundaries and he wasn't going to stalk this woman. He'd have her, but she would come to him. A woman didn't respond like that and then simply walk away and forget it. It had been the single most exciting sexual encounter of his life and they hadn't even fully fucked. He knew she'd felt the same. She wanted him.

As he made his way across town to the building, thoughts of Gabriella twisting through his mind, he firmly decided he would be patient. He'd waited this long, after all. He'd found her when he had not even been looking. It felt unreal. He had finally found his dream girl from the boathouse . . . who happened to be the same girl he had lusted after in high school. Unbelievable, but true.

He'd never subscribed to notions of fate or destiny before, but he might have to change his mind because clearly it was meant to be.

As he pulled into the parking lot of his gym, he felt the usual deep sense of contentment sweep over him. *His*. This belonged to him.

The facility was eight thousand square feet. It

used to be a distribution center for a furniture store that shut down operation in Sweet Hill. It had been vacant for years. He got it for a steal and then set to work renovating. It hadn't been too difficult to convert the space and get it up to codes. Easier than building a place from scratch. While it was technically finished and he'd opened the doors a couple months ago, there was still plenty he wanted to do. For instance, he planned to install a rock wall next month. Down the road, he'd like to install a couple indoor trampolines.

He could do that now. Build. Dream. Plan for the future.

The city had awarded him a settlement of five hundred and twenty-five thousand dollars for his wrongful imprisonment. It was a preemptive measure. He had no idea how they came up with such a figure . . . no idea what led them to believe five hundred and twenty-five K was the standard of recompense for seven years in prison.

Hale told him they feared a lawsuit. As county sheriff, his brother-in-law was privy to such information. Even if it wasn't his office that had arrested Cruz, he moved in official circles. He heard things.

The thought of suing had not even crossed Cruz's mind. Honestly, his sudden freedom was so unexpected, he was simply grateful for it.

In the seven years he was in prison he had not let himself contemplate freedom. According to his sentence, he was going to be an old man before he got out. He shifted uneasily. The prospect of that now struck cold fear through him. If things hadn't played out the way they had—if he hadn't been exonerated—he'd still be in his cell right now and Gabriella would be out in the world. Some other man would be going down on her and it wouldn't be him. She would float through her life, through relationships, eventually marrying and having babies with someone else.

The entire prospect made him feel ill. His hands clenched on the steering wheel until his knuckles turned white.

Also, he had confessed to the crime in which he was convicted all those years ago in an effort to spare his sister. Sisters, actually. No one had forced him to do that. He had no one to blame. Hale said he could probably get an attorney and press for more money. Except Cruz had confessed to the crime, so perhaps not. That would not be a factor in his favor.

True, the City of Sweet Hill Police Department had done little in the way of investigation. Once he confessed, the case was closed. After all, murder was precisely the sort of behavior expected of him.

Cruz Walsh a convicted murderer? That sounded about right to the citizens of Sweet Hill. He wasn't about to contradict the assumption.

Piper had thought herself responsible for killing Shelley Rae and he had bought into her assumption of guilt. When she woke up from a drugged sleep to find Shelley Rae dead, she assumed she had killed the girl and simply couldn't remember doing it. He'd stopped her from turning herself in. He couldn't let her go to jail. If Piper went to prison, Malia would have gone into state custody. Cruz had a record. There was no way they were going to give custody of a little girl to him.

So he had done what he had to in order to protect them. He had gone to jail for his sisters. It was the story everyone wanted. The police knew, of course, because the real killer, Colby Mathers, had confessed after all these years and they finally had all the facts. The rest of the world, however, wanted to know the details. They wanted to know *why*.

Why did Mathers kill Shelley Rae and come forward so many years later? Why did Cruz confess when he had been innocent? Those were the details the rest of the world wanted to know.

As far as he was concerned the rest of the world could go to hell.

If they wanted to be entertained they could look

elsewhere. His life wasn't going to be salacious fodder for bored housewives at the checkout stand. Sure. Media outlets were offering serious money for his story, but he could live without it.

He didn't, for one moment, regret his decision to take the fall. Not even during the seven years he was in prison. Not in his bleakest moment in Devil's Rock.

He parked his truck in the empty parking lot. This late, no one else was here. As he stopped at the door and unlocked it, a voice called out from behind him.

"Hey, y'all open?"

He turned around to spot two teenagers. One of them bounced a basketball in a steady beat over the sidewalk, his hand gripping the ball in clear expertise. Cruz recognized them as boys who had started coming to the rec center to play basketball after school.

"Little late," he commented. "Shouldn't you be home? Parents are probably looking for you."

The two boys exchanged looks and snorted. "Our parents aren't home."

Cruz grew up with a mother who was never home either. Most of the time he and his sister had to fend for themselves. He decided to take the money from his settlement and open the rec center so the kids in the surrounding neighborhoods would have a place to go. Kids like him—or rather kids like who he *used to be*. Kids that felt a little lost. When no one was at home, they would have a home at his gym.

It was a way to keep them out of trouble, but it also gave them community . . . a place where they would always feel welcome.

He assessed the boys for a long moment. One of them jutted out his chin, almost seeming to say: *Go ahead. Turn us away. Everyone does.*

"You can come in and play basketball as long as I'm here working out." He shrugged. "Should be about an hour. You can go home when I leave."

They glanced at each other and then smiled slowly. "Cool. Thanks, man."

He pushed the door open and motioned them in. They took off and headed for the side of the gym with a basketball court, the sound of the bouncing ball echoing off the far walls and high ceiling.

Cruz headed toward the weights and other various exercise equipment. He climbed up on a treadmill. After his run, he'd move on to weights. He fully intended to wear himself out to the point of exhaustion so that when he got home and fell into bed, he'd surrender to sleep instantly and wouldn't lie there for hours fantasizing about Gabriella Rossi. He'd leave thoughts of her to his dreams.

CRUZ RETURNED THE next night.

She'd spent the day cleaning house and on the phone with Nana's insurance, trying to get her physical therapy extended into a permanent home-care plan. Keeping busy mostly. It helped. She only thought about Cruz every few minutes instead of all the time.

"What are you doing here?" she asked breath-lessly, flipping out inside for multiple reasons—the main one being that Cruz Walsh was standing on her grandmother's front porch. What alternate re-ality was this?

"I thought you might not feel like cooking." He held up bags. Instantly her nose was bombarded by the smell of all manner of goodness.

Coco was distracted by the presence of food, too. He growled and yipped and whined, lifting up on his hind legs and then losing his balance as a result of his cumbersome weight. Scrambling back up to his feet, he took turns between growling and whin-ing, still torn. Clearly, he couldn't decide whether he should do his usual greeting of snarling growls when the visitor in question comes bearing food.

She actually understood his indecision.

Instead of making excuses and closing the door on him—like she probably should—she pointed to the bags. "What are those?"

"A little of everything. I didn't know what you and your grandmother might like so I got some baked ziti, barbecue and some pad thai." She looked from the bags to him and felt herself relenting.

"Gabriella! Who is at the door?"

Nana's cane thudded on the floor, drawing closer. She was only occasionally using the walker now. They made her take it when she left the house on any outings. With the help of her physical therapy, she was starting to get around well—almost like a spry sixty-year-old again. She was better than before her surgery, which had been the hope all along and the reason she put herself through the ordeal.

Gabriella looked over her shoulder, watching Nana's approach with dread, worried what she would say when she spotted Cruz. No doubt she would recognize him. She'd been in the courtroom all those years ago during his trial.

"What do you have there, young man?" Nana's gaze dropped from his face to the bags he held.

"Uhh, this is my friend, Nana. He brought us some food."

"Good. I'm starving." She waved at Gabriella. "This one here was about to make us a box of macaroni and cheese. Let's see if you can beat that. Come on inside."

Smiling in satisfaction, Cruz stepped inside and murmured to her, "Box of mac, huh? That shouldn't be hard to beat."

She shut the door after him, grumbling, "Don't act so pleased with yourself. It's not as though you slaved behind a stove and cooked the food yourself."

Chuckling, he moved ahead of her, following after Nana. Nana, who apparently didn't recognize him. God bless her cataracts.

"No, I'm just the guy who brought it."

She followed at a slower pace, taking several deep breaths to calm her racing pulse. Nana didn't know who he was. They would eat and he would leave. End of story.

She likely would never remember this night enough to piece together his identity.

Nana never watched or read the news anymore; she claimed it was too depressing. She stuck to *Wheel of Fortune* and episodes of *Law & Order*. Apparently those weren't depressing.

Gabriella couldn't argue with Nana about her opinion of the news, but she felt an obligation to know what was happening in the world. It was a requirement of the job.

Nana and Cruz continued to banter ahead of her and she forced herself to relax.

It would be okay. She just had to keep her composure.

She entered the kitchen to the scene of Nana and Cruz unloading the food onto the kitchen table like they had done the task a hundred times. Like they were old friends. Nana was chatting about *Law & Order*. It was actually a new episode tonight so she was extra excited.

Nana looked up and caught her eye. "So," she said in a jarring tone. "How long you two been dating?"

Ugh. "Nana! You know I'm not dating anyone."

"Honey, the man brought you food." Nana pulled back the aluminum foil over a tray of food and arched both bushy eyebrows at the assortment of brisket, sausage and ribs. "Meat. He brought you *meat*," she clarified.

"Nana," she groaned.

Cruz chuckled as he pulled the pad thai out of a bag. "It's okay." He leaned in closer to Gabriella, his arm pressing against hers. "I *am* kind of into her. Have been since high school."

Fire lit her face. Stupid flutters erupted in her belly. "Stop that," she hissed.

"Aww, isn't that sweet? You hear that, Gabriella?" Nana pointed at Cruz approvingly. "I like this one. He liked you even in high school and we all know how awkward those years were for you."

Nana turned to take down three plates from the cabinet.

Cruz sidled closer and murmured for her ears only, "Well, your grandmother likes me. What about you?"

She scowled. "You shouldn't have come."

"And let you eat boxed mac n' cheese?" He shook his head with a tsk.

"Let's eat in the living room." Nana returned with plates and started loading her own plate with a variety of food. "We can watch *Law & Order*. I don't want to miss it."

Nana had yet to figure out that you could record shows or pull them up to watch later.

"Here, Nana, I'll get your plate." Gabriella gestured for her grandmother to go ahead of her into the living room.

Gabriella followed and helped settle her into a chair. After making sure the plate was balanced carefully on Nana's lap, she said, "I'll get you a drink. What would you like?"

"Tea. I made a fresh pitcher this afternoon."

Satisfied she had a handle on her plate and wasn't going to spill her food, Gabriella turned to fetch her tea, but Cruz was already entering the room with it.

"Here you go." He set it on the side table beside her grandmother's chair.

Gabriella frowned, wishing he wasn't being so solicitous. It would be easier to resist him that way. If he wasn't so . . . charming.

He sent her a wink as he straightened. With a huff, she marched back into the kitchen, trying not to care if he followed.

She made herself a plate, wishing she wasn't hungry. Then she could ignore the impressive spread of food. Plate in hand, she turned to fetch a fork from the drawer only to find him directly in her path.

"Oh." She stepped back.

"Why do I get the feeling you're not happy to see me?"

"Yesterday you hid your car so my grandmother didn't see it. Now you're in her kitchen."

"Yeah. I thought about that, and I figured that since I wasn't a criminal, I shouldn't sneak around and act like one. I have a feeling I'm going to be coming around a lot to see you, and I don't really feel like being your dirty little secret. I played that role before." He shook his head and she understood his meaning.

He meant Natalie and other girls. The good girls who used him. That was a slap in the face. She winced. She didn't want to be anything remotely like them. Never.

She swallowed thickly. "You're going to be coming around . . . a lot?" Her stupid heart fluttered at that. She felt like a teenage girl who just found out her crush liked her back. God. She might be an adult now, but her heart hadn't gotten the memo.

He smiled slowly and it was lethal. She felt the beauty of it like an arrow to her heart. "Well, yeah," he said easily. Without elaborating, he moved on into the living room with his plate of food, immediately asking Nana questions about the show.

She stood in the kitchen a little longer, trying to regain her breath and composure and figure out just what the hell was happening here. Was Cruz Walsh . . . *courting* her? It didn't seem possible. It certainly couldn't be as simple as that. Not with their history . . . not with her family.

Carrying her plate of food, she joined them, sinking down on the couch beside Cruz. It was the only place to sit, but she was careful to keep space between them. Careful not to touch. They ate and watched the television. Well, she mostly just stared at the actors moving and talking.

At one point, her phone vibrated on the table beside the couch. It was from her sister.

Can you watch Noah tomorrow night?
Douchebag backed out on his night with the

kids and I already made plans. Can't find anyone else. Dakota has plans, too.

Douchebag was her sister's pet name for her ex-husband. She typed back. Sure.

Her sister was a pain in the ass, but she loved her nephew.

Setting her phone down, she noticed the episode was over and Nana was dozing in her chair. Cruz noticed, too. He moved swiftly, relieving Nana of her plate before it slid off her lap to the carpet.

Gabriella stood and gathered all three of their plates. "She ate well," she commented. "I'll have to get that baked ziti for her again. She loved it." God. She was rambling, nervous as a schoolgirl.

She set the plates aside and roused her grandmother. "Nana, come on. Let's get you to bed."

She roused groggily and reached for her cane, pushing up.

Gabriella escorted her into her bedroom. Not so much because her grandmother couldn't get herself ready for bed, but because it gave her a reprieve from Cruz. He wasn't going to follow them into Nana's bedroom. The problem was that ten minutes later Nana was in bed and snoring, dead to the world, and then Gabriella had no choice but to go out there and face Cruz again—racing heart and libido and all.

Sucking in a breath, she reminded herself that she was a big girl. If she didn't want to sleep with him, then she wouldn't sleep with him . . . even if she *wanted* to. Gah.

All the dishes were gone from the living room, ostensibly gathered up by Cruz. Great. He was helpful, too.

She moved into the kitchen and started on the dishes, super aware that he was near the table, boxing up all the leftovers. He'd brought so much. They'd have leftovers for days.

They worked in silence. Once the last dish was put away, she turned to face him, wiping her hands dry on a dish towel. "Thank you for dinner."

"Maybe tomorrow we can do this at my place. I can actually cook. Grill some steaks."

She dragged in a deep breath. A man that cooked. She thought that was a unicorn. Cody could hardly boil water for pasta.

"Tempting," she murmured. Her gaze flicked over him. *All* of him was tempting. But what was she doing here? She couldn't *date* Cruz Walsh. And she had never done no-strings sex. She didn't judge those who did . . . it just wasn't her.

"Then say yes." He shrugged like it was a no-brainer. And for him, it was. He had nothing to lose. No family members sitting in judgment. The community already judged him, so there was nothing for him to worry about on that score.

Meaningless sex wasn't anything new for him. He could get sex from anyone. He didn't need it from her. For whatever reason, that caused a pang in her heart.

She hesitated, and the longer she hesitated, the more solemn his expression became. "You can't." Not a question. A grim pronouncement.

She nodded slowly, wondering at the regret knifing through her. She was rejecting empty sex. It didn't mean anything. It didn't matter. "I can't."

He continued, "Let me guess. It's my name, right?"

"Your name?"

"Yeah. If my name was *anything* else . . . if *I* was anyone else, you'd say yes." He laughed mirthlessly.

"You can't pretend who you are . . . who *I* am . . . doesn't matter," she bit out.

"I just think you're overthinking it." His gaze crawled over her, leaving a wake of heat and longing everywhere his eyes landed. "I'm not proposing."

Humiliation stung her cheeks. Did he think she was angling for *that*? "No, no, of course not."

"You haven't just ever let yourself go? Followed your gut . . ." He inched closer, backing her up against the counter. Their bodies weren't touching, but they might as well have been for how suddenly breathless she felt. She arched away and that only seemed to thrust her breasts out. His gaze dipped down before traveling back up to her face. "You've never followed your desires? Given in to impulse?"

No. She never had. That seemed like behavior for the young and reckless, and she had never been young and reckless even when she was young. It certainly didn't seem right to behave that way now when she was thirty. That was the height of irre-sponsibility.

He closed that last bit of distance between them, aligning his body fully to hers. His deep, dark voice rolled over her. "Just fuck for fucking's sake? Because you wanted it?"

She gasped. His words were like their own aphrodisiac. No one had ever talked that way to her before (well, except him in previous days). She knew it was wicked, but his purring dirty talk shot liquid heat straight to her core and she could only think one thing: *more*.

More dirty talk. *More* him. She wanted him to follow through and fulfill on all the touching and kissing and fondling. Which was damned confusing because she was telling him the opposite, telling him that she couldn't do this.

His eyes were suddenly too much. His closeness too much. She twisted around and turned until she was facing the counter—until she had nothing to stare at except plain wood cabinets, but he was still there. She felt him behind her, radiating heat and desire.

"You've never done that?" His voice husked against the back of her head, rustling her hair.

"No," she managed to get out. She had only ever had sex within the bounds of a relationship.

"It'd be hot. Just physical. Nothing going on in your head except how I feel inside you."

Before she could stop herself, a moan escaped her lips.

His hand delved into her hair, lightly at first. She dropped her head back, her gasp ragged. His breath fanned hotly over her ear, and his touch grew firmer, fingers spearing through her hair and rubbing her tingling scalp. Still moaning, she arched her neck to the side, guided by the hard hand in her hair, granting him her neck. His mouth landed on her throat, kissing gently. At the first stroke of his tongue to her skin, her knees buckled. He caught her by pressing in closer, sandwiching her between the counter and his body.

She was on fire. She pushed back against his erection, grinding her bottom into his hardness, moaning as his wet mouth loved her neck. Her eyes fluttered shut and she bit her lip to stop from crying out loudly. It was bad enough she was already moaning like an animal.

Was it possible to orgasm with your clothes on? She felt like she was seconds from coming. God, she wanted his dirty words to become a reality. She wanted him inside her.

She inhaled a ragged breath, trying to pull herself together.

Her desire couldn't be repressed, however. Not anymore. It rushed through her like a high-speed train.

Her body ached and hummed. He felt so good against her it was frightening.

With a frustrated choke, she turned around again, squeezing between him and the edge of the counter. He looked down at her, so much taller, bigger, the dark of his eyes almost black as he gazed at her.

He braced his hands against the counter's edge, loosely caging her in.

"Cruz," she whispered, a thread of wonder in her voice that he was here, real and not a figment of her imagination conjured from the past. She flattened a hand against his chest. To push away or because she had to touch him, she wasn't sure.

"Yes?" he prodded.

She lifted her chin, grabbing for something, some lifeline to save her from sinking into the sea of him. "I'm not the same naïve starry-eyed girl obsessed with you."

He smiled. "You were obsessed with me? Interesting."

"No! Not . . . obsessed."

"No? Too bad. Because I was obsessed with you. In prison you were who I thought about when I dreamed about freedom and what I was missing on the outside."

Her heart constricted at that confession. It was too *un*real to be . . . real.

She stared up at his mouth—that beautiful mouth. She stopped just short of begging him to kiss her with it.

His heart beat hard against her palm, but hers beat harder. It was all so awkward. Almost like she didn't know what to do next, which was ridiculous. She'd done this before.

But never with him. Never with a man that oozed sex.

Maybe that was just it. She had never been with anyone like *him*. Never someone so . . . well, hot. His body was a weapon, cut and muscled, humming with strength and the promise of sexual gratification.

Her shaking hand inched its way up his shirt, stopping at the hard curve of his shoulder. Maybe just one time wouldn't hurt. They both deserved that, didn't they? Maybe once and then they would have it—each other—out of their systems. She'd be gone soon. Back in Austin. Why not?

She rose up on tiptoes and pressed her mouth to his warm neck. He tensed and shuddered as she feathered tiny kisses along the bristly edge of his jaw, reaching the corner of his mouth.

Air gusted from her lips at arriving there. She stretched higher and slanted her mouth across his more fully. His lips were firm and dry. Soft. Her chest squeezed with a desperate hunger for him to kiss her back. Finally, he did. His head dipped, swiftly catching her mouth with a growl. Taking her hand, he dragged it between them and placed it over his swollen crotch. "See how much I want you, Gabriella Rossi?"

She nodded jerkily. Somehow he did. He wanted her . . . and she believed him. She had never felt more desirable in her life.

He grabbed her by the waist and picked her up, plopping her onto the counter before she could draw another breath. The position brought their lips level. He settled a hand at her waist while his other hand sank into her hair, fingers curling around the base of her skull, pulling her in, hauling her closer until their mouths collided again.

She moaned as his tongue entered her mouth, slicked over hers skillfully, in total control. She leaned in, groaning, stroking her tongue against his, tasting the tartness of the lemonade he had consumed with his meal.

God. He tasted good. Like sex. Yes. She tasted sex on his tongue. She curled her fingers into his shoulders, clinging to him, tugging him closer, opening her mouth wider.

She was out of breath and drowning. Drowning in him. She couldn't think to form coherent words. She could only pant and gasp his name as he sucked on her bottom lip.

He made a rumbling sound in his throat and kissed her deeper, his fingers dropping to her thighs, searing her through the fabric of her leggings. She touched his face, the scrape of his incoming beard delicious against her palms.

They kissed and kissed and kissed. She didn't know kissing could be like this. Both endless and not enough. Addictive. Drugging.

One of his hands moved up and palmed her

breast. Sensation shot through her and she whimpered into his mouth, pushing into his palm.

"Bri," he muttered against her lips. His hands left her.

She mewled at the loss, but it was only temporary. He grabbed the hem of her shirt and whipped it over her head, leaving her only in her bra from the waist up on Nana's counter. God. She was in Nana's kitchen. Her family came and went through this house like it was Grand Central Station. That should have her putting this to a screeching halt.

His eyes went to her chest and she thanked God she was in one of her prettier demi cups. "Fuck." He closed his eyes in a hard blink before opening them again and fixating on her chest, a glazed quality to his dark eyes. "Do you know how many times I jerked off in high school envisioning you like this?"

"God," she gasped. The deep velvet of his voice twisted her desire into something almost painful between her legs. She should be appalled, but thinking about *him*—the boy she used to ogle—lusting after her while stroking his cock to a frenzy? It made her throb and pulse. It made her wet.

His eyes, hungry and intent on her, moved down the slope of her throat to the tops of her breasts brimming from her bra. She felt her nipples tighten under his stare.

She watched him watch her, reveling in his stark beauty, the intensity of those deep-set eyes on her, the slash of his sexy mouth. She was so caught up in the brutal beauty of him that she didn't initially realize what he was doing with his hands.

One reached for her, covering her breast. He dipped a finger inside the cup of her bra. Air hissed out of her lips when he brushed over a nipple.

She gasped.

His deep voice rippled through her. "Alone in my cell, when I'd think about tits . . . sex . . . it was your face I remembered."

She could only nod senselessly as he dipped a second finger inside her bra. He rolled and pinched the stiff nipple. Back and forth, back and forth, he toyed with the crest, making the point grow harder with every twist of his fingers.

With a choke, she dropped her head back and thrust out her chest.

"You're so hot," he growled.

Hot? Gabriella?

It suddenly occurred to her that she wasn't Flabby Gabby anymore. Not doing this. Maybe she had never been. He'd wanted her back in high school. How could he have wanted her if she was so undesirable then?

Then he moved to her other breast, rolling that rapidly hardening nipple. She felt a fresh rush of moisture between her legs. She squirmed on the counter, desperate for an end to the ache growing there.

He looked up at her from beneath heavy lids, watching her as he tugged the cup of her bra down and bared one breast. A ripe nipple popped free and he groaned, sinking down so that his hot mouth closed over the tip of her breast like he was a starving man.

She cried out as his warm tongue sucked her nipple deep into his mouth.

Her sex clenched in agony, aching to be filled.

She clutched the back of his head, urging him closer. Everything in her tensed and squeezed, pleasure fixing where his mouth devoured her, his tongue licking, his teeth scraping.

"Cruz!" she cried out again as he suddenly turned on her other breast, yanking her bra down roughly, thrusting the heavy mound high, the straps digging into her shoulders. But she didn't care. He fed on her like she was a feast spread before him, sucking hungrily, licking and nipping.

Wild, embarrassing little pants escaped her. Especially when his teeth dragged across one hard nipple and his fingers pinched down on the other one.

The pressure inside her twisted into something that she couldn't stop. She actually did push against it, too alarmed at the force building inside her, too terrified at the new sensations.

Men that cooked weren't the only unicorns. Orgasms were, too. Most of the ones she ever had were self-administered. Certainly no guy but him had ever given her one from playing with her breasts.

Tremors began to ripple through her. "Oh, oh, oh, oh . . ."

He spoke against her breast, his words muffled as his tongue played on her flesh. "That's it. Come for me."

She shook her head. She felt out of control. Out of her body.

"Take it. It's yours. Let yourself have it." His voice dropped hard between them, velvet warm, but no less than commanding. His hand flew between her splayed thighs on the counter, rubbing at her crotch. She knew she was damp and his fingers had discovered it. Mortification burned her cheeks at the truth he felt there, at the evidence of her shameless hunger. She was hornier than a hormonal teen.

Those fingers rubbed up and down and the friction was unbearable. She squirmed, the pressure acute—especially when he grazed her clit. "Oh, you're beautiful . . . so wet."

As though he said the magic words, she burst, coming apart with a cry and surging against him. She trembled, gasping, fireworks going off behind her eyes as he wrapped her in his arms.

She couldn't form coherent speech. Her muscles went limp as noodles, her legs hanging off the counter.

With effort, she lifted her head, her eyes seeking his. He was waiting, watching her. She moistened her lips, ready to invite him to join her at her apartment. It seemed the obvious next step. Just once. At least one time. She couldn't pass up the opportunity.

"Gabriella!"

She jerked at the sound of Nana's shrill voice.

"Gabriella! I forgot to take my medicine with dinner."

Cruz quickly stepped back. She slid off the counter with shaking limbs.

"Coming," she called, grateful Nana hadn't gotten out of bed to discover her half naked on the counter. She shuddered, thinking about how that could have easily happened. Anyone could have walked in on them . . . Cruz's head bent as he sucked at her breasts. Oh. God. She'd never live it down. She pressed a hand to her heart. Just the idea of it gave her palpitations.

Cruz stretched out a hand, holding out her shirt for her, his dark eyes probing, searching her face. "Here."

"Thanks." She quickly donned it, pulling it over her head, feeling much more composed. She moved to the cabinet where they kept Nana's meds. "You better go," she heard herself saying.

He didn't say anything and she sent him a look over her shoulder.

He stared at her grimly. "Now you want me to leave?"

She felt his disappointment. She even understood it. She got her rocks off . . . he hadn't. Again.

She nodded. "Yeah. Before things get out of hand." He snorted and she winced, amending, "Before they get any more out of hand. We should probably stop now, Cruz."

"Yeah. Okay." He shrugged like it didn't matter.

She turned back around and shook Nana's evening meds out of their pill bottles and into her palm. She was slacking. Nana should have taken them with her meal. When she turned around again to head down the hall, the kitchen was empty. She paused, staring.

Cruz was gone. Without a word.

She guessed there wasn't really anything more to say. She had asked him to leave. He did what she wanted.

So why did she feel like she had made a mistake?

FIFTEEN

HE RECONSIDERED THE wisdom of giving his sister a spare key for his house when he pulled up to see her car parked out front and his living room lights blazing. He didn't think she would use the key quite so freely. He pretty much thought it was a keep-this-for-emergencies type of thing.

Tonight, of all nights, he just wanted to be alone. Rebuffed by Gabriella, he wasn't in the mood to be social.

When he entered, she was watching TV.

"Hey," she greeted, reaching for the remote control and turning off the television.

"What are you doing here, Piper?"

She pushed up from the couch. "Well, hello, too. What kind of greeting is that?" She propped her hands on her hips.

He shook his head, feeling unaccountably tired

right then. It wasn't that late, but he wasn't accustomed to so much interaction with people.

In prison he had kept to himself, maintaining only the necessary friendships. You didn't want to be without allies behind bars, so he kept company with a few other inmates. Out of necessity. He made himself obliging, helping out and watching their backs. Never knew when you'd need a favor in turn. North Callaghan had been the one other inmate he trusted. Maybe the only one in there he ever fully trusted. Unfortunately, Callaghan was released before Cruz, leaving Cruz without anyone he could truly call a friend for the last couple years. Solitude had been his closest companion.

Everyday interactions took a toll on him. Or maybe it was simply dealing with Gabriella. The woman drove him mad. She wanted him. He knew it. Why was she so resistant? Was it simply who he was? He wouldn't presume to think she wanted anything serious with him. He wasn't good enough for her. He knew that. But what was stopping her from giving in to their mutual desire?

He should forget about her. He had enough on his plate getting his gym up and running. For a man not big on interaction, he was going to have to get over that to operate a business.

His sister was looking at him with such disappointment for his less-than-warm greeting, clearly waiting for him to say something. She looked at him a lot like that lately. She always wore that anxious expression. Like he might suddenly unravel, come apart into a million little pieces in front of her.

He knew why, of course. He understood her guilt even though he had said everything he could to assuage her sense of responsibility for him going to prison.

She wanted him to be okay. She wanted him whole and happy. She'd found her own happily ever after and he knew it made her feel guilty. He'd gone to prison for her and she couldn't shake that. She wanted him unbroken and he didn't even know how to pretend to be that.

"Sorry," he said. "What can I do for you, Piper?"

Her dark gaze eyed him closely. "In a bad mood?"

"Something like that." He had pretty much been in a bad mood for the last decade or more. Coming from Gabriella's place aching and unfulfilled with the taste of her still ripe on his lips didn't ease his mood.

As though he had voiced her name out loud, Piper cleared her throat, crossed her arms and said, "So the principal's sister. Um. Do you think that's such a good idea?"

He arched an eyebrow. "So the sheriff of Sweet Hill. Um. Do you think that's such a good idea?"

She snorted and shook her head with an eye roll. "Well, since I married him and I'm happier than I've ever been . . . yeah, I think it's a pretty good idea."

"But in the beginning it was a terrible idea. You were working at Joe's Cabaret. He was the sheriff." He let that hang out there. A lawman and a stripper. It smacked of bad idea.

He had never loved the idea of his sister working at Joe's, but considering he was behind bars he didn't have much say on what methods she employed to survive. The moment he learned she was getting involved with the sheriff, he had feared it would end badly. He never imagined the end result would be the two of them getting married.

"So what are you saying? You and Gabriella Rossi are like me and Hale?" Her eyes widened and her mouth worked before managing to get out in an excited rush, "Oh my God, are you in love with her?"

The words slapped him in the face. He forced a smile. "C'mon. Seriously, Piper? This isn't a Hallmark movie. I'm a felon—"

"No. You're not!" she was quick to rebut, indignation staining her cheeks. "You were exonerated."

He sighed. "Semantics in this town. I'm not

innocent in anyone's eyes, and someone like me doesn't end up with someone like Gabriella. Have you forgotten that Shelley Rae was her cousin?"

"No. I haven't . . . I was wondering if you had though." Her eyes softened, searching his face. "I don't want you hurt."

He snorted. "You don't need to worry about me. I'm not looking for forever with anyone. Not even Gabriella Rossi."

Piper stepped forward and pressed a hand to his chest. "You deserve forever with someone though."

"You're sweet." He patted her hand. "But you don't need to worry."

"If you say so." Her eyes, however, remained unconvinced. Even as he walked her to her car, she eyed him with concern. "Let's have dinner next week on one of Malia's non-practice days."

"Sure."

"The department hired a new bookkeeper. She's divorced. Very cute—"

"No," he stated flatly. "No blind dates."

"Fine." She ducked inside her car and he shut the door after her. He stood there for a moment, watching her back out and drive away.

SHE PLOPPED ON her sister's couch and helped herself to the television remote control. Her sister had every channel known to man, so channel surfing here was always an adventure.

She and her nephew had spent the evening eating pizza and playing video games. He was only seven, but he had still kicked her ass. Surprisingly, he had gone straight to sleep when she tucked him in. Surprising considering the half liter of soda she let him drink. Her sister wouldn't approve. They didn't even have soda in the house. Gabriella had ordered the liter when she called in the pizza.

She was halfway through an episode of *Fixer Upper* when the doorbell rang. She set down the bag of popcorn she was working her way through on the coffee table and got up to answer it. She took a peek through the peephole to see her brother-in-law standing there. Or rather, her former brother-in-law. She wasn't sure what to call him anymore. Tess would call him a cheating bastard . . . and she did every chance she got.

She pulled open the door. "Hey, Jason."

"Gabriella!" He blew her a beaming smile. Jason was still handsome even if he'd gone a little soft in the middle and his hair was thinning. "What a pleasant surprise. I thought I was going to have to face your sister." He mock shuddered.

She didn't grace that with a reply—it would feel too disloyal. Besides. He was the one who cheated on Tess. She stepped aside and motioned him into the house.

"I thought you couldn't make it tonight."

"Yeah, well, my date ended earlier than I expected." He grimaced and shrugged. "Didn't end as I hoped." He chuckled and added, "I'd hoped it wouldn't end until tomorrow morning."

She didn't know what to say to that. He bailed on seeing his kids because he was trying to score with a woman? She felt her lip curl in distaste. Tess wasn't wrong. He was a douchebag. More than she had ever realized. She settled for, "Oh."

He shrugged and held up both hands in the air, palms out. "What are you gonna do, huh?"

"Well, Noah's already in bed and Dakota is over at a friend's." Her gaze drifted to the door, assuming he would take his leave now.

"I'll just go take a peek at him. Give him a kiss good night." He waved a hand at her as though he expected a protest. "Don't worry. I won't wake him up."

Nodding, she settled onto the couch as he went upstairs. He returned a few minutes later. "They always look like such angels when they're asleep."

"Yeah. He's sleeping like a log. Surprisingly. I let him have so much junk food I didn't think he'd fall asleep." She cut him a warning look. "Don't tell my sister that."

Laughing, he crossed his heart. "Our secret." He lowered himself down to the couch beside her, stretching his arm along the back as though settling in for a while. "What are you watching?"

"Um. *Fixer Upper.*"

"You thinking of buying a house?"

Okaaay. So he really was staying. "Ah, no. I'll be back in Austin soon. Housing is expensive there."

They fell into silence as they watched rotten floorboards being ripped up in an old farmhouse. "You know, Gabriella, I always thought we understood each other very well."

Gabriella slid him a glance and smiled hesitantly, fully aware that her sister's ex-husband was Enemy Number One. He'd cheated on her. With multiple women. There was no coming back from that. No forgiveness for that. And yet she should be civil for the sake of her niece and nephew. Her sister struggled with that, obviously, but Gabriella could paste on a polite smile for their sake.

"I mean your sister can be pretty ridiculous. And downright mean." He grinned and winked at her in a conspiratorial manner. "Can't she? I know you've always thought so."

Her polite smile slipped a little. It wasn't that she didn't agree with what he was saying, but Tess was her sister. Family. While he was not anything to her anymore. It felt like a betrayal to agree with her former brother-in-law's poor assessment, even if accurate, of her sister.

Jason continued, "I don't know why I ever married her. I guess in the beginning that temper of hers had been kinda hot." He shook his head and released a breathy laugh. "I mean the sex . . . she was craaazy under the sheets—"

"Uh, I'm not comfortable talking about this." Yeah. TMI. She shifted her weight on the couch.

He kept on going like she hadn't said anything. "When you consider it . . . I should have ended up with someone like you." He scooted closer. She scooted away until she couldn't go any farther. She pushed right against the arm of the couch. "We're more alike . . . more suited temperament-wise." As he said this, his gaze dragged over her, lingering on her breasts. "I mean . . . you're so *sweet*, Gabby."

Why did the way he say *sweet* feel so . . . dirty?

She squirmed, her stomach tightening with discomfort. He had never looked at her like the way he was now. Never made her feel like such a piece of . . . meat. Apparently this mid-life crisis of his was without boundaries. "Well, you and Tess were in the same class. I was too young for you."

His eyes pinned her to the spot. "Not too young for me now." His hand landed on her knee. He gave it an encouraging squeeze. "You're all grown up, Gabby. And I've noticed." He shifted closer. With one hand massaging her knee, his other hand dropped to fondle his dick. "Man, I've noticed."

Oh. God. Revulsion swelled inside her, twisting her stomach into knots and she froze. Just . . . froze.

She watched in horror as his cock bulged against his pants.

She choked in outrage . . . and disgust and finally managed to push up to her feet. "Since you're here now, I can go. No need for the two of us to be here."

"Gabby." He grabbed her wrist and pulled her back down, thrusting his face close. Instantly, she smelled the beer on his breath. "No reason to rush off."

Rage started to simmer in her veins. So what? His date hadn't put out and he thought she would gladly oblige?

"I have to work tomorrow." She tried to stand again, but he had a tight grip on her.

He snorted. "At that coffee place? What can you make in a shift?" His fingers flexed around her wrist. He dragged her hand across his thigh toward his crotch. "How about you stay and I'll give you a C-note? That should cover whatever you would earn in an afternoon."

She sucked in a stinging breath. "You're offering to *pay* me . . . to stay here with you?"

He let loose a single laugh. "You make it sound so . . . cheap and dirty." His eyes gleamed at that . . . clearly he liked cheap and dirty.

"That would be because you just offered to buy me like a whore. Let go of my hand, Jason."

"C'mon. I have the money. I don't mind helping you out, Gabby. We always got along so *well*."

"I don't need your money. Now let me go."

He cocked his head and gave her a pitying look. "You're living above Nana Betty's garage. You can't even afford a house."

Is that what everyone thought of her? That she was a charity case? That she was someone to be pitied?

"I'm just asking you to stay," he went on to say. "I thought you might like to hang out. Don't make more out of it than that, Gabby. Stay." Instead of letting her hand go, he forced it over his erection and let loose a groan. "Come on. Don't you want some of this?"

"You're sick." She yanked her hand away and pushed up to her feet, but suddenly both his hands were on her, grabbing her by the shoulders. He flung her on her back on the couch and came over her, covering her mouth with a sloppy, beer-drenched kiss.

For a moment, she couldn't move. She was too stunned. Frozen again.

Then she fired to action, rage and fear fueling her. She used both hands to fight off her brother-in-law turned letch. She struggled against him, trying to speak beneath the onslaught of his lips.

"Jason, stop! No!"

She shoved hard at his shoulders. He wasn't built like Cruz but he was still strong. Stronger than she would have ever thought possible.

She managed to wedge both arms between them. She had almost succeeded in shoving him off her when a loud braying screech shattered her eardrums.

"Gabby! Jason! What the hell are you doing?"

Suddenly she was free.

Her brother-in-law sprang off her as though burned. Her gaze landed on her sister.

Tess's face burned several shades of red. She pointed an accusing finger at Gabriella. "You! How could you?"

"Me?" she squeaked. She cast an incredulous

look at Jason. He merely stood there. Mute. No explanation. No apology. Nothing close to the truth stumbling from his lips.

"You've always been jealous of me," Tess charged, her chest lifting on a ragged breath. "Is this your way to get back at me because I'm prettier? More successful? More . . . *everything*!"

"Tess—"

"I just never thought you would sink so low to make a play for my husband."

"Ex-husband," Jason chimed. "Remember? It's not as though we're married anymore. Gabriella and I are both adults and free to do what we want with each other. No reason to overreact, Tess."

"Liar!" Gabriella knotted her hands into balls to stop herself from hitting him. "There was nothing consenting about this." She turned to face her sister, beseeching her. "Tess, I didn't do this. You have to believe me."

Tess's hand lashed out so quickly, Gabriella couldn't have seen it coming. Perhaps she should have predicted it, but she didn't. The slap rang out, echoing in her ears even as the sting radiated painfully throughout her face.

She gazed at her sister in shock, one hand holding on to her burning cheek.

Tess's lips trembled, her eyes bright with emotion. Beneath the angry emotion there was a glimmer of shock, too. Like even she couldn't believe she had just struck Gabriella. "Get. Out." The words shuddered from her.

Gabriella stared a long moment at Tess as though her sister might somehow come to her senses. Then she turned her gaze to Jason, as though he might grow a conscience and speak up.

Except neither of those things happened. Nothing happened.

After a long moment, she turned away. Grabbing her bag, she slammed out of the house, stopping just short of running. She was going to be sick. Her stomach ached. Inside it felt like a flock of birds battled to break out.

Even from the driveway, she could hear them going after each other. Their shouts carried into the driveway.

Too bad they divorced. She glared back at the house. They really did deserve each other.

In her car, she eyed her stinging face in her rearview mirror. It was already puffy. Starting the engine, she backed out of the drive.

She was halfway down the street before the tears started to fall.

SIXTEEN

$\mathcal{G}$ABRIELLA TOOK AN extra-long shower. As though she could wash away the horrible events of the night. As though it could make it all go away. She lathered her body twice. Scrubbed her hair multiple times. The only thing she didn't attack with ferocity was her face. She washed it once, gently. The skin was tender and swollen from her sister's prizefighter slap.

Stepping out of the stall, she lifted her robe off the hook on the bathroom door and slipped inside it. She snuggled in close to the fabric, inhaling the fresh scent, taking solace in the worn terrycloth.

The shower had helped a little. Made her feel a little fresher, a little cleaner. A little more like the girl she had been earlier today. Before Jason assaulted her. Before her sister betrayed her and struck her.

She expelled a breath. No sense crying over what she couldn't change.

She picked up her brush off the vanity counter and moved into her bedroom. Sinking down to the edge of the bed, she started brushing out her hair in steady strokes. She'd left her bathroom light on, so a soft glow suffused her bedroom.

Even in the soft glow she could see her face—and the slight bruise in the shape of a handprint forming there. The sight of it angered her . . . brought with it a rush of emotion. Betrayal. Hurt. Why couldn't her sister just . . . love her? Believe her and take her side over a man that had hurt her, too?

She pulled her brush through her hair with a punishing yank and stopped. Staring at her face, she grazed it lightly with a trembling hand. Then her face crumpled and the tears came again. Ugly loud sobs. After a few moments, she caught herself, forced herself to stop.

Pull yourself together, Gabriella.

Pushing back wet strands of her hair from her face, she sniffed loudly. She was stronger than this. All the bullying in high school and she hadn't cried like this.

She supposed it was an adrenaline crash. Or shock, maybe.

She had been attacked, after all. First by Jason . . . and then her sister.

She full-body shivered where she sat on the edge of her bed and that didn't make much sense. The air-conditioning was running at a mild seventy-six. Her face looked ravaged. From the slap. From her bout of crying. She could feel the beginnings of a headache starting at the center of her forehead. She needed a couple Tylenol and a good night's sleep. Everything would be better in the morning.

The doorbell chimed and she winced, looking in the direction of her front door in dread. She didn't want to see Tess right now and she feared it was her.

Standing abruptly, she moved to the door, determined not to open it if it was Tess—or even, God forbid, Jason. She didn't want to see either one of those two. She didn't want to see anyone.

Taking a breath, she flattened her hands on the door, expecting a member of her family to be there. If not Tess, then someone else. Her sister had probably called everyone and told them what happened. She would want everyone to know just how badly Gabriella had fucked her over . . . just how awful a person she was.

Except it wasn't Tess or any member of her family.

It was *him*.

The one person she was okay seeing right now. The one person she *wanted* to see.

She just didn't realize it until this very moment.

HE SUCKED IN a breath when she stood in front of him in the doorway.

The apartment's living room light was off and it was damn dark, but that didn't stop him from admiring her. She looked edible in her robe, her hair darkly wet and trailing over her shoulders, her generous breasts hugged by the taut pull of terry-cloth. The robe was belted tightly, accentuating the nip of her waist and flare of her hips.

Apparently it was impossible to stay away.

"Uh. Hi." He held up a bag. "I'm always bringing you food." He shrugged, wondering why he felt so awkward. Like a boy and not a man. "My sister said you should never show up to someone's house empty-handed."

"My mom says that, too." Her gaze dropped to the bag. Her voice was a little hoarse, like she'd just woken from a nap and he felt the effect of it shoot straight to his dick. He wanted her hoarse voice filling his ears as he hammered inside her. "What's in there?"

He swallowed and fought back his rapidly growing erection. "Pecan tarts. From Eugenia's."

"The magic word. Words," she amended as she pulled open the door and gestured him inside.

"Hope you don't mind me coming by." He'd debated doing so. After his sister's visit, he felt like he should prove it to himself that Gabriella didn't mean that much to him . . . that he wasn't as far gone for her as Piper seemed to think.

"No. I'm glad." She looked away. "Which I know probably makes me really confusing since I asked you to go last time. Like I'm some person who doesn't know what she wants and sends out mixed signals." She stopped abruptly and released a ragged breath. "I just had a . . . real shit day."

"Well, I hear dessert can be a cure-all for those kinds of days." *And sex. Hot dirty sex. Lots of it. Man, get your mind out of the gutter.* She just said she had a shitty day. She didn't need him coming at her like a horny teenager—or like a man who had been locked up for several long years—with only getting in her pants on his mind.

She plucked the bag from his hand and moved to her couch. She sank down and crossed her legs. Peering inside the bag, she pulled out a tart and bit into it with a moan. He sat down across from her. She held the bag out to him and he took a tart, too.

"So tell me about your shitty day." It seemed the safest route. Innocent conversation. Her shower-fresh scent tantalized and there was still that robe. That damn robe. He knew there was nothing under it. She was so close and so naked under the fabric. He only had to reach for her. But he wouldn't. Not again. Not this time. Not without her express invitation.

She didn't look up from where she studied the contents of her bag, but he detected her reluctance in the way she lifted her shoulders in a shrug and then dropped them back down in a defeated slump.

"I'd rather not talk about it. Tell me about your day." She drew her knees up to her chest, arranging the hem of her robe, mindful that it continued to cover her. She propped her elbow on her knee and rested her face in her palm—quickly pulling it away with a soft whimper.

He frowned. "Bri?"

She looked up and that's when he noticed her face in the dimness of the living room. Her cheek, to be precise. It was swollen. He leaned forward, stroking a finger down the side of her face. The skin was heated and puffy to the touch. He knew the side effects to getting hit. Sadly, he'd lived the kind of life that made certain he knew all about such things.

She flinched at his touch.

"Bri." He said her name more forcefully. "What happened to your face?"

She shook her head and reached for the hair behind her ear, untucking it so that it fell forward in a
veil to shield her from his eyes. Too late though. He
had seen. He knew. She couldn't hide.

He took a bracing breath. Maybe it was an ac-
cident. Some mishap at work. If that was the case,
however, why didn't she just come out and say as
much? No. Someone had done this. Someone had
put hands on her.

A dangerous fire ignited inside his chest for the
bastard who had done this to her face.

He softened his voice, making sure to keep his
anger in check. He didn't want her to think he was
angry with her. "Bri . . . please tell me what happened."

"Cruz." She lifted her chin, releasing his name
in a shaky breath, her eyes wide and haunted in her
face. Now he could see that her eyes were puffy and
red. She'd been crying. It did something to him . . .
twisted his guts until they felt like a well-wrung
towel . . . and he realized with a bit of a jolt that
he didn't want this woman to *ever* hurt. Ridiculous, he supposed. No one could be one hundred
percent shielded in life. He knew that better than
anyone. But if he could protect her from the world,
he would. He *wanted* to.

"Are you all right?" That was the most important

thing. He looked her up and down as though checking for injuries. Bare skin peeked out at him between the open lapels of her robe, the V of skin threatening to distract him if he let it. But he wouldn't. Something had happened to her.

"I—I can't—" She stopped and looked down at her lap for a moment, inhaling a shuddery breath.

She wasn't going to tell him. At least not right now. He inhaled thinly through his nose. Fine. He wouldn't push, but he would find out. Eventually. And then God help the animal that dared lay a finger on her.

Composed again, she lifted her gaze back up. "I don't want to be alone tonight."

He nodded with a swift inhalation, emotion similar to both dread and elation swirling through him. "Okay." But maybe she didn't mean she wanted *him* to stay. "Do you want me to call someone?"

"Can you stay with me?"

He inhaled at the softly-voiced request. Almost as though she feared his rejection.

She wanted him to sleep over. *Hell.*

"I just can't be alone," she quickly went on to say. "I'm not asking you to *sleep* with me, not in that way . . . just *sleep* with me."

There was a distinction and she was clearly making it.

"Of course." She wasn't looking to get laid. She'd been through an ordeal and she just needed someone right now. He could do that. He could be that person for her.

She looked up at him, her eyes wide and clueless as to how much he wanted her. She'd never know how much sleeping next to her and not touching her would torment him, but he would do it so she wouldn't be alone.

"Thank you." Taking a deep breath, she stood and took the bag of pastries into the kitchen. A moment later, she was walking toward her bedroom.

He listened as the water ran in her bathroom. The sound of her brushing her teeth carried to his ears. He waited, giving her plenty of time to change out of her robe into something else.

Satisfied he'd given her enough time, he ventured to her bedroom door, knocking lightly.

"Come in." She was pulling back the covers, wearing an oversized T-shirt. He hoped like hell there were shorts underneath.

He stepped closer and pulled back his side, wondering why he felt so nervous all of a sudden. This was about comfort, not sex. And he'd slept in a woman's bed before.

Yeah, but you never were there just to sleep. You were never there for anything emotional, and what she needs from you right now is all about emotion. Christ.

She slipped beneath the covers. She looked so small and vulnerable tucked under the bedspread. He didn't like it. He wanted her to be her usual self—fiery and strong, that smart mouth of hers driving him crazy. For multiple reasons. Although he realized tonight wasn't about what he wanted.

He took off his shirt, reaching behind his neck and pulling it over his head in one sweep. Her eyes widened but she said nothing, merely watched as he stripped down to his briefs. He hastily slid under the covers, using the fabric to conceal his erection. With her, its existence was a matter of fact. The thing was a homing device when it came to her. It wanted one thing. It had one mission. Get. Inside. Gabriella.

He kept close to the edge, mindful not to touch her body, keeping as much space between them as he could without knowing for certain where she was. He was determined to hold back and not take advantage of her. Not like this. Not when she was vulnerable and shaken. He held himself still. Stiff. Probably too stiff. It was going to be a long night.

She stretched her arm toward her lamp and darkness descended on the room. It took his eyes a moment to acclimate to the dark and make out the outline of her in the bed beside him.

Springs squeaked softly and sheets whispered as she shifted her weight on the bed.

"Cruz?" The soft utterance scratched the space between them.

"Yes?"

"Thank you for staying."

After a moment, he spoke into the dark. "You sure you don't want to talk about it?" Sometimes things were easier to admit in the dark. He knew that.

She released a choked laugh. "I don't know what I'm more upset about. That my former brother-in-law sexually assaulted me or that my sister thought I consented . . . that I was a willing participant."

He sat up abruptly and leaned over her. "He did what to you?" Violence like he hadn't felt since prison, when he'd fought for his life, pumped through him.

"He touched me . . . forced a kiss on me. Tess walked in and lit into me." She stopped and he heard her heavy breathing through the dark. Ragged and wet, one beat from sobbing.

"Who hit you?" he asked, his voice surprisingly calm, in direct opposition to how very not calm he felt. His hands opened and closed into fists at his sides and he was already calculating how he could get her brother-in-law's address from Hale.

"My sister slapped me." Her voice broke and she was crying.

Cursing, he reached for her, pulling her into his arms.

"How could she hurt me like that?" She buried her face into his chest, her tears soaking his skin.

"The people we love always have that power. When they hurt us . . . it's a greater wound. If she hasn't already realized she made a mistake, she will."

She sniffed. "I'm not so sure."

There was a rustle of movement and he felt fingers brush his arm, then slide down, curling around his hand.

He'd never been a hand-holder. That was an act of intimacy he never shared with a woman. Somehow sex was easier . . . less personal than lacing fingers.

Fuck it.

He lifted her hand and brought it between them, weaving his fingers through hers, pressing their palms close. So close he could actually feel the beat of her heart through her soft skin, fusing with his own. "Try to get some sleep, Bri."

His chest swelled with something that he had never felt. Something that made him pull her closer and wrap her up in him. She sighed sweetly and melted into him, giving herself completely over to him.

He held her so close . . . so tightly there wasn't any room for air between them. As though that would somehow keep her safe. Keep her from ever getting hurt again.

There weren't two of them in this bed anymore. There was only the one.

THE FOLLOWING MORNING Gabriella woke to find Cruz gone.

Dawn barely lit the room, peeking through the blinds and painting the room in fingers of gray and pink.

She yawned and then winced. Her cheek hurt. She lifted her fingers to her face. Frowning, she swam through the fog of her thoughts, last night coming back to her bit by bit. Jason. Her sister . . . her *sister*. The slap that nearly knocked her teeth out.

She shifted slightly and turned sideways to where he had slept beside her. He had held her through the night. Even though it hadn't been sexual, it had been the most intimate she had ever been with a man.

They'd shared a bed. She had slept plastered against him. He had held her like he would never let go. But he had. He had left—and without a word.

She had asked him to spend the night with her.

At the time it seemed like a good idea. At the

time it seemed the only option considering how unbearably alone she felt.

Aloneness had never troubled her so much before, but that was before her sister turned on her in the most vicious way. Family was supposed to be better than that. Family was supposed to be there for you.

Last night she had felt so lost . . . and then he showed up at her door as if sent by angels. She snorted. She knew she was being fanciful. Even ridiculous.

Just once she had let herself cling to a man. One night the vulnerability could be forgiven.

But now she was faced with the consequence of that weakness. He was gone and she was alone again and reaching for him across her bed where he wasn't.

Where he could never be.

SEVENTEEN

SHE HADN'T SEEN or heard from him in days. *Three* days that felt like the longest in her life.

She was certain the angst she was feeling was compounded by the fact that he had slept with her, held her, all at her request, and then vanished like smoke in the air. Maybe that's what he preferred. Certainly it was the smartest, safest thing to do between two people unable to be anything more fleeting than a random hook-up.

Except nothing about Cruz felt random. Nothing about sharing a bed with him felt casual. There'd been closeness between them that night, an intimacy established. Maybe he wanted to erase that. Maybe it meant nothing to him.

It shouldn't have felt like a rejection to her, but it did. She had no right to feel this ridiculous sense of rejection. It wasn't like they'd gone out on a date and he had promised to call or text. God knew *that* scenario had happened to her before and she had never felt this level of disappointment.

It was something she knew about: going out and having what she thought was a nice time with a seemingly decent guy who then failed to call or text as promised—planting the seed in her mind that there was something lacking in her.

This wasn't *that* though.

There'd been nothing as dignified as a date between them. He brought her and Nana dinner. They watched TV. That wasn't a date. He spent the night and cuddled with her. She winced. That wasn't a date either, to be truthful.

They'd been locked in a closet and they made out.

He'd showed up at her place and they'd made out.

That was the extent of it. They'd hooked up. Fooled around. No promises made. Contrary to what her heart was telling her . . . it *was* casual. She needed to put her big girl panties on and face that fact.

But he had said they would be seeing a lot of each other and he had kept true to that vow— except for these last three days.

She shoved the voice aside. She couldn't put any stock into that utterance. Because she wasn't needy or desperate or delusional.

This was Cruz Walsh, and she shouldn't be longing for the man to make love to her.

After the things he did, how can you not?

Telling her internal voice to shut up, she turned and greeted a customer, taking her coffee order. Fortunately it was something complicated and required her concentration for the next ten minutes.

When that order was complete, she went back to the sink to rinse out the blender. Her mind strayed into Cruz territory again. It couldn't be helped.

Apparently he had given up his pursuit of her. Maybe he had just decided he didn't want to hook up with a journalist he believed was after his story—a story he was determined not to give.

Disappointment lanced through her chest.

It wasn't, however, because his rejection hurt. It was not because she didn't get to have that wicked mouth again and all his other wicked parts, the sexual promise of which had been *epic*.

"Someone is requesting your presence," Jabal leaned in to whisper near her ear.

Gabriella twisted around where she stood at the sink, instantly tense. Could it be . . .

At the sight of her bright-eyed niece, her shoulders slumped a little. No. Not Cruz. She should be glad and relieved because she didn't have to come face-to-face with him in her workplace where she would probably turn into an awkward, bumbling idiot. And there was her manager who always frowned on fraternization.

"Hey!" Dakota waved enthusiastically as she and her friend stopped in front of the pastry case.

"Hey, sweetie." At least Dakota didn't seem aware of what went down between her aunt and her mother. Gabriella moved away from the sink, sending a look of appeal to Jabal. "You mind?" She nodded to the sink.

"Sure." Jabal nodded. "I guess I like you enough. Go ahead and take their orders."

Swapping spots, Gabriella squared up in front of her niece. "Sorry I didn't get to talk to you the other night. Congratulations."

"Oh." She shrugged in dismissal. "No big deal."

"Well. What can I get you?"

"Um." Dakota looked over the assortment. "What do you think, Malia?"

The name hit her with a jolt. Malia? As in Cruz's youngest sister? Gabriella turned to look at Dakota's friend for the first time to be sure. It was the same girl from the other day at the high school. Her face was softer and feminine but the resemblance to Cruz was absolutely there. The same dark hair. The golden skin. The dark eyes were the same, too, fringed with lashes even more lush than Cruz's.

"The lemon cake." Malia pointed, her fingertip tapping the glass. "That looks good." She lifted her dark eyes to Gabriella's.

Gabriella could only stare. A few seconds ticked by before she realized the girl was waiting for her response. "It is," she blurted, nodding. "It's my favorite."

"Great." Malia smiled.

"I'll have the chocolate croissant," Dakota said. "And an iced white mocha."

Gabriella snapped her attention back to her niece. Shaking her head, she smiled. "Your mother would have a fit if she heard you order that."

Dakota grinned. "Good thing she's not here."

"I'll have an iced white mocha, too," Malia said as Gabriella opened the case and selected their desserts. She placed them on plates for the girls, trying not to gawk at Malia and pick out all the similarities she shared with her brother. The girls waited, chatting as Gabriella prepared their drink orders. She managed to get their drinks right even as she eavesdropped on their conversation. It was mostly about their upcoming dance and whether or not they would go with a group or dates.

"Here you go," she said, passing over the iced white mochas.

"My treat," Dakota announced as she dug out her wallet. "You can get me the next time."

"Aw, thanks." Malia bumped hips with Dakota in a friendly thank-you and Gabriella had to wonder how long these two girls had been friends. Tess had never mentioned the friendship, and it was the kind of thing her sister would have mentioned because she would not have approved. That went without saying. Her sister was overly concerned with appearances and connections. In Tess's mind, Malia would always be a Walsh. Bottom line. Her sister would never forget that.

"Thanks, Aunt Gabby." Dakota made an exaggerated show of sticking a few dollars into the tip jar.

Gabriella chuckled and shook her head. "You're too much." Dakota probably knew her mother wouldn't leave Gabriella a tip. They'd been in here together countless times and Tess never left her a tip. Apparently sisterly love didn't extend that far.

"Sure thing, girls. I made them extra tasty for you." Which essentially meant she loaded them up with extra whipped cream. She winked at the girls and watched as they headed to a table near the window.

She must have been staring too long and doing nothing in the process. Jabal sidled up beside her and nudged her with an elbow. "Get moving. The boss is watching."

She didn't even glance where she knew Bianca was standing, but she felt her laser stare on her back. Sighing, she got busy again, making sure to look industrious.

The girls seemed content to park themselves for a while, talking and looking at their phones together, heads bent close as they laughed at whatever it was they were watching.

In fact, her attention was so focused on them that she didn't notice a new customer had entered the café. Not until he was standing in front of the counter, waves of testosterone pulsing off him and extending to her, wrapping her in some kind of web.

"Holy hell, that's a gooey cinnamon roll of a man," Jabal murmured appreciatively.

Gabriella's gaze swung and collided with Cruz's. Apparently Jabal fit into the five percent of the Sweet Hill population that didn't recognize Cruz Walsh.

Her coworker stepped up to the counter, angling her head in what Gabriella knew was the beginning of her flirt game. "Hi there. Welcome to The Daily Grind." Yes, she did use a little breathy inflection in the word *grind*. "Can I get you something?"

Gabriella stood frozen, staring unblinkingly at him, her muscles locked up tight, an animal caught in the crosshairs.

His gaze fixed on her with sole-focused intensity over Jabal's shoulder. "Hi, Gabriella."

"Hey there," she said, her voice croaking out. She swallowed and tried again. "Hi there."

Jabal swung around and mouthed widely, "OMG. You know him?"

She ignored her coworker and kept her gaze glued to Cruz.

"How's it going?" he returned.

Their manager decided at that moment to make her presence felt. She cut directly in front of both Jabal and Gabriella to stand in front of Cruz. "Can I help you?" she asked sharply.

Gabriella frowned at the back of her head, wondering if her sharpness might be indicative of something besides her annoyance with Jabal and Gabriella. Might it be because she recognized Cruz from the news?

Gabriella moved forward slightly, forgetting about the fact that she should be working so that she could better observe Bianca's pinched expression.

Cruz tore his gaze from Gabriella to answer Bianca. "I'll take a cup of coffee."

"Just coffee?" she asked in faintly accusatory tones, as though he should order a scone, too.

"Yeah," he replied evenly. "Plain coffee is fine."

Bianca moved to pour the cup of coffee. Gabriella decided to step up in that moment and collect his money from him.

"That's three seventy-eight."

He handed her a five-dollar bill with a faint smile. It made her stomach flutter. He wasn't much for smiling. "Expensive cup of plain coffee," he remarked, his gaze crawling over her face, leaving a path of heat everywhere his gaze touched. How was that possible? How did one ignite fire with a mere glance?

"Yeah. It's cheaper to make it at home." She sent a quick glance over her shoulder, only half caring if Bianca overheard her. "Probably tastier, too."

A corner of his mouth lifted in definite amusement and the flutters in her stomach turned into full-on somersaults.

"Gabby!" The manager snapped her name and stalked over with Cruz's steaming cup of coffee. "I got this."

Bianca looked back and forth between them suspiciously. As though they had done something wrong. Gabriella bristled at what felt like clear injustice in the works. Save her from small-minded people. She and Cruz were only talking and being friendly. She had done the same with countless customers. It wasn't as though her manager could read her mind and know all the X-rated thoughts flashing through her head when she looked at Cruz. Stubbornly, she stayed put. She was an adult. She did her job well. Bianca had nothing to complain about on that score and she didn't get to boss Gabriella around simply for the fun of it. Simply because she thought Cruz Walsh was an unsavory individual—for that was clearly what was tracking through her mind.

Holding her ground, she took Cruz's change from the cash register and handed it back to him, her skin sparking where his fingertips brushed her palm. "Thank you. Enjoy your coffee."

Nodding, he glanced at her manager and then headed over to where his sister sat with her niece. Malia's face brightened upon seeing him. She patted the seat of the chair beside her for him.

"Gabby," the manager snapped. "Quick. Get on the phone with the sheriff's department."

She looked back at her manager, shaking her head in confusion. Bianca's face was splotchy red with hot emotion. She glared at Cruz where he sat across the café.

"What for?" Gabriella asked.

"Tell them Cruz Walsh is in our place of business and he's harassing two of our young female customers."

Oh my God. She gaped at her manager for one long moment, certain she had just fallen down the rabbit hole. Was this woman for real? She pointed to where Cruz sat with the girls, certain that she could clear up this nonsense. "Uh. That's his sister and my niece."

Bianca scowled, processing this for a moment before answering, "*Your* niece? So you're okay with your niece fraternizing with a known murderer?"

Jabal stood closely behind Bianca, waving her finger in a little circle near her head to demonstrate just how crazy she thought their manager really was.

"Firstly," Gabriella began, "he's not guilty of any crime. Secondly, he's not harassing anyone. He's just having a cup of coffee."

Her manager propped both hands on her hips. "You're paid to do what I tell you to do."

"That's actually not my job description," she countered. "Nowhere is your name even mentioned in my job description. I show up on time, keep the place clean, prepare drinks and food and serve customers with a smile."

Bianca's face burned even brighter. "Do what you're told. Call the police."

She held her ground and didn't look away. "No. I will not."

"If you value your job—"

"If my job requires me to follow your asinine instructions and persecute that man over there, then you can stuff your job."

She must have spoken loudly. The entire place seemed to have fallen quiet.

Jabal's mouth fell wide open behind Bianca. With a small shake of her head, she snapped out of her shocked stupor and grabbed the arm of the other barista on duty, making sure he didn't miss any of the show. The pair of them gawked behind the manager's back, Jabal nodding her head in support.

"You can get your things and go," Bianca announced. "You're fired."

EIGHTEEN

SHE WAS FIRED.

It clicked in her mind that she had never been fired. Deep inside she was still the good girl who turned her homework in and got straight As. She didn't get fired. Not even from part-time jobs at a coffeehouse. She was Gabriella Rossi, grade A over-achiever.

Nodding her head jerkily as though she accepted the verdict just rendered against her, Gabriella's shaking hands went to the ties of her apron, stupid emotion clogging her throat as she unraveled the bow behind her back.

She was never good at confrontation. Flabby Gabby never did confrontation. She simply kept her head low and survived.

"Sounds good to me," Gabriella got out. "If I

had to work for you another minute I might have had to become a raging alcoholic just to cope."

Jabal let loose a loud snort of laughter.

Without another look, she stalked to the back where all the employees kept their things. She grabbed her stuff from her locker and then headed back out to the front of the café—and instantly felt all eyes on her. Both employees and patrons watched her. Her niece and Cruz's sister . . . and *Cruz*. Of course. He watched her with his dark, unreadable eyes, his mouth set into a hard line.

She readjusted her grip on her purse strap and marched across the seating area.

Dakota rose to her feet and started in her direction. "Aunt Gabby . . ."

She forced a bright smile. "Do you need a ride?" She tossed a glare over at Bianca. "I'm sure you don't want to stay in this shithole. There's a better coffee place five minutes from here. They don't burn their beans there."

Bianca's face reddened. Good. She heard her.

"Oh. I was going to hang out a little longer with Malia. Some other kids from school might pop in, too. You don't mind, do you?" She sent a wary glance in Bianca's direction.

"No worries." She gave Dakota a kiss on the

cheek. Her issues didn't belong to Dakota, after all. The girl should be able to stay with her friends. "I'll see you at Sunday dinner."

"Sure. Bye, Aunt Gabby."

Acutely conscious of Cruz's eyes on her, she wended her way between tables and out of the shop. She didn't want to explain anything to him.

She didn't want to suffer condolences for her sudden loss of employment.

Adrenaline still pumped through her from her clash with her manager. She just needed to get back home where she could punch a wall or something. Maybe scream into a pillow over the injustice of it all. Part of her still wanted to march back in there and inflict her wrath on Bianca.

Instead, she walked outside and blinked into the sunshine. When she came into work this morning it had still been dark. She glanced at the time on her phone. Nana would be working with the in-home care therapist for another hour, and then her parents were supposed to be coming over to grill fajitas and play Monopoly with her tonight. Nana was in good hands. Gabriella had the rest of the day to do whatever she wanted.

She was almost to her car when she heard her name. "Gabriella?"

She stopped and turned. Holding a hand up to

shield her eyes, she watched as Cruz walked across the parking lot, his long strides swift, eating up concrete as though he were a man on a mission and that mission was Gabriella.

Her mouth went dry. She shifted on her feet uneasily. So much for a clean escape.

He stopped in front of her. "You just got fired." It was more statement than question, but his eyes still searched her face, seeking verification.

"Um." Her head fell back slightly to look up at him. "Kinda. Yeah." She shrugged uncomfortably. "I guess so."

"Because of me?" Again, more a statement of fact than question.

"Um." Her mind turned that over. She didn't want him to feel like she had made some grand sacrifice for him. Her awkwardness only increasing, she shifted her weight on both feet. "No. Not really. I—"

The rest of her words were cut off. Apparently, he'd heard enough.

His hand shot out and curled around the back of her neck. The sensation of his warm fingers at her nape sent a shock wave through her. Instantly, she came awake, her body alive, all her nerves singing hallelujah.

He hauled her in against him, his hardness

pressing into hers, melding into her generous curves. She whimpered. She could feel every inch of him—his firm chest, his washboard belly and Thor-like thighs. Sensations flooded her. He was so much bigger . . . taller and muscled. He always made her feel small, like a petite, treasured thing. His fingers flexed on the back of her neck, the blunt tips singeing her skin, burning deep past skin into muscle and bone.

When his mouth finally slanted over hers hotly, his tongue licking his way inside her mouth, it was like sinking into chocolate. Rich and decadent and just *sin sin sin*.

His fingers tightened, burrowing into her hair, caressing her scalp as he kissed her. His teeth gently tugged on her bottom lip and desire coiled tightly in her belly. He released her bottom lip and gave it a long, savoring lick. She sighed, and he took advantage, slipping his tongue inside her mouth.

After a long moment, he lifted his head and growled in that gravel and grit voice of his, "No one has ever taken a hit for me."

Apparently he didn't believe her denial.

His eyes glowed darkly, crawling over her face, lingering on her tingling lips. Her mouth probably looked puffy and bruised from his kiss. He looked at her like she was the most incredible thing he had ever seen . . . which wasn't a totally comfortable sensation. Not for a girl who couldn't even take a compliment with any measure of grace. "I've pretty much gotten used to trouble. It's followed me my whole life. You didn't need to stick your neck out for me. I guess I owe you one now, Rossi."

She shook her head. "It was no big deal. Just a crap job that paid nine dollars an hour," she attempted to say, but his head swept back down and he kissed her again, shutting her up.

They must have moved . . . or the force of his kiss propelled her backward because suddenly she felt a vehicle bumping into the back of her.

She fell back limply, indifferent to the cold metal at her back. She lost all ability to care about her surroundings. She only cared about him. About his hard, delicious body fused to hers. About his lips, both hard and soft, rough and gentle—his tongue inside her mouth, stroking her tongue, exploring and tasting and making her want to crawl inside him and stay there forever.

Her fingers dug desperately into his shoulders. He slid one hand down her back, between her body and the car to cup her ass, gripping it in his broad hand. And then her feet were off the ground.

She wasn't sure what happened first. Whether she jumped up against him or he simply lifted her.

Her legs wrapped around his waist. Incredibly he supported her weight. Incredibly she didn't feel any self-consciousness over it.

Their mouths fused together. Everything was desperate and hungry and *oh-my-God-oh-my-God-oh-my-God*. A car honked and she gasped, pulling away. Blinking, she looked around, dazed, suddenly remembering where she was—and how this shouldn't be happening here of all places. Her niece was feet away . . . as was his sister, and her crazed manager with a finger hovering over the keypad, ready to dial 911.

With a growl, he dragged her mouth back to his and they started all over again.

Screw it. She let herself have this kiss . . . have *him.* She had never felt more on fire in her life. It was hard and fast and she felt like she was drowning.

"Gabriella!"

She jerked at the sound of her name. Somehow it didn't register on Cruz.

"Gabriella!"

She pushed at his shoulders, ending their kiss. Still pinned to the car, she looked wildly around him, spotting her sister charging across the parking lot, her stylish white coat, à la Meghan Markle, whipping around her svelte body.

"Oh God . . ." She closed her eyes in one long

blink of misery. She hadn't seen her sister since the night of the slap and now she had to see her . . . like this?

"What are you doing?" Tess glanced around the parking lot, obviously concerned they were attracting an audience. "Are you out of your mind?"

Without answering—because it seemed obvious what it was she was doing—Gabriella slid her legs down to the ground. With a ragged breath, she stepped around Cruz, smoothing shaky hands down the front of her shirt.

Tess came to a hard stop, her slim, toned calves braced in a militant stance. Just beyond her the door to The Daily Grind swung open. Dakota and Malia stood there, watching the little drama unfold with bright curiosity in their eyes.

"Really, Gabby?" Tess propped a hand on her hip, indifferent to the girls several yards behind her. "I mean I get that he's fucking eye candy, but where's your dignity? First Jason and now *him*?"

She felt Cruz stiffen. They weren't even touching but he radiated tension. She sent him a quick glance.

His expression was empty as his lips peeled back from his teeth to say, "She didn't want your fucking ex to touch her."

"I beg your pardon?" she raged.

"You heard me. Wake the hell up. Your ex assaulted her . . . and then you did the same when you slapped her."

Tess gasped, her gaze flying to Gabriella. "You told him?"

She lifted her chin. "Yes. We're . . . friends."

A dangerous tension radiated from Cruz. "Go ahead and tell your ex that if he ever touches her again, I'm coming for him."

Tess's big brown eyes flew wide in her face.

"Tess." At the sound of Gabriella's voice, her sister looked to her. "If you *ever* hit me again . . . I won't roll over and take it like I did last time. I'll hit you back. And I can't promise I won't ruin your perfect nose."

Tess's mouth sagged open. It was a moment before she found her voice and then she was yelling, "I'm not going to stand here and let—"

"Keep your voice down," Gabriella snapped, her gaze drifting to the girls. Tess followed her gaze and spun around.

"Dakota!" Her gaze flitted from her daughter to Malia next to her. At the sight of Malia, her eyes narrowed in displeasure. "Dakota . . . come here."

Dakota's face reddened and she sent an apologetic look to her friend before walking with clear reluctance across the parking lot toward her mother. She stopped before Tess, scuffing her shoe on the ground. "Yes?"

"Dakota," she said in a voice that was full of reprimand. "Did you forget the conversation we had?"

Dakota lifted her chin defiantly. "No."

"So you're saying you just decided *not* to obey me. You chose to deliberately defy me."

She sighed heavily. "Mom, there's nothing wrong with—"

"You are not allowed to associate with that girl, understand?" Tess stabbed a finger in the air for full impact. "I don't want to see you with her again."

Gabriella sucked in a sharp breath, ashamed that this was actually her sister. This was even worse than Tess slapping her. That had been an attack on Gabriella. She was the only hurt party then. This she was doing to Dakota and Malia.

"Tess," she said sharply.

Her sister swung on her, her eyes blazing. "Don't! She's my child. You don't get to lecture me . . . and you're hardly in a position to do so anyway." Her scathing gaze flipped to Cruz.

Dakota's face burned a deep tomato red and she looked down, suddenly extraordinarily focused on her shoes.

Malia's eyes welled with moisture and she looked at her brother as though beseeching him for rescue.

Cruz muttered a profanity and then strode forward, shrugging past Gabriella and Tess and grabbing his sister's hand. "Come on, Malia. Let's go. We'll go get some dinner. What do you feel like?"

Relief flashed over Malia's face the second before she turned away.

Bleak frustration and regret welled up inside her as she watched the brother and sister walk away. She wanted to call them back. Go after them. Make everything that just happened . . . not happen.

She wanted this world to be a better place and not brimming with narrow-minded people like her sister.

Gabriella turned on Tess. "How are we even related?"

"Oh, don't get so self-righteous with me."

"You're such a bitch!" Dakota burst out and then ran back into The Daily Grind. Presumably to the bathroom where all teen girls fled in moments of distress. Gabriella knew that firsthand.

"Nice." Tess shook her head. "Thanks, Gabby."

"Me?" She flattened a hand to her chest. "How am I responsible for this?"

Tess started stalking toward the café, calling out over her shoulder, "Maybe when you're a mother, you'll understand."

Understand that her sister was mean and judgmental? She didn't need a kid to see that.

She looked back out at the parking lot, her gaze searching for Cruz and Malia. They were already gone. She exhaled, an awful, sinking feeling coming over her. She knew she wasn't responsible for her sister, but that didn't mean she didn't feel the blame. That didn't mean she didn't regret it and wish she could do something to take it all back.

CRUZ KEPT THE conversation light, deliberately trying to cheer his sister up. She didn't need to know that he was furious. As in want-to-drive-a-fist-through-a-wall furious. It was one thing when people treated him like shit but another thing when people hurt his sister.

She started crying the moment she got into the car. He sent a text to Piper that he was taking Malia out for nachos. That's what they settled on after five minutes of driving around. Nachos and queso and guacamole. Pure comfort food. By the time their Cokes arrived, her tears had dried and she was laughing as he told her a story about a kid at the gym who had gotten tangled up in a volleyball net and it took Cruz and another member of his staff half an hour to free him

"You should have just cut the net."

"Those nets cost good money," he protested.

"Well. You should put in an indoor soccer field,"

she suggested, swirling a chip through the queso, making sure every inch of it was covered.

"The place isn't big enough for that, but I'm still planning to add more features. There's room for a soccer field out back, and I'm thinking about some batting cages outside, too."

"That's so cool." She nodded. "Everyone is talking about it at school."

"Yeah?"

"Yeah." She fiddled with her straw. "There's not a lot of places for kids to go after school and on weekends. The summers are the worst. There's nothing to do in this town."

"Well, that's what I was hoping to provide."

She grinned. "And all the girls keep telling me I have a hot brother."

He shook his head. "I'm sure when they see me they think: *old man.*"

"Hardly," she replied. "You're not *that* old."

He guessed he should be glad they weren't harassing her because of him—especially considering how many people disliked him in this town. Gabriella's sister and manager were prime examples of that. Maybe the younger generation would be more open-minded.

He could only hope for her sake. He had thicker skin and couldn't care less. He wanted to think that his sister wasn't being penalized for having him for a brother . . . for having the last name Walsh.

"Sooo . . ." Malia began as she lifted a chip laden with meat and cheese from the platter they were sharing. "Dakota's aunt. She's cute." She waggled her eyebrows suggestively at Cruz.

He chuckled and shook his head. "There's nothing there, Malia." And really, there wasn't. They'd fooled around. As kids and again recently. Sure. He'd made her come multiple times. Orgasms he could still feel. Still taste on his tongue. Still dreamed about and had him waking with a boner.

But they were nothing.

"Didn't look that way to me."

He shifted in the booth. Getting grilled about your love life by your fifteen-year-old sister wasn't exactly comfortable.

"Your imagination is getting carried away."

"Really? I thought you were going to eat her face in that parking lot."

He stilled. "You saw that?"

She shot him a disgusted look. "The Daily Grind has wall-to-wall glass windows."

He winced. Yeah. He should have exhibited better control. Although with Gabriella he wasn't exactly a model of self-restraint.

"*Everybody* saw," she added.

"And did you see her sister?" he countered with a shake of his head. "That pretty much sums up why there is no me and Gabriella Rossi."

It had never been clearer to him that he and Gabriella came from two different worlds. They were incompatible. She'd called him a friend in that parking lot. He didn't see how they could even be that. Not in this town. Not in this life.

He couldn't believe that earlier this week he had entertained thoughts that they were meant to be. Such thoughts smacked of permanence and wedding rings and minivans. Shit. What had he been thinking? That wasn't him. That wasn't even a future him.

As far as the town of Sweet Hill was concerned, he was a felon. Felons did not settle down with good girls like Gabriella Rossi.

"That bitch? Uh. Yeah. She was kinda hard to miss. Poor Dakota. How'd you like that for a mother?" Malia stabbed a chip viciously into the bowl of queso. "*But . . .*" She whipped her chip and held it aloft. "I also saw Gabriella get fired for sticking up for you. She seems pretty cool to me. So who cares what kind of sister she has? Just because her mom is terrible doesn't make me stop wanting to be friends with Dakota. You judge people on their own merits."

If only everyone in the world thought the way this fifteen-year-old kid did.

Yeah. Gabriella had defended him and gotten fired as a result. He would never forget that. No one had ever stuck up for him before. It kind of made him all the more desperate to have her. But that actually only convinced him he needed to leave her alone. He could bring nothing good into her life. He had gotten her *fired*, for God's sake. If that wasn't a sign for him to stay away, what was?

"She might be a decent person, Malia, but that doesn't mean we're right for each other. It's complicated. We would never work."

She bit into another nacho and chewed, looking unimpressed with his answer. When she finished her bite, she asked, "I don't think it's that complicated. You're a guy. She's a girl. You're both single. You're clearly into each other from the way you were making out—"

He snorted. "It's that clear, huh? When did you get so good at relationship analysis? Are you thinking about becoming a therapist or something?"

"Yes, it is *that* clear. And stop deflecting, please."

He shook his head. When he'd left for prison his sister was just a little girl watching cartoons and now she was this too-smart-for-her-own-good individual capable of looking after herself. "I'm not even looking for a relationship."

"You're such a liar."

He straightened, offended. "Why do you say that?"

"No one *isn't* looking for love. It's part of the human condition. We want love and companionship. Not everyone finds it, but we want it."

He was quiet for a long moment. He took a drink from his glass, wondering if he had ever been so optimistic and full of hope. His sister was a sweet kid. He didn't want to crush her by informing her that he had given up on the idea of love and happily ever after pretty much by the age of twelve. Her brother was a broken man and no woman was ever going to fix him.

He decided to humor her instead of dropping that truth on her. "Well, I might be looking for love." Somehow he managed not to choke on the words. "But I'm not looking for it with Gabriella Rossi."

Even as he said the words, his throat tightened against them. He felt something for Gabriella. He couldn't deny that. He certainly wanted her like he had never wanted another woman. No woman had come close to affecting him the way she did.

But that wasn't love. He was certain of it.

NINETEEN

A DAY PASSED WITH no sighting of Cruz. She occupied herself, deciding it was time to declutter Nana's house. Not exactly a wild Saturday, but then Gabriella never was one to have too many of those.

Her grandmother never tossed out a magazine and she subscribed to several. Convincing Nana she needed to get rid of some of the magazines was a real chore. Gabriella had to hold each one up to her and half of them Nana insisted on looking over again to make sure they could be trashed. It made for a very long day and four very large garbage bags sitting at the curb. Both she and Nana were wiped out by dinnertime, so they just ordered a pizza.

"I like you not working and staying here with me," Nana announced as Gabriella finished washing their dishes.

"Well, unfortunately it doesn't pay the bills.

You're getting around much better. I'm going to have to head back to Austin soon." She stacked the last plate in the dish rack. It was true. Her time here was dwindling. She hadn't been simply trying to make Cruz feel better when she told him she didn't care about losing her job. She didn't care. She would have had to turn in her notice soon anyway.

"Bah! Why do you want to do that?"

"Because I have a job there, remember, Nana?"

She waved another hand in dismissal. "You can work here. I just saw Clint Brown the other day. He brought up you working for him. Said he'd like to retire soon and he needs someone to take over the paper when he does." She stabbed a finger in Gabriella's direction. "He meant you, Dumbo. That's what he was implying. You could have your own paper. Imagine that, Gabriella!"

She had to admit it did sound tempting. Her own paper to run . . . she alone would make all decisions, decide on the staff and what to print, decide on what sponsors and advertisers to work with. Except it was Sweet Hill. The *Sweet Hill Recorder*. It wasn't exactly the big times. And she had always vowed to leave this place and never look back. If she stayed here it would be like nothing had ever changed. Wouldn't it?

No, she couldn't do it. She couldn't be that girl

again . . . that girl *still*, that girl *forever*. Her life would consist of running into people like Natalie who would gush over the past like those were magical times and not the darkest days of her existence.

"That's very kind of him, Nana . . ."

"But?" Nana supplied accusingly.

"But my home is in Austin."

Nana shook her head in disgust. "You're going to regret it."

Well, that was a little dramatic. "Regret not taking Mr. Brown up on his offer? I think—"

"No. Regret running from yourself. You been doing that ever since you graduated high school."

She flinched. That's not what she was doing this time. She needed to live elsewhere in order to find herself and shed the trappings of the past. At least that's what she always told herself.

Except you haven't done that yet in the years you've been gone. If you were truly different would you be so bothered when you ran into the Natalies of the world?

Deciding a change of subject was in order, she asked, "Nana, I'm running to the dry cleaners and to pick up my last paycheck. You want me to take anything for you?"

"Nah. I'm fine." Nana stood and, ignoring her walker, headed into the living room to continue work on the puzzle of Big Ben they'd started. It was a sign. Nana didn't even need the walker anymore. Gabriella really did need to start making arrangements to go back to Austin.

Even if she did feel a little pang around her heart because that meant leaving Sweet Hill. No, not Sweet Hill. The pang was for leaving Cruz.

When she was eighteen she had been in a rush to get out of this town. Up until recently, she'd still been in a rush.

That had changed though . . . because Cruz had happened. Because she'd met him again. Because he set her on fire. Because he had actually remembered their kiss in the boathouse. It had meant something to him, too. Unbelievable as that seemed.

She still burned for him. That fire had never gone out. Not since she was fifteen years old. It never would go out. She knew that now. Her desire for him would always smolder within her.

Maybe if she had him just once . . . the fire could be banked. She would feel closure. Yes. Clearly she couldn't go until that happened.

NOW THAT SHE had made up her mind that she wasn't leaving Sweet Hill without first sleeping with Cruz Walsh, she was at a loss. How did she find him?

She conveniently pushed aside the whole prospect of seduction. Seducing a man wasn't something she had ever done before, but she would just trust that she would know what to do in that moment, when the time came. The real question was how would she even find him?

He didn't have a cell phone. She already knew that. She knew he bought a house outside of town and she knew he had opened a gym across town.

She could find the gym easily enough. She didn't have the address to his house, however.

The man had been pursuing her. Who knew getting him into bed would be so difficult to orchestrate? She supposed it was easy to get a man into bed when it was just any man. When she added a *specific* man to the criterion it complicated things. She didn't want just any man. She wanted Cruz Walsh in her bed. Or she in his. She wasn't picky.

She said good night and left her grandmother and dove straight into the shower where she lathered, buffed and loofahed every part of her body, followed by a very thorough shaving of her legs and bikini area. After her shower she lotioned herself until her skin felt new. Dressed in a simple T-shirt dress, she pronounced herself showroom ready for sex.

She made a brief drop-off at the twenty-four-hour dry cleaners, and even though she didn't feel in the mood to face Bianca, she stopped at The Daily Grind to pick up her last paycheck. It turned out she didn't have to worry because Bianca wasn't working. It was a different manager, and this one looked vaguely embarrassed about the whole situation. When he started to offer an apology and suggest that maybe she wanted to appeal her termination to the owners, Gabriella cut him off. "Don't worry about it. I'll be moving back to Austin soon. I'm fine with it."

She was heading across the parking lot to her car when Jabal called her name and raced to catch up with her. "Have you seen my Twitter?" she asked with a breathless laugh, pulling out her phone from her apron.

"Um. No."

"Check this out," she said tapping on her phone. "I've never gotten so many likes or retweets in my life and I owe it all to you. I gained like three hundred followers."

"What are you—" she started to say and then stopped dead as her eyes clapped on the video that Jabal was showing her. It was of Cruz and Gabriella making out in the parking lot yesterday. They were leaning against a car and she had her legs wrapped around him. They were going at it like it was the last minute of their lives. The camera zoomed in to get a clear shot of their profiles.

"Jabal!" She snatched the phone so she could watch the horrifying video up close. The caption read: *Girl, get it . . .* followed by several hashtags. One hashtag was actually #CruzWalsh.

"What the fuck?" she exploded. "How did you think this was okay?" She looked closer at the tweet. "And you tagged me?" Her gaze landed on another of the dozen or so hashtags. "#hottiefelon?"

Jabal's smile slipped. "What? What's wrong?"

Gabriella shook the phone at her. "Why would you post this? How could you think this was okay?"

"Um. 'Cuz he's hella hot and like a celebrity."

She closed her eyes in a miserable blink and then shook the phone at her friend again. "Take it down. Delete it now. Now!"

For all the good that did. She was a journalist. She knew better than anyone that once something was out there it was out there forever.

"Fine." Pouting, Jabal took her phone back and deleted the tweet. "I think you're overreacting. It's not like you were naked or something or actually fucking."

Gabriella fanned her suddenly hot face with her hand and immediately began telling herself that

Jabal was right. It wasn't *that* big of a deal. She didn't need to freak out. A video of her kissing Cruz Walsh wasn't that interesting to people. So yeah, it had been retweeted a couple hundred times in the last twenty-four hours. It's not like it had gone viral or anything. That hardly qualified.

Additionally, it wasn't as though it were a secret she was keeping from her family anymore. Her sister had seen them so that cat was out of the bag. Both her mother and her brother had shot her several texts—all of which she had yet to answer—but she would have to face them eventually whether they saw this video or not. She grimaced. Sure video evidence wasn't great, but they already knew.

She shook her head. That was just family drama. Everything was going to be fine. Like Jabal said, it wasn't a sex video.

"It will probably be okay," she agreed, willing the queasiness in her stomach to quell. She stopped fanning her face and pressed a hand to her rolling stomach.

Jabal continued to watch her like she was being totally ridiculous. "It's fine," she assured. "What are you worried about? You know how many videos and photos are floating around of me? Even if this blew up you should totally pat yourself on the back. I mean, he's gorgeous."

She exhaled and didn't bother explaining that it wasn't as simple as that. She didn't *want* videos of herself making out all over the Internet. She didn't want that kind of attention, and she knew Cruz didn't either. The guy was media shy. He didn't do interviews. He wasn't on social media, period. For God's sake, he didn't even own a phone. He was a very private person. Or at least he was trying to be.

Suddenly she knew she had to tell him about this. She had to let him know so he wasn't blindsided. Turning, she made her way to her car.

Once in her car, she pulled out of the parking lot onto the main road in the direction of his gym. Hopefully, he wouldn't care and they could just move on to more fun things . . . like the real reason she wanted to see him tonight.

TWENTY

GABRIELLA ACTUALLY DROVE around aimlessly in her car for a while, gathering up the courage for what she was about to do. Approaching a man for the sole purpose of sex was bold, and bold wasn't exactly her MO. Additionally, she had to tell him about the video and he probably wouldn't love that.

At one point, her phone went off and she glanced down in the cup holder where it sat. It was a FaceTime call from Cody. Deciding to answer, she pulled over into a Whataburger parking lot.

She accepted the call and Cody's face appeared on the screen with his large office window behind him that overlooked downtown Austin. It was a familiar and yet oddly *un*familiar sight. Like something from a long time ago. Another life. Something . . . she didn't even miss. Before she could examine that and all its implications too closely, Cody was talking.

"Hey there, wasn't sure I was going to catch you or whether you were going to be out busy with your new boyfriend." He leaned back in his reclining desk chair, tapping a pencil against his palm.

"Uh, what do you mean? I'm not—" She was about to say she wasn't *seeing* anyone but those words stuck in her throat. "I don't have a new boyfriend." That much was true. Cruz was something to her—she couldn't deny that—but a boyfriend he was not.

"Huh. So what are you doing with Cruz Walsh? Just having a fling then? I never thought you were a fling kind of girl. Could have saved us the trouble of a relationship."

The heaviness in the pit of her stomach turned into a full-fledged boulder.

His face zoomed closer as he dropped forward in his chair. "Hey, you looked pretty hot against that car. How come you weren't that adventurous with me? Never knew you were into public displays."

Her face burned and she glanced away beneath his scrutiny, searching for her composure. She resisted the impulse to slam her phone shut. He was still her boss. Well, technically he was her team leader. He led four other journalists. The first year she had been on his team their relationship had been strictly professional. They had started to evolve into something more about a year and a half later once she started working with him.

It had seemed like a good idea to date him. He had been sweet. Complimentary of her talent . . . of *her*. They had a lot in common. He was a professional, too. The kind of man she thought she *should* be dating. She had decided to risk it, telling herself she would never find Mr. Right if she didn't take any chances in life. Yeah. Mistake.

"Yeah, well, there are a lot of things we never did, Cody."

He frowned, clearly trying to figure out just how much she was insulting him. "I guess I underestimated how far you would go for a story, Gabs."

"That wasn't about a story," she snapped, her face and ears hot.

He snorted. "You're telling me you're into this guy . . . a felon. Man, you really are slumming it." His lips curled into a sneer.

"My personal life is none of your business. Should I ask HR what their position is on you voicing an opinion on what I do in my free time?"

His lips flattened into a hard line. He was well aware of HR's position. They'd been up front with HR when they started dating . . . and when they stopped. She knew the head of HR had warned

Cody to behave himself . . . not in those precise words, but that was the gist.

She continued, "And I changed my mind about doing the story. He doesn't want to give an interview. I'm not going to force him into it."

"God, you're really into him." He tsked and shook his head. "Thinking below the waist. That's a rookie mistake and rookie you are not. You've been in this business long enough to know better. I expected better of you, Gabs."

"You know what, Cody. I really don't care what you expect of me. My job doesn't require me to squeeze an interview out of an unwilling subject. I'm not you."

"That's right. You're not. And that's why I'm leading my own team and you're still a staff writer— exactly where you were when you were hired on three years ago."

The reminder stung. It was the truth, however, and not one she hadn't thought about. She'd felt stuck in a rut lately. She'd blamed it on turning thirty, but that was only a number. It was the fact that she thought she would be further along in her life by now . . . that she would be *someone* else. Someone who felt pride and a sense of accomplishment in what she did.

When she learned of Nana Betty's surgery it had been the perfect excuse to take a break and figure out her next step in life. She had been telling herself her next step was to return to her life in Austin.

Now that no longer felt right. She knew, especially in this moment staring at Cody's face, that she needed to get her resume out there. No sense prolonging it.

"You know what else, Cody?"

He arched an eyebrow. "Enlighten me."

"I quit."

IT WAS LATE when she finally parked her car in front of his gym. She knew it was well after hours and the place was probably closed and she had missed her window of opportunity.

Except she then recognized his parked car.

She took a steadying breath and flexed her grip on the steering wheel, stretching her fingers and then settling back into a tight grip. The lot was empty save his car. He was still here and alone apparently. *You can do this. You can do this.*

With that mantra rolling around her head, she stepped out of her car.

She eased open the door and stepped into the well air-conditioned space. She inhaled the crisp aroma of fresh paint and sweat. The renovations were still fairly recent. That explained the fresh paint smell. She knew that the place had opened with a splash. People had been interested, both because Cruz Walsh was the owner and because the gym offered free after-school programs to kids that lived in the surrounding communities—surrounding neighborhoods that consisted of a lower socioeconomic population. The closest neighborhood, in fact, happened to be where Cruz Walsh grew up. She might have made a point to know that fact in the days she was obsessed with him. When she got her own car in high school, she might have even driven past a few times. Stalkery behavior, sure.

It seemed clear to her why he picked this location. He wanted to give something back to the community where he grew up. He wanted to help kids like himself, kids who didn't have a lot of resources. It seemed proof enough that Cruz Walsh was a decent person. She didn't know why other people didn't see that. People like her sister.

The door might have been unlocked, but it was clear that the gym was closed for the day. Most of the lights were off.

Except someone was here. Guns N' Roses pumped at a low volume from some hidden speakers and the main office light was on. She stepped up to the open door of the main office and peered inside. Giant post office tubs of mail blocked her from making it very far into the space. The envelopes inside the tub caught her eye. How could they not? So many of them were brightly colored shades of pink. Coral pink. Magenta. Mauve. Lilac. Fuchsia. Watermelon. Bubblegum. They were decorated with stickers and hearts.

She lifted one letter and a cloud of glitter gusted out from the thin paper. She read the addressee's name. *Cruz Walsh, Man of My Dreams*. Just that. No address.

She bent down and browsed through the rest of them. None of them had Cruz's physical address, but several had little epigraphs and notes in addition to his name.

Cruz Walsh, future husband.
You're the butter to my bread.
To the most beautiful man alive.

She gasped. Realization dawned. *Oh my*. They were love letters.

Various fragrances wafted up from the plastic bin, and she realized that several of them were perfumed. The different perfumes battled with each other for dominance to create an overwhelming mélange of scents. Holding her breath, she eyed the three bins. There were hundreds of letters here. All unopened. The senders were females from all over the country. She even spotted a few return addresses from Canada. One from Germany!

"What are you doing?"

She whirled around with a gasp, feeling caught. Like she was up to no good.

Cruz stood framed in the doorway, his dark eyes intent and burning as they fixed on her. His mouth was frowning. She could only stare at his frown and feel unsettled by it. Not that he was the smiley sort, but that frown made her stomach twist. He most definitely did not look happy to see her.

"Uhh . . ." Her gaze flicked to all the bins of mail rather guiltily.

He followed her gaze and his nostrils flared in clear annoyance.

"You have a lot of mail," she remarked.

"Yeah, I haven't bagged them up and taken them to the trash this week yet."

"Women write you love letters?"

He grunted. "If you could call them that. I guess. I don't open them."

Her mind processed that. If this was what he got for not even granting interviews, she couldn't even imagine what would happen if his story got picked up on any major platform.

"At least they don't know where you live," she offered.

"Small blessings." His lips twisted wryly. "What are you doing here, Gabriella?" The question sounded tired and she felt very unwelcome . . . and *very* foolish standing in front of him.

She shifted uneasily, smoothing a suddenly sweating palm down over her hip and telling herself not to read too much into his behavior. So he was rather abrupt. She could understand that. Her sister had been awful and not just to him but to his sister, too. They hadn't parted on very good terms yesterday.

"I wanted to see you." She let that hang out there, hoping he would say something. Fill the awkward space between them.

Nothing. He turned and looked away from her, staring at the wall as though he saw something there of interest . . . or maybe he just didn't want to look at her face.

She started to suspect he was gathering his thoughts to come up with a polite rejection.

She knew all about rejection. It was something she could practically smell on the air.

She moistened her suddenly dry lips. This wasn't like him. Ever since their time locked in the storage closet he had come on strong. He didn't mince words. He wanted her. He'd been clear about that. Even her self-doubts and self-consciousness couldn't deny that.

And yet right now she felt like she was standing in front of a different man. "Cruz?" She whispered his name as though she needed to say it out loud to confirm this was him. *Her* Cruz. The same man who had said: *We started something years ago. You think I'm gonna let another twelve years go by?*

This man seemed like a stranger.

He looked back at her, his expression resigned. "You should go."

She flinched like he had slapped her. He wanted her to go? She held his dark gaze, words winging through her mind but none surfacing on her tongue. Shaking her head, she pushed past him out of the front office.

She guessed the scene with her sister yesterday had really turned him off her. Maybe it was for the best.

Except she couldn't *not* acknowledge what her sister had done. She couldn't leave without apologizing for her behavior. "I'm sorry for what my sister did yesterday. She was cruel and vicious. I hope Malia isn't too hurt. She's a very sweet girl. She didn't deserve that . . . neither did you." There were so many things he hadn't deserved, and it killed her to know that she might heap any more suffering upon him.

He stopped and looked at her. "Family is everything to me. I'd do anything for them."

She nodded, understanding. He was that kind of person. Family first with him. Of course, this would make him even more wary of getting involved with her. Why should he want the trouble?

"I understand." Exhaling, she turned and marched out of the building, her arms swinging fiercely at her sides.

She hadn't even told him about the video. That would probably be the icing on the cake for him. Another thing to blame her for. But was that really her fault? Sure, Jabal was her friend, but Gabriella could hardly be blamed for her ex-coworker's poor choices.

She made it to her car and then stopped. She stood there, fuming, stupid tears pricking her eyes.

She knew what this was. She knew what the crushing weight on her chest was about. She liked him. She *really* liked him and she had never stopped liking him. Not even when she was in her twenties and he was only a memory and an unattainable one at that—even when it had been wrong on every level to like him, she had.

He was the dream she never forgot.

Then suddenly, impossibly, she saw him again and he wanted her. By his own admission, he wanted her. HER. He'd made her feel things. Made her crave him like air. Of course, she was a hot mess right now. Damn him for changing his mind. She came here ready to bare herself. Ready to strip down before him, both literally and physically.

She wasn't running away this time.

Before she quite knew what she was doing, she pushed away from her car and swung around. She marched back toward the gym and pushed inside the double doors, glad that he had not yet locked them.

A quick glance verified his office was empty. He wasn't there. She stepped forward into a main area that was divided into sections. There was a basketball court, a volleyball court, and an area with a giant colorful tower of blocks and tunnels for younger kids to climb.

She peered through the vast space, searching. Meager light glowed on the far side of the gym. This single light saved the interior from complete blackness. She stalked across the floor toward it, crossing the basketball and volleyball courts.

Thwack. Thwack.

The sound rang out in a steady staccato, echoing through the cavernous building. "Paradise City" ended and Aerosmith rolled on.

If she had to guess, the heavy thuds were Cruz

beating a punching bag. She tried not to let that vision take over her mind—tried not to see Cruz's impressive body straining and working out. Although she was too angry to let that idea distract her.

Rounding a corner, she spotted him on a wide matted area. There was, in fact, a ring for boxing and he stood just outside of it, attacking a punching bag as she predicted.

At the sight of him, she stopped cold.

He bounced on the balls of his feet, legs apart, knees bent. He was beating the hell out of a punching bag, taking his time between blows as though assessing the bag, measuring where he wanted to hit next and how hard.

He landed a shuddering hard hit. Each blow landed deep, swinging the bag from where it hung from the ceiling. She wondered if this was his pent-up aggression and if it had anything to do with her. She wouldn't mind taking a few whacks at the bag. She itched to take a swing at it. She guessed they all had their demons, but tonight he was hers.

Maybe she should get something like that for herself. Hang it in her spare bedroom and attack it any time she was in a mood. It might be the kind of workout she had been looking for.

She watched him, enjoying the sight more than she should considering he had just dismissed her.

Rejected her. He was shirtless, of course, his bare chest on full unabashed display. He really was something off the cover of *Men's Health*, and that only fueled her anger.

He'd always had a great body—even in high school, but this was just . . . just ridiculous. Was this what prison did? Gave you a body that could be weaponized? He should offer the prison work-out experience. The hard-core gym rats would show up in droves.

A pair of athletic pants sat low on his hip bones and she couldn't do anything but look at those bones and the indentations and feel her mouth sali-vate. Suddenly she had an image of herself strad-dling him . . . of her hands right *there*, gripping each side of his hips, her mouth pressing directly over his navel, following that subtle happy trail down, down, down . . .

Heat swarmed her face.

If her nephew hadn't interrupted them the other night, she could have already done that. As it turned out, now Cruz wanted her gone.

She must have made a sound that alerted him to her presence. He swung around, his eyes snapping to her.

Again, she felt caught. Like she had done some-thing wrong. Like he could take one look at her face and know all the wicked things she had been thinking as she admired his body. If possible, her face flamed hotter.

"What are you still doing here?"

She hated the question . . . hated him right then. "You made me like you," she accused. He blinked. She continued, gaining steam. "I'd managed to put you behind me." She was stabbing the air with her finger now. "I'd forgotten you—" Not exactly a lie. She had *mostly* forgotten him. "And then you kissed me in the closet and came to my house and the coffee shop and you made me start wanting you all over again." Her chest lifted high with angry breaths.

He said nothing but came closer, ripping the Velcro free on his gloves.

She kept on talking in the face of his steady advance. "I came here to apologize to you about my sister, but that's not the only reason—"

"Why are you sorry for your sister? You didn't do anything."

"I know that, but she is my sister—"

"Is that what you do?" He tossed one glove angrily to the mat and then the next. "Go around apologizing for your sister?"

"No," she snapped.

"As far as your family is concerned, I will never be *right* with them."

She swallowed. He spoke the truth, but she didn't care what her family thought. She couldn't always claim she felt that way, but she felt that way now. He shouldn't care either.

"I'll never be good enough for you," he added fiercely. "And your family is not wrong. Fuck, Gabriella. You were fired because of me!" He waved a hand in the direction of the door. "So why don't you go? Leave and stay away from me. You've apologized for your sister. Duty done. You can go now."

She sucked in a sharp breath. She'd been dismissed.

"Why are you being such a jerk?"

Where was the Cruz from before? The one who couldn't stop kissing her?

He leapt toward her and gripped her arms. "Because I'm trying to do the fucking right thing."

And casting her from his life was the right thing? "So damn noble. Isn't that what you always do? You went to prison for a crime you didn't commit." Her gaze flicked around her. "Then you opened a rec center for all the kids in your old neighborhood instead of leaving this town where people treat you like a pariah. When do you ever just do something for *you*? Something that might not be the right thing but it's what *you* want? Something that makes *you* feel good?"

His hands dropped from her arms. His jaw tensed, a muscle feathering along his cheek. "You don't know anything about me."

"I'm right about this." She nodded with certainty. "You went to prison for years. You're accustomed to self-denial." She lifted her chin and took a risk, saying, "You wanted me before. Now you don't."

He stepped back, eyeing her warily, and she was convinced. He hadn't stopped wanting her. He just decided against it. She had to remind him that he still wanted her.

She continued, "You're scared."

He shifted on his feet and snorted as if that was the most ridiculous thing he had ever heard. "I'm not."

She glanced around, taking stock of their surroundings and what was available to her. With a fortifying breath, she stepped forward. A wary look came over his face. She walked past him and approached a pair of dangling gymnastic rings anchored by chains to the ceiling. Kicking off her flats, she let her feet sink into the soft mat.

"What are you doing?" he called.

Holding his gaze, her hands reached for the hem of her T-shirt dress.

His expression went from wary to alarmed. "Are you trying to goad me into . . ."

The rest of his words died a swift death as she pulled her dress up and over her head and tossed it several feet aside. Teenage Gabriella Rossi—hell, even Gabriella from a month ago—would never have been able to do such a daring thing. She wouldn't have had the confidence.

But now she stood before him on full display in her bra and panties. True, they were a good bra and panties set. One of her best. She felt pride and no small relief over that.

The lacy black demi-cup cut really close to her nipples and did great things for her girls, thrusting them up and out. The matching black panties were little more than a lacy scrap of fabric and showed a considerable amount of ass cheek.

Reaching for the rings, she turned so that he could appreciate the cheeks peeking out of the lace.

She pushed out her ass and snuck a look over her shoulder at him, not sure what she would find. Hopefully, he wasn't still glowering . . .

He came up fast behind her with a growl, one of his hands going to her breast, sliding right inside the skimpy cup so that his hand covered the entire globe. His other hand grabbed hold of her ass.

He groaned and the sound was pure animal. "You're going to kill me." His hands squeezed her breast and ass and she moaned, her hands slipping from the rings, ready to let go, unable to hold on.

"Don't move your hands. Keep them on the rings." He nipped her earlobe as though to emphasize the point and she whimpered as lust shot straight to her sex.

She tightened her grip, fastening her suddenly sweating palms around the rings. He circled around her and buried his face between her breasts as both his hands simultaneously slid inside her underwear to mold and squeeze her ass. "Your fucking body destroys me." He punctuated each word with a deep rolling massage that blasted sensation straight to her clit. "It's insane how much I want you."

"You told me to leave," she panted, reminding him that he had said that . . . still hurt over that fact. It had stung and she wasn't above flinging that at him.

He lifted his head and stared down at her with liquid dark eyes. "I didn't want you to leave," he confessed. "I've always wanted you, Gabriella Rossi. In the boathouse . . . I didn't know it was you, but I wanted it to be. In prison, in the dark of night, when I dreamed of the girl I kissed in the boathouse she didn't have a face . . . so I gave her yours."

TWENTY-ONE

𝓕OLLOWING THAT MIND-REELING confession, he dropped, pulling her panties down in one sweeping move. They fell to her ankles. She didn't even have an opportunity to kick them aside before he lifted both her legs and draped them over his shoulders. Her feet were off the ground and his face was buried between her thighs, his mouth fast on her pussy. She wanted to process his shocking words, but there was that distracting, wondrous mouth of his.

She tried to think about the significance of what he said—*he had always wanted her?* She wanted to ask him, but he was devouring her. Licking and sucking. She wanted to grab hold of his hair for support, but she couldn't let go of the rings.

Every once in a while the sensation of his tongue rubbing her clit was too much, too intense, and she would use her grip on the rings to pull her body up and away. Growling, he would clamp down on her thighs, tug her back, and mouth-fuck her harder. Until she was coming. Screaming as a climax rolled through her.

Her vision was unfocused but she gradually realized he was standing in front of her again. She was shaking as he peeled her hands from the rings and unhooked her bra. The straps fell down her shoulders, leaving her naked in front of him. His eyes traveled over her. Over *all* of her. "The reality is so much better," he said thickly. "Better than anything in my head."

He acted as though he had wanted her for always and always—and after his unbelievable words she wondered if maybe he had. *I've always wanted you, Gabriella Rossi.*

Could he have noticed her in high school? Could he have crushed on her, too? Like she had crushed on him?

But she couldn't contemplate that right now. She couldn't even think at all in this moment.

His gaze fixed on her breasts. She tried not to squirm under his scrutiny. "Such pretty tits." She moaned and arched as one of his big hands palmed her breast. "I could spend hours just loving these."

His touch grew almost rough as he handled her.

She relished it, arching her spine, thrusting her chest out. He fondled a heavy globe, pinching her nipple between thumb and forefinger. His other hand followed suit so that he was squeezing both mounds, lifting them and pushing them together while tweaking the tips.

Suddenly she couldn't stand anymore. Her knees gave out and her legs buckled. He caught her, lowering her to the ground gently so that she didn't just drop. His mouth found her breasts. He sucked a nipple deep into the cavern of his mouth. He used his tongue and teeth, and she arched on the mat, pushing her flesh into his greedy mouth. Her breasts had never been lavished with such attention. She felt owned. Marked and possessed.

He settled his hips between her legs, forcing her legs wide. He only wore his pants, but she felt him, rock-hard, prodding into her bare sex. He pressed down to grind against her and it was amazing. She was ready to come again, and he hadn't even penetrated her.

She buried her fingers in his hair and held him close, content to keep him there forever as he ground his cock into her, the barrier of his pants something she hated and wanted gone. Her hands flew to his waistband, tugging them down.

"I need a condom," he growled around one distended nipple, scoring it with his teeth. "But I can't bear to stop . . ."

"I can't bear for you to stop either." But they needed a condom. She knew that.

He lifted away and she watched hungrily as he quickly stood and discarded his pants. And then he was naked. Gloriously naked. Oh. My. The man was a god. Especially *that* part of him. There was nothing earthly about it. His member looked like a heavenly instrument as far as she was concerned.

She pointed a finger rather desperately, her sex clenching in near pain to be filled. "My purse."

He followed the direction of her hand and was there in a flash, bringing the bag back to her just as quickly. She dug through the contents until she found the condom she had packed. She handed it to him with a smile. "I came armed."

Smiling, he took it. "Fuck, my hands are shaking."

He wasn't lying. His hands were shaking. For her. Because of her. How could that be? This was Cruz Walsh. Sure, he'd been in prison for seven years but she knew the man was no monk. He'd been with scores of beautiful women.

Her gaze roamed over him. He was so beautiful. His erection bobbed between them and she reached for it with both hands, and she realized she would need *both* hands.

He groaned as she wrapped her fingers around him. He was big. Bigger than anything she ever had inside her. She stroked him in awe, touching the fat crown reverently. She traced the slit, rubbing in the pre-cum that leaked out, gratified as another groan shook him. The head of him swelled and grew tighter under her fingers. "Damn it, Gabriella. How am I supposed to open this when you're touching me like that?"

Touching, she realized, wasn't enough. She bent her head between them and licked him once, twice, and then she fully pulled him into her mouth.

He fell back on the mat with a strangled cry, arms spread out in surrender at his sides. She leaned over him, lavishing her mouth up and down his engorged cock.

"What are you doing to me?" he gasped, his hand burying into her hair, not guiding her, just holding on to her as she worked over him.

"Stop." He sat up and rolled her onto her back on the mat. He hovered over her, his elbows propped on either side of her head, his dark eyes locked with hers. "I've waited half my life to be inside you."

The words jarred her. *Half* his life. Since they

were fifteen. She gulped, holding his gaze, lost inside his eyes.

"The feeling is mutual." She needed him inside her now. More than she'd ever needed anything on this earth she needed to feel this man buried deep in her.

The condom crinkled near her head. Her gaze drifted to the side. It was still in his hand. She reached for it. Took it from him. She tore it free from the package and lowered it between their bodies. He watched her as she rolled it down the hard length of him. She couldn't resist. She wrapped her fingers around the girth of him and gave him a good squeeze.

A shudder racked him and he choked out a profanity.

Surprisingly, her fingers were steady and sure. Finished, she gripped him again and brought the head of him to her opening, dipping the tip of him and gliding it over her wetness.

Shoulders shaking from strain, he looked down, watching as she slowly guided the crown of him inside her, just a fraction.

Then she was shaking, desire and anticipation overwhelming her. With his elbows still propped on either side of her head, he framed his hands along either side of her face, fingertips brushing her hairline. "Look at me, Gabriella. I want your eyes on me as I enter you."

She looked at his face, inches from hers, and she didn't blink.

It should have embarrassed her, but everything about this moment was so right and long-awaited. She burned for him.

Tension rippled over his jaw and then he let go. Shoved inside her with one slick thrust, filling her completely, stretching her deliciously.

She threw back her head and a sob broke from her lips.

"Gabriella," he commanded. "Look at me."

Her gaze whipped back to him.

Eyes on her face, he thrust again. Harder.

She squirmed against the invasion, her hands pushing at his corded shoulders as if needing leverage. "Oh," she gasped. "You're big . . ."

"You can take it." He brought his mouth to her ear, biting down on the lobe sharply, sending a rush of moisture to her sex. "Oh, you just got really wet. You feel amazing." Another thrust. "Like you were made for me."

She cried out at the fullness of him sliding in and out of her, the friction shooting sparks through her. She lifted her hips greedily, taking in more of him.

His mouth claimed hers, swallowing her cries.

He kissed her senseless, his tongue rubbing against hers, arousing her on a whole new level and sending another rush of moisture to her sex.

"How do you feel this good?" Breathing raggedly, he pulled back to thrust even deeper, harder, shoving her higher up the mat. He followed, driving into her. A small scream escaped her.

"That's right. Scream for me, Rossi."

Her nails dug into his shoulders, hanging on for dear life. It was incredible. She didn't know sex could be like this. Rough and hard and fast. She didn't know she could want it like this.

She was shaking and wild, her body not her own. She came in a violent burst. She went limp, his name on her lips as she quivered in the aftershocks. Tears sprang to her eyes from the miracle of it. It might be sacrilegious, but it did feel like a miracle. A miracle fifteen years in the making. For fifteen years she had wanted this and dreamed of it like one did the lottery—a lovely fantasy that was never expected to come true.

He didn't stop though.

He continued riding her, pumping ceaselessly. His hands dug into her generous hips, lifting her up for his thrusting cock. "Again, Rossi."

"Can't," she gasped, shaking her head. It was too

much. There was no way. He could not possibly wring out another orgasm from her.

He was unrelenting. His thrusts fell faster, harder, pushing her again to the edge of another climax.

She clutched his shoulders, his back. Her hands skimmed down and gripped his tight ass, reveling in how it flexed as he pumped in and out of her.

Then he launched her over that edge again.

A keening cry escaped her—a sound that should have embarrassed her if she could form coherent thought. Tears streamed down her face.

He lost all restraint. He became an animal of instinct, fierce and intense as he worked into her body, taking it and claiming it for his desire.

She'd never felt so desired. So inherently female. So strong and powerful.

A few more plunges and he stilled, throwing back his head with a groan as he came.

Her breasts rose and fell in heavy gasps. She couldn't slow her breathing.

He lowered his hot-liquid gaze back to her and she knew she looked as shell-shocked as she felt. She wet her bruised-feeling lips and fought to regain her breath. "That . . . I . . ."

"Come back to my place," he said thickly, his thumb brushing over her moist lip. Sensation shot through her at the contact and she marveled that that simple touch could affect her after everything—after all the far more intimate things they had just done. Would this man never not reduce her to a pile of goo with a touch? "I don't want you to leave me tonight."

She didn't want to leave him either. Not tonight. Not *ever*.

And that was ridiculous. Clearly her sluggish brain was clouded from too many orgasms.

She tried to think of why going home with him was a bad idea. She knew there was a reason she should say no. There were *many* reasons. Several.

Her family. The fucking world. She would be going back to Austin soon.

This thing between them could never go anywhere. Never be permanent.

But all those reasons seemed insignificant.

"Okay. I'll follow you in my car."

TWENTY-TWO

*T*HEY SHOWERED WHEN they got back to his place and he took her against the tiled wall with soapy water sluicing down her body. Her curves were slippery in his hands, but he was convinced shower sex, something he had actually never had before, was his new favorite thing. Her tits tasted better wet and with the faint aroma of his soap on her glistening skin.

Cruz knew he should let her sleep, give her some relief from him, but he had spent seven years dreaming about this woman in a prison cell.

He couldn't be satiated.

Of course, if she had protested or complained he would have restrained himself, but the fact that she was so into it, sometimes even reaching for him first and climbing on top of him in bed, only fed his hunger. Gabriella astride him was something that went beyond fantasy.

And there was that sense of a clock ticking, that this was all about to go away, vanish like smoke.

It filled him with a sense of urgency.

It made him desperate and greedy.

He had to make it last. He had to mark her. Had to ruin her for another man. Just the thought of another man in her future had him reaching for her, kissing her. He almost didn't even stop for a condom in his haste to slide inside her.

Of course, he realized, belatedly, he was marking himself.

Ruining himself.

No woman would ever be enough. Because she would never be Gabriella.

At dawn, he actually fell asleep with one arm wrapped around her waist, her body pulled close to his chest. She wouldn't sneak away without his knowledge. There would be no disappearing like smoke. Not yet.

His phone started ringing insistently a little after eight. He blinked bleary eyes, startled to realize the bed was, in fact, empty. He sat up abruptly, glancing around wildly. Then the sound of running water penetrated. She was still here.

He was debating joining her in the shower again

when he recalled his phone had been ringing. He checked and saw he had a missed call from his sister.

He called her back. "Hey, Piper."

"Cruz? How are you?"

"I'm fine." He sat up, leaning his back against the headboard. Better than he had ever been, in fact. "Why?"

"Of course, you haven't seen it," she said with an indulgent sigh. "You really should join the twenty-first century, Cruz."

"What are you talking about?" he snapped.

"Go look at your computer. Type in your name."

He pushed back the covers, taking the phone with him, and strode naked across the room. He typed in his name and countless URLs popped up featuring him.

He clicked on the first one and it took him to the website of the *Austin Daily Reporter*.

His stomach bottomed out. No way. *She didn't.*

He clicked on the video beneath the header: *Undercover Reporter Goes Deep Under Covers . . .*

And there was a video. Of course. He played it, watching himself make out with Gabriella in the coffeehouse parking lot.

"Shit," he breathed.

"You found it."

"Yeah."

"Clever wordplay," she offered weakly.

"I can't believe she would do this." He scanned the article, his heart seizing on the line: *Investigative reporter Gabriella Rossi promises details to come as she peels back the layers on the man, the mystery, Cruz Walsh.*

"Jesus," he muttered, his gaze swinging toward the shower. The door was open and Gabriella stood there, smiling at him. She looked beautiful, her skin pink from the shower, his towel wrapped around her. He felt it like a blow to his gut.

She only looked at him and saw him as a story. Not a person. That had always been in the back of her mind, but he never had to face it until now.

As she took in his expression, her smile faltered. "Cruz?"

"I gotta go, Piper." He hung up on his sister even as her voice continued to talk.

He turned his laptop screen around, gesturing at it. "You've been busy. I'm surprised you didn't leak any photos from last night. You're clearly resourceful enough."

Clutching a towel to her chest, she stepped forward and scanned the screen. Color blossomed in her cheeks. "I didn't have anything to do with that!"

"That's your paper, isn't it? The one you work for?"

She closed her eyes in a long blink and then opened them, her velvet eyes the perfect picture of anguish. "My coworker, Jabal, posted the video to her Twitter. My paper must have found it and picked it up—"

"And just posted this without you knowing?" He motioned to the screen with a disbelieving snort.

"My Copy Editor is a pit bull. The more salacious the headline, the better. He's not big on journalistic integrity."

"And you are?" he shot back.

Her cheeks flamed hotter. "I don't deserve that!" She moved to her discarded clothes. Dropping the towel, she began dressing herself, her breasts jiggling with her movements and damn if he didn't get hard watching her. Even angry, he wanted her.

As she wrestled to turn her dress right side out, she kept talking. And he kept watching her, wanting her.

God, he was messed up . . . or he just had it really bad for this woman. Both, he guessed.

"He's been pushing me for your story. You *knew* I wanted your story. I never hid that from you—"

"Yeah. I just didn't think you would stoop to this."

She stopped, flinging her dress down and glaring

at him. "I wouldn't! I didn't!" Her gaze lowered, colliding on his very erect cock.

Her face only reddened further. She reached for her panties and stepped into them. His dick wept at the sight. He stepped up behind her, his hands landing on her hips. "So you're done then? No more undercover work? I mean . . . I enjoyed your methods. I wouldn't be opposed to another round." Even as the words escaped him, he couldn't believe he was saying them.

She turned to face him, her eyes raging bright. "Go to hell," she spat, hastily donning the rest of her clothes. "You just want to believe this so you can fuck up whatever it was *you* thought was happening here between us."

"And what did you think was happening here, Rossi?" The question came out perfectly bored even though his blood was pumping hard and fast through his veins.

"Nothing," she snapped. "Absolutely nothing. We were just two consenting adults having sex." Dressed now, she clutched her purse to her chest. "So you didn't really need to pick a fight, Cruz. Don't worry. I would never dream of falling in love with you."

He told himself that was a relief. There would be no tears. No awkward professions of love.

She nodded sarcastically, her brown hair flowing wild all around her. "You're safe from me."

She stormed out of his bedroom. He followed at a more strolling pace, wondering why those words felt like another slap to his face.

He didn't want her love. That would give way to things normal people had—marriage, kids, retirement plans—and he wasn't a normal person. He never would be. So he let her go.

He'd lusted after her for years and now he had her. It should be enough. It had to be.

He stood on the porch and watched as she stalked angrily to her car, her steps wobbly over the gravel. His hands clenched the wood porch railing as though he needed something to hold on to. From inside he heard his phone ringing, undoubtedly his sister calling back to check on him. She always worried. What she didn't realize was that some broken things could never be fixed.

He didn't move though. It felt important that he should watch, that he should have this final glimpse of her.

He trained his expression to reveal nothing as he watched Gabriella Rossi climb into her car and drive out of his life.

SHE DIALED CODY the instant she pulled out onto the highway. "How could you do that to me?"

"Hey, what's on the Internet is fair game for all."

"You wrote lies!"

"I call it like I see it, Gabs. But not for nothing, you looked pretty hot up against that car. Made me think of old times."

She was going to be sick. "You're a pig. I quit."

He laughed. "You already did that."

"Well, I'm saying it again because it feels so fucking good to say it!"

He was still talking as she ended the call and then gripped the steering wheel, gulping back sobs and feeling very much like she was on the verge of hyperventilating.

She was out of a job twice in one week . . . and it wasn't exactly easy to get a job in media in this digital age, but she couldn't summon the will to care about that at this moment.

She was breaking inside. Cruz was right about one thing. She was a liar.

She hadn't been telling the truth when she said she would never fall in love with him. Because she had. She'd always loved him . . . first as a myth. A fantasy. The larger than life dreamy boy in high school.

Then she had fallen in love with the real Cruz. The noble man who went to prison for a crime he didn't commit and then stayed in the town that persecuted him. He stayed and opened a place, a community for disadvantaged kids.

She pounded the steering wheel. She loved his stupid face.

She pulled onto Nana's street and winced when she noticed the news van. *God, no.*

Trent was there with Nana, but it didn't appear he needed to do much. Nana had things well in hand, stabbing a broom at them and backing them up toward their van.

Gabriella eased off the gas and waited for them to drive away before pulling into the driveway.

Trent's eyes danced with delight as she got out of the car. At least someone was enjoying all the drama. "Of all the people in this family to be caught in a sex scandal, I never thought it would be you, Aunt Gabby." He held up his phone. "Seriously though, a lot of my friends want to know if you're free this Friday night."

"Trent!" She nodded toward Nana, conveying that he should be more circumspect.

Nana waved a hand dismissively. "It was only kissing. What's all the fuss?" She shot Trent with a look of disgust. "And why would she want some teenage boy when she has a man like that?"

Heat swamped her. "Nana, he's not my man."

"Well, why not? You better lock that in. That fella is a man's man. A regular Paul Newman."

Trent looked at her as though bewildered.

"Before your time," she supplied.

Nana focused her attention back on Gabriella. "Don't let Cruz Walsh slip away, my girl. He's a keeper. A man like him doesn't come along two times in a life. Sometimes he don't come around at all."

Gabriella started. "I—uh. Nana . . ." She shook her head. "How did you know? How did you know it was Cruz Walsh?"

"Agh." She waved one of her heavily veined hands. "I've known it was him the moment he showed up here with food. You think I don't remember what he looks like?"

"But your . . . cataracts . . ." she said lamely.

"Ack! I'm not blind. He's quite memorable."

Gabriella gaped, speechless for several moments. "You knew it was him when he came over here and you said nothing?"

Nana shrugged. "You seemed to want to believe I didn't recognize him. Who am I to shatter your delusions?" Nana's cloudy gaze narrowed on her. "That's for you to do."

Yes. Yes, it was. She had been living under a number of delusions. Primarily, that she wasn't good enough. For most of her life, she had thought her life would be better if she was somewhere else. If she had the right job. If she met the right man. If she was the right dress size. If others accepted her. None of that mattered now. She didn't care about any of that.

She would decide what her happiness would be. Her life and the happiness she found in it was entirely up to her.

Another vehicle approached, sliding up to the curb and giving a light honk in greeting.

"Who's that?" Nana demanded. "Another one of those news people?" She tightened her grip on her broom, clearly ready for another go.

Her chest sank. "I wish." It was Natalie. Ugh. She'd rather face a mob of paparazzi than Natalie.

She rolled down the window and waved her hand. "Gabby!"

Dread consumed her as she walked toward Natalie's SUV. She stopped on the sidewalk, not getting too close. She angled her body toward the house, trying to convey that she wasn't up for a long chat.

Nana and Trent stood near the front door, watching across the distance.

"Gabby," she said in a heavy breath. "Are you okay?"

"I'm fine. Thanks for asking," she said numbly,

hoping she now felt satisfied with *not* minding her business and drive away.

"Wow. You weren't kidding. You certainly do take your career seriously." She shook her head, her wide eyes mocking as they fixed on Gabriella with false solemnity. "I had no idea journalists went to such lengths to get a story. You certainly are dedicated. Hats off to you, girl."

Well, Natalie certainly took the prize on subtext. "Oh, fuck off."

Trent hooted and applauded from where he stood.

Natalie's mouth gaped. She sputtered like a fish. "What did you say—"

"I said fuck off. You're not my friend. You never have been. Why are you even here? Don't you have any friends? Go away and bother them. Stop trying to torment me. It doesn't work anymore."

"Well." She took several gulps of breath. "The years haven't been kind to you."

"They have, actually. They got me to this moment . . . to finally being someone I like. And that someone isn't afraid to tell you to get the hell out of here."

Her sister suddenly whipped into the driveway. *Great.* Tess was the last person she wanted to see right now. Natalie was easy to handle, she realized. There was no investment. Tess, on the other hand, was family. She couldn't tell her to get out of her life with any expectation of success.

Tess hopped down out of the driver's seat and slammed the door. Dakota was with her, too. Her niece rounded the front of the car and went to stand beside Trent.

Tess marched over with swift, purposeful strides.

"Oh, hello there, Tess," Natalie called. "I was just stopping by to check on poor Gabby here." She pulled an exaggerated pout and tsked her tongue. "You know . . . all things considered . . . and you can't imagine how rude she's being to me."

Tess looked Natalie over coolly. There was no telling what she was thinking. The shiny lenses of her glasses blocked her eyes. "Fuck off, Natalie."

Gabriella snorted. Well, then. She hadn't seen that coming.

Natalie's face went from smug to astonished in one second flat. Gabriella could understand the astonishment. She felt a similar sentiment.

Tess continued silkily, "Anyone can see through you, Natalie. You're so jealous you can't even stand it."

"Jealous? Me?" Her gaze shot to Gabriella. "Of fucking Flabby Gabby?"

Gabriella rolled her eyes, for once feeling very unaffected by that slur.

"First of all, don't call my sister that ever again." Tess stepped off the curb and placed a hand rather menacingly on the roof of Natalie's SUV. "Gabriella is getting laid by Cruz Walsh while you're married to a man who can't even see his shoes anymore." She fluttered her fingers in a shooing motion. "Get off our street."

"Bitch! Both of you! Bitches," Natalie spat, slamming the gear into drive and hitting the accelerator, narrowly missing a neighbor's car parked across the street.

"Bye!" Stepping back onto the curb, Tess waved cheerfully. "See you at the next PTA meeting."

They watched Natalie drive like a bat out of hell down the street.

"Thanks." Gabriella looked over at her sister like she had never seen her before—and she hadn't. At least not this version of her.

"Sure." She shrugged. "We're family. I know I've kinda failed at acting like your family lately, but I'm going to try and do a better job."

"Well, thanks, but I'm not sure it's going to make a difference. Natalie is only going to hate me more and now it made the two of you enemies—"

"Her? *Pfft.* No one likes her. *I* don't care about her." Tess leveled her a look. "I know it doesn't always seem like it, and I suck at showing it, but

I care about you." She sent a glance at where her daughter stood, watching them. Clearly they had had some manner of heart to heart. Gabriella was glad for that. Mothers and daughters should be close.

Tess continued, "I have issues. Jason, the divorce, other things . . ." She shook her head. "Not important. They have nothing to do with you. They're my burden, but I've been taking it out on everyone. I took it out on you the other night." Her chest lifted on a breath. "I do love you and I promise to do better at showing it." Emotion thickened her voice. "I'm sorry I hit you. I know it wasn't your fault. I'm sorry Jason hurt you."

It took her a moment to reply. "Wow. Thanks, Tess. That actually makes me feel better." A sob thickened her throat that she managed to hold off. After her miserable morning with Cruz, this helped. "I've actually had a pretty crap day."

"I can imagine. I saw the article. So what are you going to do about it?"

"Do? What can I do?"

"Oh, Gabby. You're the smartest person I know. You can figure your way out of this. You like Cruz Walsh, right?"

Gabriella hesitated, staring at her sister uncertainly.

Tess rolled her eyes. "C'mon. You've always liked him."

"You knew that?"

"We lived in the same house, Gabriella. I may not be as smart as you, but yeah. I knew how you felt about Cruz." Tess gazed at her pensively. "Are you in love with him?"

After a moment, she nodded and the sob she had been holding back broke through. Tess stepped forward and wrapped an arm around her shoulders. Together, they started walking toward the house. "C'mon. We'll get your man."

"No. He's done with me." She wiped at her eyes. "I'm moving back to Austin," she said, even though she wasn't sure about that or anything anymore. She'd just quit her job she had waiting there, after all.

"I don't think either of those things are true," Tess remarked.

She mulled that over. Could she stay here? In Sweet Hill? Where people still thought of her as Flabby Gabby? As soon as the thought entered her mind, another one immediately popped up.

I'm not Flabby Gabby.

The voice wasn't loud or even insistent. It was just a fact.

She had never been Flabby Gabby.

Cruz had liked her back then. There had been

nothing wrong with her when she was a teenager. There was nothing wrong with her now.

She looked at her sister and then her gaze drifted to where Nana stood on the porch, Trent and Dakota beside her. She had family here who loved her. They weren't a perfect family, but they loved her.

And she loved Cruz.

She wasn't going anywhere. Whether Cruz loved her or not, she was staying right here.

This was home.

TWENTY-THREE

$\mathcal{T}$HE FOLLOWING MORNING, Gabriella woke up early. She showered, dried and styled her hair, and actually wore clothes that made her feel like a human being again. A human with purpose.

Nana was already up and eating breakfast. Gabriella pressed a kiss to her papery-thin skin. "I'll text you and let you know when I'm going to be home."

"All right. Knock 'em dead."

A smile quirked her lips. "I'll try." She gave her lipstick a check in the hall mirror and then headed out.

She drove past The Daily Grind, noticing Jabal's car in the parking lot. She'd pop in on the way home. She was craving her signature drink and she wanted to make sure Jabal knew she wasn't mad at her.

She turned into the parking lot of the *Sweet Hill Recorder* and took the same parking spot beneath the old oak tree where she had parked every day of summer when she worked at the *Recorder* in high school. Only a few other cars were in the lot, but she recognized Mr. Brown's PT Cruiser.

She walked through the front door, marveling how her life had come full circle.

"Gabby Rossi!" Mr. B rose from his desk where he was working at his computer. "How lovely to see you."

"Hello, Mr. B." She inhaled and glanced around the building before meeting his gaze again. "I'm ready to work."

CRUZ'S FRONT DOOR flung open and slammed shut. He emerged from his bedroom just as Piper blew into the room, waving a newspaper above her head.

"Hey there, Piper. I guess you never heard of knocking."

"Cruz, Cruz!" She brandished the paper above her head.

"Piper," he returned evenly, unmoved.

He'd been fairly *unmoved* for the last week. Ever since Gabriella left. Correction: ever since he ran her off.

"You have to see this."

She slapped the paper on the table, her finger stabbing it repeatedly.

"Right now? I need to head to the gym."

"Cruz!" She propped both hands on her hips. "Sit down and read this paper right now!"

With a sigh, he sank down and dropped his gaze to the paper she shoved toward him.

Instantly the very professional-looking photograph of Gabriella in the top corner caught his eye. He tensed. "Really, I don't want to read any more stupid—"

"It's not stupid!" she shrieked. "Just shut up and read it, you big dumb man!"

Scowling, he returned his gaze to the paper and read with great reluctance, thinking as soon as he finished, he could get Piper out of his hair.

Dear Sweet Hill:

I grew up in this town. Some of you might remember me as Flabby Gabby. That was my nickname in high school. My peers would gleefully call me this to my face. As you can imagine, high school wasn't the best time of my life; some days it was a nightmare, but I survived it mostly because of Cruz Walsh. That strong, silent boy, elusive and beautiful in every way, gave my heart a reason to beat.

Most of you know him because he was convicted of a crime he did not commit and recently exonerated. Many of you don't believe in his innocence. You judge him for his name. You judge him for his past.

I know the real Cruz Walsh.

I know him as noble. I know him as a man who endured seven years in a cell for a crime he didn't commit and he doesn't begrudge anyone for it. I know him as the man who created a place for the children of Sweet Hill, a place where they can come together, where they can always feel safe, where Flabby Gabbys like me can feel hope.

I know the real Cruz Walsh and I'm in love with him.

Sweet Hill shaped me into who I am, but because of Cruz Walsh I can now forgive and love this town and myself in a way I never could before.

Until next week,
Gabriella Rossi
Copy Editor In Chief, Sweet Hill Recorder

He couldn't look away. He read it again and then again, just to make sure his eyes weren't deceiving him. No, those words there. Gabriella Rossi was in love with him. She had just admitted it to the entire town . . . along with baring her soul about a whole bunch of other baggage. The confession had been raw and honest and he felt every word of it in his soul.

"Say something, Cruz." Piper looked at him earnestly, her dark eyes bright and eager. "Please." She angled her head in a motion of appeal. "Don't be an idiot."

He opened his mouth, but nothing came out. He blinked through his suddenly blurring vision.

"Cruz! What are you going to do?"

He rubbed at his eyes, wondering at their burning sensation.

"Cruz? Are you . . . crying?"

He looked up at her, startled. He never cried. Not even when he had stood up for his sentencing in the courtroom and the fact that he was about to go away for a very long time had loomed undeniable and inescapable and glaring before him. He had never felt more alone than he did in that moment. Still, he had not cried.

And now Gabriella Rossi loved him and it broke him. Truly broke him. He blinked and swiped at his eyes. Straightening, he snatched his keys off the table.

"Cruz . . . where are you going?"

He stopped at the door and looked back at his sister. "I'm going to find a closet."

SHE RETURNED FROM her lunch break to find the office conspicuously empty. Mr. Brown was there. That was normal, but Daisy, one of their part-time staff writers, was gone. Friday was her day to work, but it looked like her desk was cleared off already—her laptop gone.

"Mr. B? Did Daisy go home already?"

"Daisy?" He blinked at her as though he had never heard the name.

"Er, yes." She pointed to Daisy's desk. "Daisy?"

He followed her gaze and looked at the desk like he had never seen it before either. Okay, maybe Mr. B needed to think about retiring sooner than the year out he had decided upon.

"Gabriella, would you take this to the archives room?" He extended an envelope toward her.

"Sure, where do I file it?"

"In the file cabinet to the left, there's a folder labeled *fan mail*."

"Fan mail?"

"That's right. Feel free to read the letters first. These keep coming in about your Copy Editorial. And the phone has been ringing off the hook." He grinned then, his chest puffing up like a proud

papa. By Copy Editorial he meant her letter to
Sweet Hill. He had loved the piece and been in
full support of her publishing it as her first piece as
Copy Editor In Chief. She had suspected he would
be in support of it. The man was a romantic and he
loved this town. In his eyes, it was a win-win.

She'd needed to do it. It felt necessary to purge
herself and start on the right foot at the *Recorder*.
She was done running away. She realized she would
have more influence running this paper than she
had working anywhere else . . . and that's all she had
ever wanted. A platform for her voice.

As for letting the world know she was in love with
Cruz? Well, that felt right, too. There was nothing
wrong or dirty or sinful about loving someone . . .
about loving *him*. Love was love. It was everything.

She knew he didn't feel the same, but he had her
love nonetheless.

Her family was thrilled that she had decided to
stay in Sweet Hill . . . and she was actually thrilled
to be close to all of them. They might drive her
crazy, but they were there for her. Their love was
unconditional.

Her mother might have grumbled about her declaration of love for Cruz Walsh, but, surprisingly,
her brother and sister had shushed her on the matter.

When she entered the archives room, she blinked

against the sudden darkness. She tried the switch, but nothing. The bulb must be out. She turned back around for the door. It had shut behind her and it took a moment for her hand to unerringly grip the knob and turn it.

But . . . nothing. She tried again, rattling it. Nothing. The door wasn't opening. It must be jammed. She pounded on the door. "Mr. B! The door is locked."

Sudden light filled the room. Not as bright as the bulb had been. This was more of a romantic glow.

She turned around and gasped. Cruz stood there, settling a lantern on top of a file cabinet.

"Cruz . . . what are you doing?"

"I'm locking us in a closet."

She looked around. The room was, indeed, similar to a closet. As she processed that, shifting on her feet, looking at the door and back at him, she asked, "Is Mr. B in on this?"

"He is." He nodded. "I like him."

"I guess so," she said slowly, continuing her assessment of their surroundings. There were blankets and pillows on the floor. A cooler. He watched her take everything in and pointed to the far side of the room. "Bathroom."

Yes, she was aware the archives room boasted a bathroom.

"This time we won't need a bucket."

"This time?"

"This time getting locked in," he clarified, but she was pretty much piecing it together. He'd arranged this. He'd arranged for them to get locked in for the weekend.

"Are you worried you have to trap me to get me alone?"

"Maybe a little," he admitted. "I do have this habit of running you off."

She ducked her head, looking away so that he didn't see her smile.

"What's in the cooler?" she asked.

"Roast chicken, Caesar salad, lemon bars. Fruit. Sandwiches . . . basically anything we might want to eat over the weekend." He shrugged. "Or however long you want to stay in here. With me." His eyes looked suddenly vulnerable right then. Like she might not want to be locked in together with him anywhere or for whatever length of time.

"I read your article."

She nodded. "Most everyone has."

"You meant all that?" His voice was gruff. "You're in love with me?"

She sighed and shook her head, wondering why this was so much harder to do in person than when putting pen to paper.

"Yeah."

"You sure about all that stuff you said? About me?"

"Do you think I changed my mind? That I'm just some naïve starry-eyed girl obsessed with you?"

He stepped forward. "Good then. Because I'm obsessed with you. In prison you were who I thought about. When I dreamed about freedom and what I was missing out on in life . . . it was you I thought of. Now that I know you . . . you're better than any dream I had back then. The reality of you is . . . *everything.*"

He stopped directly in front of her.

She gave her head a small shake. "When you say things like that, I fall in love with you all over again."

He slipped his arms around her and lowered his forehead to hers, their lips practically brushing as he spoke. "I don't want to miss out on life anymore. I've already missed seven years. I love you . . . and I want you even though I don't deserve—"

She kissed him, cutting him off. Coming up for air, she breathed against his lips, "I said you were a noble man in that letter because that's what you are. I see you, Cruz Walsh."

"And I see you, Gabriella Rossi," he replied. "I didn't take a chance with you when I was a kid, but I'm not going to make that mistake again."

When they finally pulled apart for a breath, she saw that they had managed to lower themselves down to the mound of blankets and pillows he had locked in the room with them. "You are quite the clever man, Mr. Walsh . . . arranging all this."

"I promise, I will always make time to find us a closet. It's where I do my best work."

EPILOGUE

Eight months later . . .

$\mathcal{I}$T HAD BEEN a late night. One of Gabriella's reporters called in sick, so she had to cover both the school board meeting and the girls district volleyball playoffs. Still, it was a good feeling—being exhausted doing something you love. And it was Friday. She had nothing to do over the weekend except laze away the days with Cruz.

They didn't go out much. She'd moved in almost eight months ago, and they kept to the house, preferring to stay in with each other when they weren't working. They couldn't get enough of each other.

She had thought that might slow down, but not yet. Apparently, he hadn't been lying when he had told her they had years to make up for. She smiled goofily. They were still going at it like a couple of kids.

Life was good. Her love life was truly rich . . . as was her career.

The paper had taken off. They'd doubled their number of subscribers and people treated her and Cruz like local celebrities, waving at them whenever they were out. Apparently everyone loved a star-crossed lovers story and that's how the town of Sweet Hill now viewed them—as underdogs to root for.

The house was dark when she entered it, but the place smelled delicious. She inhaled, identifying the aroma—sayory roast beef and potatoes. Her stomach growled. She couldn't even recall if she ate lunch today.

She fumbled for the light switch, but suddenly there was a flare. Her gaze moved to the table and the candles Cruz was finishing lighting.

"Cruz." She sighed his name like a benediction. She'd woken up beside him that morning, but she had still missed him. Her heart leapt at the sight of him.

He grinned at her, his lips curving slowly. "Welcome home, baby."

"What's this?" She eyed the elegantly laid table.

"I've made dinner."

"Oh . . ." She spotted a fresh loaf of bread on the table, along with a bottle of wine. "Is that . . . china? And crystal glasses?"

He nodded. "Your grandmother's dishes. She insisted I use them."

She shook her head. "I'm sorry. I don't understand. Why are you using Nana's—"

"I wanted this evening to be perfect."

She cocked her head. "Annnd why is that?" She had figured they'd eat a pizza, watch TV and then go to bed early where they would spend the next couple hours wearing each other out. Like most Fridays.

"Because you deserve perfect, Gabriella."

She sighed. "Ohh."

He stepped forward and pulled her into his arms, kissing her until she melted against him. Until she forgot everything.

Then he was pulling away suddenly, loosening his arms from around her.

She frowned at the loss of him, bewildered as to why he was pulling back from her . . . why he wasn't still holding her. Why weren't they shedding their clothes and making their way to their bedroom?

"Cruz," she panted. "Where are you going? Come here."

He took a deep breath and actually looked . . . nervous. One emotion she had never seen from him, and *that* made *her* nervous.

Then he went down, balancing on one knee. She ceased to breathe. Her hands flew to her face. She peered down at him from between her fingers.

There was a ring in his hand. Oh. God. Oh. God. Oh. God. There was a ring in his hand!

"Gabriella . . . Rossi . . . will you marry me?"

She realized both of her hands had now descended to cover her mouth, muffling her response. She dropped her hands. "Yes! Yes, yes, yes."

He took her hand then and slid a breathtaking solitaire on her finger.

"It fits," she breathed, gawking at it.

"Your sister may have helped with that."

"My sister? You went to Tess?"

"And your niece. And Nana. And my sisters. Oh, and your nephew and his boyfriend."

"Trent and Derek? Does everyone know?"

Nodding, he rose to his feet and swept her back up in his arms, kissing her until she lost all sense of time and place.

Later, they would dine and drink and talk about all the particulars of his proposal. They would talk of their families and the future . . . and the present. Because neither one had ever been happier than they were in this moment.

And don't miss the rest of Sophie Jordan's unforgettable Devil's Rock novels!

ALL CHAINED UP

Some men come with a built-in warning label. Knox Callaghan is one of them. Danger radiates from every lean, muscled inch of him, and his deep blue eyes seem to see right through to Briar Davis's most secret fantasies. But there's one major problem: Briar is a nurse volunteering at the local prison, and Knox is an inmate who should be off-limits in every way.

HELL BREAKS LOOSE

Shy and awkward, First Daughter Grace Reeves has always done what she's told. Tired of taking orders, she escapes her security detail for a rare moment of peace. Except her worst nightmare comes to life when a ruthless gang of criminals abducts her. Her only choice is to place her trust in Reid Allister, an escaped convict whose piercing gaze awakens something deep inside her.

FURY ON FIRE

After years in prison, North Callaghan is finally free. But the demons haunting him still make him feel like a caged beast. He loses himself in work and hard living, coming up for air only to bed any willing woman to cross his path. So when his new neighbor snares his interest, he decides to add another notch to his bedpost. The only problem? Faith Walters is a white picket fence kind of girl.

BEAUTIFUL LAWMAN

From the wrong side of the tracks and with most of her family in jail or dead, Piper Walsh is used to everyone in town thinking the worst about her. So she isn't surprised that when she comes into contact with Sweet Hill's wildly irresistible, arrogant sheriff, Hale Walters, they're instant adversaries. Piper has nothing in common with the town golden-boy-turned lawman—and she refuses to be a notch on his bedpost.

*G*ive in to your Impulses!

**These unforgettable stories only take a second
to buy and give you hours of reading pleasure!**

Go to *www.AvonImpulse.com* and see what we
have to offer.

Available wherever e-books are sold.

AVONIMPULSE